Royal House of Leone

A PRINCE FOR CHRISTMAS

&

THE PRINCE'S SECRET BABY

by Jennifer Lewis

All Rights Reserved.
Published 2017 by Mangrove
25883 N Park Ave
Suite 521672
Elkhart, Indiana, 46514, USA

ISBN 978-1-939941-36-7

1

A scraping sound woke Serena from a deep sleep, and she sat up in total darkness, heart pounding. "Who's there?"

She hoped like heck that the answer was *no one*.

She'd rented this big beach house to get away from everyone and lick her wounds in private. Suddenly, being all alone in the middle of nowhere didn't seem like such a brilliant idea. Groping around, she realized she'd fallen asleep on the living room sofa and dropped her ereader on the floor.

Boom. Boom-boom.

Someone was banging on the door. Terror streaked along her veins.

No one knew she was here. There weren't even any neighbors that she'd noticed. The remote property was surrounded by dunes and woods.

A serial killer?

Pulse racing, Serena sprang off the sofa and fumbled for her phone on the nearby coffee table. Hiding the glow of the screen with her hand, she dialed 911 and crept into a corner while listening for the ring.

Just outside the room, she heard the front door creak open.

JENNIFER LEWIS

Her blood froze. The call wasn't connecting. Why? She fought the urge to wail in desperation. She had no bars because the cell service here on the Georgia sea islands absolutely sucked.

I'm all alone in the dark, miles from civilization, with a home invader. She'd thought it bad that her heart was broken and she'd have to be alone for Christmas. Now, to top it off, she was going to die.

Not if I can help it.

Her eyes had adjusted to the semi-darkness enough for her to see an orchid nearby in a tall vase. She tipped the orchid out—it was fake—and gripped the vase in her hand like a club. Staying low she scuttled across the carpet to hide beside the arched entrance to the foyer. She rose up, praying her knees wouldn't creak, and gingerly lifted the heavy vase high over her head. She could hear footfalls on the carpet. If he came this way...

A big shoe landed right in front of her, and she brought the vase down on his head with every ounce of force she could muster.

"What the—?" The man crumpled to the floor as chunks of ceramic scattered. Quick as a flash he was on his feet again, big hands gripping her upper arms.

She screamed and beat him with her fists. "Get your hands off me! I'll call the police." Her useless phone had fallen to the floor.

"Who are you?" he asked coolly, deep voice rough.

"None of your damn business. Get out of my house this instant!" Adrenaline surged through her and she struggled to free herself, but his hands were too strong.

2

"Your house? This house belongs to my friend Zadir."

Zadir Al Kilanjar. That was the owner's name on the short lease she'd signed. She stopped struggling. Maybe this man wasn't a crazed killer. "I rented it from him for two weeks."

"I saw a light upstairs. That's why I knocked. Zadir told me it was empty and that I could have the place over Christmas."

"Clearly he was wrong. I'm here, and I have a signed lease. You need to leave." Her terror was starting to subside into irritation at being scared out of her wits in the middle of the night. And embarrassment at the realization that she might have overreacted.

He took one hand off her long enough to switch on a nearby light. A blinding burst of light revealed that in addition to his impressive strength, the intruder was tall and broad with a bold handsome face.

Where a trickle of blood flowed from one temple.

Maybe news of that would get him to let go of her. "You're bleeding."

"Perhaps you shouldn't have smashed my friend's china on me." His dark eyes glittered a challenge. His grip didn't soften. "That's assault."

She could almost swear she saw a hint of amusement in his expression.

She felt her dander rising. "I rented this house legally, and you have invaded in the night and scared at least five years off my life. Unhand me, sir!" She hoped the formal command would get his attention.

3

It worked. Slowly, and with apparent reluctance, he pulled his fingers from her arms. His gaze rested coolly on her face for a moment, then dropped to appraise her body.

Extreme self-consciousness washed over her. What was she even wearing? She refused to look down. He was elegantly dressed in dark pants and a subtly checked shirt, the sleeves rolled up over muscular, tanned arms.

They're just arms, Serena. She wasn't attracted to him anyway. His looks were too flashy. She preferred someone more...subdued. Like Howard.

Ouch. It had been almost three weeks since Howard dumped her, and it hurt like he'd just told her five minutes ago.

"Are you okay?" His brow furrowed with concern.

"I should be asking you that. Don't get blood on your friend's carpet." Her heart rate slowed. Now that the threat of gruesome death was subsiding, she started to relax. "You really should go."

"But I have friends meeting me here tomorrow."

"Then you'll have to get in touch and tell them to meet you somewhere else." She crossed her arms over her chest. Which reminded her that she had on a college sweatshirt over her blue-striped pajamas.

Cringe.

At least he didn't know who she was. Probably no one would even recognize her from her publicity pictures right now.

"It's three a.m." He cocked his head and rested his dark gaze on her face. "And now I've been assaulted. Can I at least have a cup of coffee first?"

"No." She wanted to get him out of there before he could figure out she was alone. Since her twelve-week stint on *Good Morning,* people were way too curious about her personal life, and so far she'd managed to keep her humiliating breakup out of the public eye. "Please leave."

He reached a finger up to his injured temple. "A Band-Aid, perhaps?"

"I don't know where they are." Who did this guy think he was? "It's not a bad injury." With an attitude like his, he deserved to get blood on his expensive-looking shirt.

"I'll call and ask Zadir."

"Never mind." She didn't want anyone else in on this. "I'll check the bathroom."

She could swear a slightly wolfish smile of triumph tugged at one side of his broad mouth.

Which made her want to hurl another vase at him.

She turned and walked toward the powder room off the foyer, sure she could feel his eyes on her. Probably laughing at her pajamas. Heck, it was nighttime! She should be in pj's. He was lucky she didn't sleep in the buff.

She pulled open the cabinet under the painted porcelain sink. "You're in luck. There's a first aid kit down here."

"Doesn't surprise me. Zadir is one of those people who have people who think of everything."

"Except double booking his beach house." She handed him the gray plastic box, careful not to touch his fingertips. He had big hands, with long, strong fingers.

5

"Most likely his very capable staff booked it to you, and he just offered it to me without checking with them." He opened the box and pulled out some gauze and a tiny brown bottle of peroxide.

"Which means that I have the legal right to be here and you need to leave."

He looked up, and his dark eyes flashed. "Impossible."

2

Sandro moved in front of the mirror and applied peroxide to a small cut near his hairline. He winced as the wound smarted. The beautiful, angry woman still stood in the small powder room with him, and he suddenly realized something. "I don't know your name."

He frowned as he fiddled with the Band-Aid, trying to get the paper strips off. His fingers were too big "I am Sandro Leone." He put down the bandage and extended his hand.

She didn't lift her hand. "What do you mean impossible? Of course you have to leave. I have the rental until January seventh."

"I have two friends meeting me here tomorrow. It'll be Christmas Eve." It had been hard enough to convince them to come in the first place. Any hint of chaos and they'd both cancel and be on their own.

"Go to a hotel." Her big dark eyes gleamed with determination. Which sparked a flare of heat in his gut. He liked a woman with fire. And the way she'd attacked him suggested that she had more than a few sparks.

"There aren't any. And who wants to stay in a

7

hotel over Christmas?" He softened his voice. "It's a big house—ten bedrooms—how many are there in your party?"

She stiffened and pushed an imaginary strand of hair off her forehead. "I'm here on a sabbatical. To write a book."

"Over Christmas?" He couldn't keep the disbelief out of his voice. "You can't be alone on Christmas."

"I can be alone whenever I want, thank you very much." She crossed her arms over her chest—which threw it into tempting relief. She was pretty, with a high forehead, big dark eyes with long lashes, a proud mouth and smooth brown skin.

And she was here all alone? Over Christmas? He snuck a glance at her ring finger—empty.

Interesting.

And sad. She was far too lovely to be alone. And though she wore a baggy sweatshirt and what looked like men's pajamas, he had enough experience with women to predict that she had the kind of body that would stop traffic.

"Since it's such a big house perhaps myself and my friends—there are just two of them—could take over the third floor. The more the merrier, right?"

She lifted her chin. "The third floor has the best view."

He felt like he was making headway. "Okay, then you have the third floor and we'll have the second-floor bedrooms."

"Wait a second, I didn't say you could have any bedrooms. Call Zadir and tell him he made a mistake. Let him find somewhere else for you." She handed him another Band-Aid. He took it, deliberately brushing his fingertips against hers. Heat flashed between them—as he suspected it would. From the way she snatched her hand back, he could tell she felt it, too.

"He's in Ubar. It's in the Middle East, and there's a big time difference."

"That's a plus. It's the dead of the night here."

"And it's right before Christmas. I'm sure he has his hands full with family and other obligations."

"Since when do they celebrate Christmas in the Middle East?" This woman seemed remarkable unsusceptible to his usually robust charms.

But he didn't give up easily. He made another attempt to peel the paper backing off the bandage. These things were made for people with tiny, delicate fingers.

"They had the Christmas party of the century last year. I was there. I know, how about if I pay your rent, so your stay here is free?"

Her eyes sparkled with indignation. "I don't need your money, thank you." She picked up the Band-Aid he'd discarded, deftly peeled off the paper and stuck it to his forehead, then pulled her hand back with lightning speed before he could enjoy the heat of her fingers. "What I need is peace and quiet."

"We'll be very quiet. My friends are both total geeks. That's why they need someone like me to make sure they're not alone at Christmas. I make a pretty decent Christmas dinner. I've done it before." He shot her a winning smile.

She stared at him. "What if I want to be alone at Christmas?"

He studied her face for a moment and saw the hesitation in her eyes, the trembling frustration in her lips. He spoke softly. "Nobody really wants to be alone at Christmas."

On her blog Serena wrote a lot about "turning frustration into determination," but she was beginning to hate this guy. "I do. Your wound is bandaged. Please get in your car and leave."

"But I just drove three hours from the airport and that was after a connecting flight from Atlanta and a nine-hour flight from Zurich. I'm not sure I'm even safe to drive at this point. Can I crash on the sofa until daylight?"

He probably had no idea that *she* had been sleeping on the couch when he showed up.

Could she really send a stranger out onto the unlit backcountry roads with no sleep? That was not how she was raised. She softened. "Okay. Just until you get enough rest."

His mouth creased into a smile broad enough to be a little cocky. "I appreciate it. I'm sorry for inconveniencing you."

She shrugged. It wasn't his fault. "A misunderstanding. Are you hungry?" She started to feel like she'd been a bit harsh. Perhaps she should have tried communicating with him before smashing a vase over him. Still, he'd half frightened the life out of her.

"I ate on the plane so I'm fine, but thanks."

He had a nice face. Too handsome for any sensible purpose, but a warm, open expression.

Sandro, wasn't it? He didn't seem like a total jerk. "I'm Serena."

She decided to keep her last name to herself in case he was into Googling people. Hopefully, tomorrow morning he'd disappear and no one would be any the wiser that the *New York Times* best-selling author of a book on *Living Your Best Life* was holed up on the Georgia sea islands, wishing she could figure out how to follow her own advice.

She turned and left, partly driven by a desire to pick up the shattered evidence of her overreaction and partly to get away from that penetrating gaze.

She hoped the blue porcelain vase wasn't a priceless antique, because it definitely wasn't fixable. She collected the pieces in a bag from her trip to the local market on the way here. Sandro crouched down and plucked a large piece from the other side of the arched doorway. "I guess I'm lucky this thing wasn't made of steel. You packed quite a punch with it."

"You took me by surprise. I assumed the worst." She felt kind of embarrassed now. "I'm glad I didn't have a gun. I'd probably have used it. I've watched too many scary movies."

"It is lonely out here." He picked up some more pieces and cupped them in the palm of one big hand. "I didn't realize how far the house was from everything."

"Not many people know about this area. Most of the locals are Gullah people. This house and two others like it are the only new ones out here." She'd learned that while looking for the most remote rental house she could find.

"Who are the Gullah people?"

"You've never heard of them?" Other people's ignorance often annoyed her.

"In my defense, I'm from Europe." A wry smile crinkled his eyes. "A tiny country called Altaleone."

"Oh. You do have a slight accent now that I think about it. The Gullahs are descendants of African slaves who've lived in this same isolated spot for centuries and retained aspects of their traditional culture. It's a unique and fascinating place."

"I look forward to seeing it in daylight. I noticed there were few lights between here and the highway."

She stood up, her bag now full of all but the smallest pieces. Hopefully, she could find a vacuum cleaner somewhere. "Thanks for helping. That was kind of you. Does your forehead hurt?"

He shrugged. "Not much." His eyes twinkled. "I think I'll survive." He emptied the shards from his hand into her bag. "If you don't mind I'm about to fall asleep standing up."

"Oh, of course. Do take the sofa." She gestured toward the one she'd just been sleeping on. She didn't want him settling into a bedroom. Then she'd never get rid of him. "I'll be upstairs. Please don't do anything to frighten the life out of me."

His apologetic smile disarmed her. "I'll do my best. See you in the morning."

An alarming prospect.

3

Serena muttered to herself under her breath while she applied mascara. And lipstick, and a hint of contour and highlighter.

Really? She was putting on makeup for a random stranger who'd made her jump out of her skin?

Apparently so. Maybe she just needed to paint on her game face. Especially since she wanted him out of here as soon as possible so she could get back to licking her wounds in peace.

Dressed and with her hair in a neat bun, she ventured downstairs. A quick glance at the sofa showed it empty. Had Sandro left already?

Her hopes were dashed when she heard the fridge door close in the kitchen. "Good morning," she called. Was he rifling through her newly purchased food? This man had a nerve.

"Good morning, Serena." Sandro looked deliciously rumpled, his dark hair tousled and his expensive shirt crumpled. "What would you like for breakfast?"

"Uh…I can help myself."

"Why don't you relax and let me cook you something? A friend I shared a flat with in Paris now owns a string of gourmet restaurants. I picked up a few tricks from him." He grinned, then turned back to the fridge.

"Are you serious?" Now she was intrigued. Could a man this gorgeous and confident really cook?

"Try me." His eyes twinkled with mischief, suggesting that she try more than his cooking. She resisted the urge to roll her eyes and fought the smile tugging at the corners of her mouth. "Do you like frittata? I see you bought eggs, onions, spinach and parmesan cheese." He looked at her expectantly.

"Mmm, that sounds delicious." And she'd get to sit here and watch him make it? "I'll take you up on your offer. And I hope you're making enough for yourself as well."

This might even make a good blog post— perhaps with mention of a handsome man cooking but no information about his identity. She hadn't yet revealed to her audience that her engagement was over.

Still, she didn't want Sandro to get the idea that he was staying. "Did you get in touch with your friends?"

"Not yet. They're on the West Coast so I need to wait a while longer before it's morning there." He was already breaking eggs into a bowl, big tanned hands moving with deft ease.

Yum.

This was an excellent way to get her mind off Howard, who didn't know how to boil an egg, let alone make a frittata with it.

"You probably shouldn't be alone here anyway.

The car rental place told me there's a big storm coming." He sliced into the onion, and she braced herself not to cry. She didn't even need an excuse lately. "I had to promise them I wasn't going anywhere near the ocean."

"So you're a liar. That's encouraging. But how can there be a storm? It's not hurricane season."

He shrugged. "I guess this storm didn't get the memo. And there's also a winter storm coming down from the Great Lakes. They're supposed to meet up somewhere right around here. Wind, snow, ice and who knows what else. You might need help shoveling out afterward."

She shrugged. "I'm from Virginia. I've seen snow before, and I'm stronger than I look."

"I'm from the Alps. I've seen snow higher than my head." He flashed that disarming grin, and her insides did a weird flip-flop thing.

"What country did you say you were from?"

"Altaleone."

"Never heard of it." Maybe he was making it up. He'd already confessed to being a liar.

"It's tiny. In between northern Italy and Austria."

He must be pulling her leg. She'd been skiing in Austria and visited Italy twice. "I don't believe you." She picked up her phone and searched for the name using the house's Wi-Fi. Sure enough, there it was. Total population twenty-nine thousand. Ruled by the Leone family since a.d. 800 and known for producing fine champagne and cut diamonds.

Wait a second.

"What did you say your last name was?"

"Leone. Sandro Leone." He smiled before stirring chopped onion into the egg.

"Any relation to the royal family of your country?" She lifted a brow, now sure he was lying to her.

"My brother Darias is the king." He said it softly, matter of fact. "It's a beautiful country. You should come visit."

She scanned the wiki page and saw the name Sandro Leone listed as a member of the royal family. "So if your brother is the king, you must be…"

"A prince? Yes." He chopped the spinach with speed and skill.

"Show me your passport."

"What?" He looked up from his chopping.

"If you arrived on a plane you must have it with you. Do you expect me to just believe you're a royal prince?"

He walked to the sink and washed his hands, then dried them. She followed him into the living room, where he fished into an outside pocket of his bag and pulled out a passport. He handed it to her with a lifted brow.

The passport was burgundy in color and had a hard cover. She flipped it open and the colorful pages revealed a photo of Sandro and the name he'd given. "This could be fake."

"It's real. I swear it." His eyes glimmered with humor.

Damn it, she believed him.

She shoved the passport back at him. "We don't really believe in princes in America." She wanted him to know she had no intention of calling him your majesty or any such nonsense.

"I don't take it personally." That warm smile again. He led the way back to the kitchen and resumed his chopping. "I'm just a regular person. I'll never be king."

Sure. The wiki article had referred to the ancient family's great wealth in land, art and plain old money. "Just a regular Joe, huh?"

"A regular Sandro." He scraped the spinach into the eggs and whipped the mixture with a fork. His rolled-up sleeve gave her a tantalizing view of his muscled forearm. "At your service."

"You're too much. You still need to find somewhere else to stay, though. I'm here to write."

"What do you write?"

She hesitated. "Nonfiction."

"What kind?"

Gulp. "Self-help books. Giving people life strategies, that kind of thing."

"Like how to spend Christmas alone in the middle of nowhere?" The way he glanced at her, laughter dancing in his dark eyes, made her chuckle in spite of herself.

"Exactly. I can show people how to have a wonderful holiday by themselves."

He poured the egg mixture into a baking dish. "Where is your boyfriend or husband?"

She gave him credit for not staring awkwardly at her while he asked such a personal question.

She gave herself credit for not flinching before answering. "I had a recent breakup. To be honest I couldn't face going home to my family alone. My sisters and my brother are all married and happy. I'm the odd one out."

"You do seem pretty odd." He closed the oven door, opened the fridge, poured two glasses of her orange juice, and sauntered over to where she stood by the island. "But I like that in a woman."

She took the glass from him. "Are all royals as confident and obnoxious as you?"

4

Sandro shrugged. "Probably."

"It figures." She sipped the juice, fighting the urge to smile. He stood far too close, and she could smell the last traces of some kind of yummy expensive cologne clinging to him. When she told people this story none of them were going to believe her.

"Why didn't you buy a goose?" he asked.

"Why would I?"

"It's the traditional Christmas bird. You didn't buy a turkey, either."

"I bought a rolled turkey breast with stuffing in it."

He grimaced. "I saw that in there. Sorry, but no."

She stared. "What? It's not any of your business what I eat."

"Indeed it is." He polished off the last of his glass and put it in the dishwasher. "I have fallen into your life, and I intend to save you from yourself."

"I don't need saving, thanks."

"Because you already figured everything out and wrote a book about it?"

"Pretty much." Strange feelings built in her chest. A mix of hurt and anger and humor at her own ridiculous predicament. "And since that's how I pay my bills, I need to write another one. And I can eat a rolled turkey breast while I'm writing it if I want to."

He chuckled and turned on the oven light. She could see the top of the frittata already beginning to bubble.

She frowned. "You preheated the oven?"

"Of course."

"So you were going to make a frittata whether I wanted one or not?"

"If you wanted something else I'd have made that. Just getting prepared. Speaking of which, we need to hit the local stores before the storm rolls in. I started writing a list."

"There's only one store, and I don't think they're going to have goose. I went there in daylight, remember. I wanted to buy feta cheese, but they didn't have anything that exotic. They have a lot of different cuts of pig." She shuddered at the memory.

"Excellent. My chef friend I told you about is from the Deep South. New Orleans, to be precise. His name is Louis DuLac."

"I'm not eating pigs' feet. Or intestines. I'm not wild about the rest of the pig, either."

"Shame. We'll make do with turkey. If you rub butter and herbs underneath the skin it stays juicy."

"You really do love to cook, don't you?"

He'd turned away to remove the dish from the oven using one hand and the dish towel. "It's a useful hobby."

"I agree. I wish more men could cook." She wasn't much of a cook herself. She liked reading cookbooks and watching cooking shows, but even when she used all the right ingredients and followed the directions to the letter, nothing ever came out quite right.

Kind of like her life lately.

Her stomach growled. "That smells wonderful."

Enjoy life's unexpected blessings. Hadn't she used that as a chapter heading once? "Let me get the plates. If I can find them."

It didn't take long to get two places set at the large stone island. She even found some ironed linen napkins.

"Coffee?" He put freshly cut slices of frittata in both places.

"I thought I smelled coffee."

"I'm glad you thought to shop ahead."

"I try to think of everything."

"Is that something you recommend in your books?"

"Absolutely. The power of making lists." She smiled. He was so easy to talk to that she couldn't be mad at him right now. Even if they were blowing through all the ingredients she'd bought for her holiday for one. "But seriously, where will you stay? Is there a hotel? Or another rental?"

"Milk? Sugar?"

"Just milk." Was he ignoring her questions? Just because he was royal didn't mean he could do whatever he wanted.

"Say when." He poured in a trickle of her one percent milk.

"When."

"I hardly poured any."

"I like it dark. So when are you leaving?"

He put the milk back in the fridge. "About that." He turned and put his hands on his hips. "Wouldn't you enjoy a multi-course, expertly prepared Christmas dinner with all the trimmings? And I brought some Christmas music. You'll like Zach and Ajay. They're super nice guys even though they're geeky shut-ins a lot of the time."

The frittata looked so delicious that she didn't feel like arguing right now. Maybe the eggs would give her the strength she needed to put her foot down. She decided to ignore his question.

His phone rang, and she heard someone talking on the other end.

"Just a few gusts of wind, nothing serious." He sat down on the stool near hers. "We're not going to get snowed in. We're at the beach! Who ever heard of getting snowed in at the beach. Don't worry. You'll be back in time for your meeting."

He hung up and shook his head. "It's hard to get these workaholic types to take a break. He's trying to use the storm as an excuse to cancel."

"You were trying to convince me only a few minutes ago that I might need help shoveling out. I take it you're the kind of person who says whatever they think will win."

"Do you warn about people like me in your books?"

"Not yet, but I'm considering this breakfast as research." She shot him an arch look.

He had the audacity to look pleased. "I hope they don't cancel. Then I'll be all alone for Christmas." He looked up at her with sad eyes.

You're the kind of person who says whatever they think will win.

"You could fly back to...Altaleone."

"It's too late already. By the time I fly from here to a hub, then from there to Austria, or Switzerland, and drive through the mountains—which are heavy with snow at this time of year..."

"That would be sad, wouldn't it?" She tried to sound sarcastic. "You could use the time to write a book. What do you do, anyway? Or is being a prince a full-time job?"

"I'm a mechanical engineer by training. I invent things by inclination." He sipped his coffee.

"Like what?"

"Right now my main focus is on portable solar panels for smaller applications like a single laptop."

"So spoiled executives wouldn't have to worry about running out of power on the train."

"You'd be surprised by how much of the world is still off the grid. Picture someone in rural Africa being able to connect to the Internet via satellite and share or retrieve information a hundred miles from the nearest lightbulb."

"Okay, that does sound pretty cool." Great, he had to be smart as well as handsome. And his bringing power to African laptops made her posts on how to organize your closet seem a bit lame. "Did you bring a panel or two with you in case we lose power during the storm?"

He laughed. "Nope. I'm like the shoemaker's children who have bare feet. But knowing Zadir, this place probably has a full backup generator. How do you like breakfast?"

"It's very good," she admitted reluctantly.

He looked pleased again. "When you're done we should hit the store. No sense waiting until the weather gets really bad."

She heard a text come in on his phone. He muttered a veiled curse and dialed someone. "Zach, it's just a storm. The airports are not going to be shut down for days." He rose and paced while listening impatiently. "And being Jewish is no excuse to be alone on one of the most festive days of the year. Jesus was Jewish, remember? And it's his birthday. If the local airport gets snowed in I will personally drive you to Atlanta. Or Charlotte. Or somewhere bigger, anyway." He paced some more. "They always overestimate these things. The house is gorgeous—right on the beach! And the weather here is perfect right now."

Serena glanced at the kitchen window, where rain spattered gently against the glass. It was kind of adorable that Sandro wanted to give his non-Christian friends a festive Christmas so they wouldn't be alone. Then again, it was pretty obnoxious, too.

He put his phone down, looking annoyed. "Some people are so pessimistic."

"He's not coming."

"Nope. Ajay should be getting on his plane any minute, though. He's only in Philly so he'll be here in a few hours."

His phone pinged with an incoming text. He picked it up and peered at it. "Quitter." Then he turned to her. "I guess it's just you and me, after all."

5

Sandro insisted that Serena drive with him to the grocery store—firstly, because he had no idea where it was; secondly, because he was afraid she would somehow change the locks while he was gone.

Still, he could tell she was beginning to like him. He steered the rented car, laden with the local store's very meager provisions, along the narrow beach road. And threw her another winning smile, just to help his cause.

Serena was beautiful, with a body to die for. Hopefully, their growing mutual intimacy would allow him to enjoy the pleasures of those full lips and full hips. He grew hard thinking about the possibilities.

Stay in the moment, Sandro. "At least they had a fresh chicken, and my stuffing will be way better than the boxed stuff you bought. Trust me."

"It's hard to trust you now that I know you'll say whatever you think will win me over. But since you're so terrified of spending Christmas alone, I will let you spend it with me."

He wanted to laugh. She seemed almost more

arrogant than him, which was saying something. And she still acted like she couldn't care less about him. Which, of course, only made the challenge of seducing her more exciting.

"We should go to the beach." He could see glimpses of the ocean through the trees on his side of the car.

"That chicken needs to go in the fridge." She kept her chin at a jaunty angle, as if ready to deflect all blows.

"True, but once it's safely tucked away, let's go for a walk."

"I actually have a lot of work to do." He could tell she still wanted to wall herself off in her room and mope.

He couldn't stand that kind of waste.

"We can talk about your work." He shot her a winning smile. "Maybe find you some inspiration."

The rain had cleared up and the sun peeked through the clouds, dusting the beach in pale light. Serena kicked off her sandals at the edge of the dunes. It couldn't hurt to go for a walk with him, right? She might as well make the most of this beautiful location.

The invading winds so far were tropical, so it was warm enough to wear only a sweater over her T-shirt and khakis, and the ocean breeze was refreshing rather than chilling. Sandro wore faded jeans with a hole in one knee—rather an affectation for a wealthy prince—and a dark blue sweater. With his tousled hair and dark, flashing eyes, he looked like an Italian fisherman, and the effect was unfortunately enchanting.

Maybe she'd get a blog post out of this one day when she had more distance.

He rolled up the bottom of his jeans. "How did you get started writing books?"

The sand felt cool between her toes as they walked toward the shoreline. "The two I've written so far have been compilations of my blog posts. I started a blog in my senior year of college, and it caught on. I expanded into writing magazine articles, making YouTube videos, and one day I decided to put a bunch of my blog posts together into a book and publish it myself."

"You found readers?"

"Yes. I'm sure some of them were people who read my blog, but I was able to use my magazine connections to get publicity and it ended up hitting a best seller list for several weeks."

"What was your book about?"

"I called it *Living Your Best Life*. It's a bunch of articles based on experiences I had as I looked for a job, rented my first apartment, figured out how to deal with a demanding boss—just living as a single girl in the city."

"Did you talk about dating?"

The ocean lapped in and touched her toes. "Ouch! That's colder than I expected." The water was a dark gray-blue. She didn't want to talk about dating. "Sometimes."

"You must have men flocking around you wherever you go." His eyes rested on her a little too long as he said it.

"Hardly." She tried to sound breezy. "Not any I was interested in, anyway. I ended up having so many articles about my dating misadventures that I compiled them into another book called *Waiting for Mr. Right*. A publisher gave me a big advance for that one. It comes out next month."

"*Waiting for Mr. Right*. Did you find him?"

She reached up to tug at her sweater, and for a second she could swear she felt his eyes on her ringless ring finger. The book wasn't even out yet, and already Mr. Right had cut and run.

"I thought I had. We dated for two years. We were engaged, even." She shuddered. Suddenly the weather seemed less tropical. "It's cold. Do we really want to do this?"

"We'll warm up if we keep walking." He switched places with her so that he was on the ocean side, water lapping around his ankles and wetting the rolled bottom of his jeans. "What happened?"

Shame gripped her—for the umpteenth time. How did you explain it? She didn't even know how to explain it to herself. The whole thing hadn't sunk in yet. "He decided to go...in a different direction."

"He turned out to be gay?" He looked curious.

She laughed in spite of herself. "No. He just said he didn't want to get married. He's still single as far as I know."

"How odd." Sandro frowned. "He probably is gay and hasn't admitted it to himself yet."

"I think I was too demanding." She sighed. "Howard said it wasn't easy living in a blog post. Too much pressure to do everything by the book." She laughed again. "It is ridiculous, isn't it? Even as we set out on this walk I wondered if it would become a post."

One side of Sandro's broad mouth hitched in a

smile. "I'd love to be one of your posts."

She blew out. "You wouldn't really. He said it was like swimming around in a fish bowl."

"Sounds a bit like being royal." He grinned.

A smile snuck across her mouth. "I suppose it does. People watching everything you do, expecting it to be fabulous."

"So I do my best to make sure it is."

"Fabulous?"

"Of course."

His dark eyes drifted lower, and she felt the heat of his gaze roam over her breasts, her belly, her khaki-clad thighs. She had not packed for elegance on this trip, and right now she wasn't sure whether to be horrified or pleased by his bold appraisal.

She decided to turn the tables on him. "Maybe you could give me some tips on living a fabulous life. I could share them with my readers."

"You are always writing a blog post, aren't you?"

She shrugged. "Occupational hazard."

"I only have one tip—surround yourself with good people."

"I guess I broke that rule by coming here alone."

"Luckily I turned up." He smiled. "And I'm so glad you were here. I'd have spent my holidays in an airport, trying to fly back to some friends somewhere."

"You don't like to be alone?"

"Not all that much. I'm from a big family. I have nine brothers and sisters."

"Wow! That's unusual these days."

"My mom loves children. She's waiting with bated breath for one of us to give her a grandchild."

"Luckily, my siblings have jumped in early to save me from that pressure. It's bad enough with them wanting me to get married."

"Did they like your ex?"

"I don't know. I'm not sure they did."

"Were they glad when you broke up with him?"

"I haven't told them yet."

6

Sandro stared. "That's why you couldn't go home for Christmas."

She nodded, recrimination clawing at her heart. "Breaking up with your fiancé is bad enough, but when you're always telling people how to live their life, including how to handle relationships, it's hard to admit you failed."

"Who says you failed? If it didn't work out, he was wrong for you."

She swallowed. "I've tried to convince myself of that, but it's not working too well. According to all my social media, he was perfect and we were supposed to live happily ever after."

Sandro had the gall to laugh. "I guess you'll have to post some updates. Did you love him?"

"Of course! Do you think I'd marry someone I didn't love?"

"Perhaps, if your reputation depended on it." He spoke slowly, studying her face.

Her skin heated under his curious gaze. "I'm not that shallow." She stared out at the ocean. "I admit that it took me a while to fall in love with him, but I could see that he was a good match and over time I grew to really dote on him."

Sandro lifted a brow. "I don't think that's how it's supposed to work."

"Says who? People these days rush into relationships with the wrong person. Everything's about sex. They don't even take the time to figure out if they're compatible before they start living together."

"And you recommend a more clinical approach."

"Absolutely." Was he poking fun at her? She couldn't tell. "You should look at a relationship like buying a new car. Does it have the features I want? Is it going to hold up under the conditions I'll be driving it in? Will it hold its value? Will it protect me in case of disaster?"

"Will it give me a jolt of adrenaline when I take it on the autobahn?"

She laughed. "That one wasn't on my list. But of course your partner should excite you."

"Did Howard rev your engine?"

"Absolutely. He was very handsome." *Damn him.* "I got him working out four times a week and drinking a raw-juice smoothie every day. He looked like an Olympic athlete."

Sandro laughed again. "Maybe he didn't want to look like an athlete. Maybe he wanted to have a beer belly."

She blew out. "For all I know you could be right. Not my problem anymore." She looked at him walking beside her, the wind whipping his clothes against his hard body. "Besides, I can tell you work out. Keeping fit is important."

"I'm a crazy adrenaline junkie. I can't sit still. The muscles are simply a side effect."

"That sounds dangerous."

"Only when you're doing it wrong." His dark eyes glittered. Or was it simply the ocean reflecting in their depths? "Do you ever do anything reckless?"

"Not really. Unless you count attempting to have a relationship with another human being," she said ruefully.

"I guess you won't be making that mistake again." Mischief played around his mouth.

She stared at him for a moment. "Maybe I won't."

"You could get a cat instead."

"Then I'd have cat hair on my clothes."

"True." He seemed to be fighting the urge to laugh. "Maybe you could get a stuffed cat."

"It's not funny!" Emotion welled in her chest. "Maybe I am impossible. Maybe I'm incapable of having a relationship with anyone." Tears blurred her eyes.

"I didn't mean to make you cry." He had the decency to sound remorseful. "Let's sit for a minute. There's a sheltered spot here in the dunes."

He slid his arm in hers and led her up the beach, which was lucky, as the combination of tears and salty beach air had half-blinded her. She let his strong presence guide her until they were sitting next to each other on the cool sand.

She swiped at her tears. "I did try hard to make him happy."

"He was a lucky man."

"Don't patronize me!" She hated the whiny sound of her voice. "I'm not a child. I'm a grown woman, and I need to face up to my mistakes."

"We all make mistakes," he said again in that infuriatingly therapeutic tone.

"Do we? I bet you don't ever make mistakes." She couldn't get herself to sound calm. Emotion that had built up in her in the last few weeks, heck, maybe the last year—or maybe her whole life— exploded to the surface. "Why would you? You're the handsome prince—the knight in shining armor—who any girl would welcome into her life. I bet you've never experienced a single moment of rejection."

He watched her, bemused, and she fought a powerful urge to slap him hard across his handsome, arrogant face. "Have you?"

Her answer came in the form of a hard, hot kiss.

Sandro's lips crushed over hers, and her protest evaporated instantly in the fire of his kiss. Her limbs grew weak as his big, strong arms wrapped around her. The warmth of his body enveloped her, and his musky, masculine scent overwhelmed her senses.

For a crazy instant she was able to just let go— of all the pain, the embarrassment, the disappointment, the secrecy, the uncertainty about herself and her future—and lose herself in the fierce intensity of his kiss.

A sudden gust of wind threw sand against them and stung her cheek hard enough for her to pull back. She stared at him, blinking, for a moment. Then her heart sank and shame flooded through her. "I guess you just proved my point."

"There was a point?" A smile tugged at his wet lips.

"That you've never experienced rejection. I'm

guessing you assumed I'd reject you and that you could say that, yes, you had been rejected and that we all...that you...that I..." The rush of tears overwhelmed her again.

How could she have been such an idiot? Of course he didn't actually *want* to kiss her. No man wanted another's unwanted castoff. He wanted to give her a chance to reject him so that she could feel.... Who knows what he wanted her to feel.

And now she'd just shown him what a total fool she was.

"My kisses don't usually have this effect on women."

"Really?" she spluttered through her tears. "What kind of effect do they have? I'm sure you've had opportunity for extensive scientific study." His lips touched her forehead, and she fought a powerful urge to sink into his strength. "Stop toying with me."

"I'm not toying with you." He took hold of her chin in his finger and thumb. "I'm very, very, very attracted to you, and on top of that I find you fascinating."

He spoke so seriously she was almost tempted to believe him.

"You try so hard to do everything right, to be strong, and you can't stand for a second that anyone would think that you're not perfect. Even your own family."

"I suspect that makes me crazy, not fascinating." Her voice shook a little.

"I find it absolutely irresistible."

7

Another gust of wind picked up sand and flung it at them. Sandro noticed dark clouds gathering inland, behind the dunes. He wanted to kiss her again, but common sense prevailed. "I think we should head back."

"Of course." Serena leaped to her feet and brushed sand off her gorgeous behind. Clipped and brusque in her movements, she probably took his suggestion as a rejection.

Once they got back to the house, he intended to let her know it was anything but.

"Is that a dog?" She turned to face the dunes, where the gusts now flattened the gray-green dune grass.

"I think it's the wind."

"I thought I heard barking." She started to walk back.

"Maybe you're right." He lingered behind, unable to resist a glimpse of the view. "And I think you're onto something," he said, resisting the urge to brush a last sprinkle of sand from her pants.

"What do you mean?"

"Coming here by yourself. Taking a break from reality."

"If only I could take a break. My readers expect new content every other day. Something uplifting and entertaining, preferably with an artistically styled yet candid-looking photo."

He chuckled. She wasn't laughing. "You put a lot of pressure on yourself."

She looked right at him. "I invited it willingly. I worked hard to build my audience and encourage their participation. I guess I thought I'd be going from strength to strength, leading and guiding. It never occurred to me that I'd want to go hide under a rock."

The sadness in her eyes tugged at his heart. They walked along the beach, swift gusts now whipping at their clothes and a sting of cool rain on the back of their necks. "Your pain will give you perspective in time."

"I suppose so."

"It'll make you more compassionate, more understanding when things go wrong for other people."

She glanced up at him. "Do things ever go wrong for you, or do you just jet around jumping off mountains, wearing a coronet?"

He drew in a breath. "That assumption is my biggest hurdle in life. People assume I live to entertain myself and never experience defeat or disappointment or yearning."

"Are they right?" She lifted a slim brow.

He squinted against a gust of sand-laden wind. "I'm smart. I work hard. I do my best to think of others and put their needs first. If no one's interested in listening to my first-world problem, I suck it up and move on."

"I guess a prince would have only first-world problems." She laughed, shielding her eyes from the sand. "I suppose mine are, too. I bet you've never had a broken heart, though."

"Don't be so sure." The rain picked up, big droplets now hitting them hard. "Let's run."

Back at the house, Serena toweled off her face and hair, surprised at how quickly the weather had turned. "I guess this is the edge of the tropical storm. Are we supposed to put storm shutters up or something?"

"I don't know. Let me call Zadir." A minute later Sandro frowned and looked up from his phone. "I can't get a signal."

"I haven't been able to get one since I arrived." She tried again, to no avail. "The coverage is horrible out here and now the Wi-Fi is gone, too. I think the dish isn't working because of the weather. I've been grateful for the solitude so far, but now it's making me nervous. We're so close to the beach. Should we be worried about a storm surge? It's been raining off and on since I got here."

"Possibly." Sandro looked grim. "At least this house has upper floors."

"As long as the whole thing doesn't get washed away." Her stomach clenched at the thought. Which at least gave her some distraction from the much more disturbing feelings happening just below it—especially when she had the misfortune to look at Sandro.

How had she let him kiss her? He'd obviously had second thoughts about it pretty fast, getting them up and headed back to the house, but the effect on her had been hot and heavy and intense and almost frightening.

Overwhelming.

No doubt it was all on her side, like her feelings for Howard and her foolish assumption— encouraged by the simple but elegant engagement ring he'd given her—that they'd live happily ever after.

Boy, was she wrong.

Sandro had moved on and was preheating the oven and rubbing the chicken with butter. The wind had picked up and was whistling through the trees outside, while rain pelted against the large windows.

She tried to distract herself with peeling the potatoes, which he intended to toss with herbs and roast. "I don't believe you've ever had a broken heart."

"Maybe not broken." He looked up, dark eyes warm. "Perhaps just badly bruised. It was a situation where she meant a lot more to me than I did to her."

"Sounds familiar." Suddenly she felt a little better. "She was your girlfriend?"

"I thought so. I was young, maybe eighteen, and she was a sophisticated older woman of twenty-five or so."

"A cougar." She smiled, cutting the eyes out of a potato. "I can see you falling for a cougar."

"She taught me a lot." His slightly lifted brow suggested that much of what she'd taught him happened between the sheets. "Which any eighteen-year-old would be grateful for. But I fell hard. She seemed so wise and interesting. She'd traveled a lot by herself, backpacking around Asia and Africa, meeting all kinds of people, and she had such great stories. I envied her freedom and anonymity. Everywhere I go there are paparazzi waiting to catch me doing something stupid."

"First-world problems," she teased.

"Indeed." A slow smile crossed his broad mouth. "But it became more of a problem when she wouldn't be seen in public with me. She didn't want anyone to know about our affair. She was embarrassed to be involved with a royal."

"That's different. I'd think you'd have more trouble with people wanting to date you because you are royal."

"True. She was repulsed by all the wealth and privilege and entitlement. All the stuff that gets other women excited was a turnoff to her."

"I'll give her credit for being original."

"Yup. And it made me adore her more. I wanted to spend my life with this woman, sharing adventures at her side, but she only wanted me under the cover of darkness. Eventually she got annoyed with me pushing for more and called me a spoiled princeling. She left for a trip to the Caucuses region and I never saw her again."

"She died?"

"No, she married someone else. A much older man, from Georgia." Noting her amusement, he added. "The Georgia where people speak Russian."

"Oh. But you recovered."

"Did I?" He looked wistful, his fingers plunged underneath the skin of the chicken. "I suppose I did, but I've never felt the same way about anyone else."

"I'm sure you will one day." Clearly the kiss he'd given her hadn't distracted him from his long-lost love too much. Still, she was the one who'd asked him about his ex. "I appreciate your sharing. It makes me feel better."

"You're better off without him. He wasn't right for you." Sandro basted the outside of the skin and tucked herb leaves into it.

"So I guess the woman who bruised your heart wasn't right for you."

"Clearly not. And there can't be much worse than being stuck with the wrong person. I think we should break open your champagne and celebrate our freedom."

Her face heated at the realization that he'd found her bottle of champagne in the fridge. What kind of loser brings champagne to a weekend alone? "Why not?"

He washed his hands, put the chicken in the oven, then uncorked the champagne and poured it into two flutes that they found in a kitchen cabinet.

He handed one to her. "Here's to love."

Serena blinked. *He doesn't mean between the two of you, dummy.* "Of course, to love." Her voice sounded a little more nervous and forced than she'd hoped. She sipped quickly to cover her embarrassment, and bubbles went up her nose and made her sneeze.

Lucky thing her skin was dark enough to hide the flush rising up her neck. Why did he have to be so gorgeous? He probably kissed every woman he met. He'd probably forgotten all about that kiss, while the memory of it was growing and blooming in her mind, occupying her thoughts and stimulating her senses.

This was going to be a very long holiday.

She attempted another sip and managed not to splutter it out. Her ears pricked up. "There it is again, I swear I hear a dog."

"I think there's another house in that thicket of trees next door. I saw a roof when we were out on the dunes.

"But is the dog outside in this weather ? That seems dangerous." The wind whistled audibly in the trees, which creaked and groaned under strong gusts. Her fears compounded when suddenly a huge crash sounded from the living room and the lights went out.

8

"That's not good." Her voice sounded thin. It was still daylight, but the sky was black with clouds and the kitchen had only one small window, so they stood in almost darkness.

She heard Sandro put his glass down on the stone countertop. "It sounded like a window breaking." He hurried into the living room, where, sure enough, one of the tall French doors was smashed in, bisected by a palm whose wet grayish fronds now rested on the beige rug.

"Oh, my gosh." She stared at the tree. "That tree wasn't even near the house." The upended roots were out by the road, at least fifty feet away across the lawn. Tiny square shards of glass sprinkled down onto the floor from the smashed door.

"Safety glass." Sandro picked up a piece. "I wish it was impact glass. That stuff won't break even under hurricane-force winds."

"The opening is compromised. Wind and rain can come into the house, and under the right conditions wind could even rush in and blow the roof off." She'd seen a documentary about that.

"We need to board it up."

"They might have hurricane shutters or plywood somewhere. It's a shame we can't get hold of Zadir." They both tried calling the management agent she'd rented from, but her phone couldn't find a signal, and though Sandro managed half a bar standing at the top of the staircase, no one picked up at the other end.

"I'll feel bad if Zadir's house blows down." Sandro looked annoyingly unworried. A tornado would probably just leave his royal hair looking artfully ruffled. "But I imagine it's insured."

"I'm sure it is, but I have another idea. Is there a control panel of some kind?" She began looking around the front hall and kitchen, opening closets and feeling inside the cabinets. At least she came upon a sleek electrical panel tucked discreetly inside the pantry. "I think that I saw signs of roll-down shutters on the outside of the windows."

"Except that now there's no power to roll them down." He leaned against the island as if nothing could bother him.

"Damn, I forgot about that. But didn't you say there's a generator?"

"If there was it should have come on by now. Maybe it's out of gas."

"Or maybe it needs to be switched on manually. Come on, let's find it."

In less than five minutes they'd found a power panel for the generator, and all systems were up and running. But they couldn't lower the shutters on the broken French window as the tree still penetrated the opening.

They had to brave the rain and thunder and lightning and haul with all their might before they finally got the treetop out of the window. Rain streamed into Serena's eyes as she surveyed the scene. "The roots are sticking out into the street. It's a traffic hazard."

"There isn't any traffic."

"Someone might drive by."

"We'll have to turn it." Sandro hauled the heavy root end while she attempted to lever the frond end around until the tree lay across the increasingly sodden lawn.

"Do you hear the dog now?" Arms aching, Serena strained to hear through the pelting rain. Thunder rumbled overhead, and lightning illuminated the house as it struck nearby.

"I think it's just wind in the chimney. We'd better get back inside."

By the time they staggered back in, they were drenched with both rain and perspiration. Serena lowered the electric shutters with a sigh of relief. "We're lucky to have light. I wonder how long before the gas in the generator runs out."

"There'd better be enough in there to cook my chicken." Rain dripped from Sandro's chiseled features. "I take my Christmas dinner very seriously."

"I'm glad they didn't have a turkey at the store. At least a chicken doesn't take that long."

"With any luck there's a huge fuel tank buried underground somewhere."

"I don't usually like to count on luck, but in this case we don't have much choice." Serena felt self-conscious in her wet T-shirt. "I'm going to go change."

"Wait." Sandro said the word quickly, his eyes

focused on hers. Then they drifted lower, to her mouth. Her lips twitched under his bold stare. Should she really just stand here because he'd commanded her to? How did women usually respond to a royal command?

Her thoughts scattered as he tugged her close and pressed his lips to hers.

A shudder roamed through her body, and goose bumps spread down her arms. She'd like to blame the combination of rain and cool air-conditioning for the shiver of excitement coursing through her, but she knew it came from deep inside.

From Sandro.

Chemistry flashed between them like the lightning outside. Her fingers, acting of their own accord, pushed into his damp hair, and a moan escaped her mouth as he deepened the kiss.

When he finally pulled back enough for their lips to part, she was panting slightly, her heart pounding.

Eyelashes half lowered over desire-darkened eyes, he rested his gaze on her face again. "I think we should go upstairs."

9

"Uh, yes." She croaked, barely able to make a sound. "I need to change." Was he suggesting that they climb into bed together?

Her body responded very enthusiastically to that idea—her fingers itched to peel his wet clothes off his strong body—but her mind screamed at her to be sensible.

"Me too." His response came after her thoughts had already run away from her, and she struggled to think what he'd agreed with.

"Oh." So he did just want to change. Fine. "Let's go." She peeled herself further away from him, straightened her T-shirt—he'd fisted his hands into it—and headed for the stairs.

Her insides pulsed with arousal, calling to her.

She tried to settle herself. It wasn't as if she'd gone years without sex. Or even months.

Her body didn't care. Her nipples tingled against her wet bra, and her pants chafed wetly against her trembling legs.

Sandro must be used to women melting under his gaze and turning into quivering Jell-O of need at his touch. Gorgeous and royal? It was a deadly combination.

Not that she was usually susceptible to such superficial qualities in a man.

She was emotional, though, with this whole Christmas-in-hiding thing. Her recent breakup had crushed her confidence and left her worried— would she now be alone forever? Would all her followers decide she was a fraud and desert her?— so maybe she was more vulnerable than usual to the attentions of a practiced player.

"Good lord." The gruff voice behind her made her turn as she walked up the stairs. Sandro's eyes rested on her behind. She blinked. That was crude. She didn't like that. It wasn't gentlemanly.

Still, her body responded with a flush of heat.

How did he do this to her?

She could tell he was attracted to her. Very attracted. She could see it in his hot, steady gaze and feel it in his touch.

But he probably felt the same way about half the women he met.

Did she want to be another notch in his bedpost?

Yes, some traitorous part of her body answered swiftly.

No! She tried to reason. Besides, she'd gone off her contraception so she couldn't, even if she wanted to.

Which she didn't. How would she feel in the morning if she slept with a man she'd just met?

She headed into her bedroom. Sandro followed. "Uh, what are you doing in here?"

"I'm here to help you undress." Mischief danced in his eyes.

"I can handle that all by myself, thanks."

48

"Wet clothes can be quite difficult to remove." His dark gaze drifted to her breasts, where her damp T-shirt clung to the outline of her bra. "I'm sure I'll need some help myself."

Her heart beat faster. "I don't think this is a good idea."

"We're both single, we're stuck here, there's an attraction between us strong enough to light something on fire." A smile tugged at one side of his mouth.

"But…" *This isn't going anywhere. It would just be a fling.* She prided herself on not jumping into pointless dalliances. On saving herself for Mr. Right.

Except that he'd turned out to be Mr. Wrong.

The sound of her own voice surprised her. "You do make some good points."

He took her in his arms. "I'm smarter than people give me credit for."

She giggled as her chest crushed against his. "I might be less smart than people give me credit for. If my readers knew what I was doing right now…" The thought made her stiffen. "I can count on you to be discreet?"

"Of course."

Should she? Temptation clawed at her. Then she heard it again. "The dog. Listen."

This time it was unmistakable. A bark, followed by a long howl of desperation.

"Poor thing. It might be chained outside."

Serena pulled from their embrace and hurried to the window. "I can see the house from here." From the look of its rusting metal roof, it was an older house, wood and rather ramshackle, with a front porch half hidden by a clump of trees. "There it is. It's chained to a porch column. Oh, my. It's soaked." Even from up on the second floor, she could see black and white fur plastered to its skin. "Let's bring it inside."

"Sure." If Sandro was annoyed by the interruption to their almost tryst, he didn't betray it. He was out the door and down the stairs before she could gather her thoughts.

"What if the owner is home?" she wondered aloud as they reached the foyer. "I hope we don't get shot."

Sandro chuckled. "We'll call out first."

They headed out into the blasts of wind and rain. "Ugh, this is nasty." Rain slapped her in the face, and the gusts were distinctly colder than before. "Oh, no, look at the road."

Its bumpy unpaved surface was slick with water—moving water.

"My God, it's a river."

The water was already creeping up onto the lawn. "Quick, let's get the dog."

10

Serena hesitated for a moment. Sensible people didn't step into floods. This was the kind of thing you saw people doing on the news, then getting swept away in water far deeper than they'd expected.

Still, the dog couldn't be more than a hundred feet away. Now that she knew the house was there, she could glimpse it past a thin clump of trees. Sandro was already splashing across the puddle-strewn lawn.

"There's a fence." Sandro climbed over a crumbling picket fence, then helped her over. The property next door was lower, and already water crept over their shoes.

They hurried to the porch. Up close the house was small, old and poorly maintained. Not a safe place to ride out a storm. "If there's someone in here, they should come into our house. A flood could wash this one away." She cleared her throat and called, "Hello!"

The dog barked like crazy, straining at its leash, which was a steel cable like a bike lock.

"Is anyone home?" shouted Sandro. He strode up to the door and banged on it with his fist.

"Come next door with us. The street's flooding."

Serena approached the dog, which had started growling and snarling. "It's okay, sweetheart, we're here to help." She spoke softly, trying not to sound too nervous. Dogs could pick up on that. The steel cord attached to a rusted metal ring screwed into the porch column. "I'll have to detach it at the collar." There was a carabiner clip there. "But I need a leash so it doesn't run off."

"I'll grab it." Sandro rushed over.

"It might bite."

"I'll take my chances."

Oddly, the dog quieted, turning submissive as they both loomed over it, and Sandro took it in his firm hands. She unclipped the leash, and he clutched the stunned dog to his chest.

"No one's home. No lights, no answer," he said through the rain. "Let's get out of here."

The rain and wind together were blinding, and water now lapped at their ankles as they struggled back over the ramshackle picket fence and up across the soggy lawn of the newer house.

Serena battled the wind, trying to get the door closed behind them. When she finally slammed it shut she turned the dead bolt. "The water is rising." Her voice shook. "What if it gets really deep?"

"This house is sturdy. It'll hold." He stroked the dog, which now shivered in the cool air that lingered even though they'd turned the air-conditioning off.

"Let me get a towel." She grabbed the hand towel from the powder room and quickly ruffled it through the dog's soggy fur. Now longer growling or even barking, the dog stared at them with wide blue eyes. "I think it's saying thank you."

"It should. It could have drowned out there."

"We should get upstairs."

"You go on up." He handed her the dog, which settled into her arms. She expected it to be heavy, but it barely weighed anything. "Let me check on the chicken and potatoes."

She laughed. She'd forgotten all about them. "Okay. I guess we'll be having a picnic up there."

She held the little dog close. He was black and white with longish hair, probably fluffy when dry, and he had big, mournful blue eyes. She'd always wanted a dog when she was little. Her parents were far too sensible to get one. Just like she was too sensible to get one now. A dog was a big responsibility.

She couldn't believe someone would leave this one out on the porch in a big storm. It had a bowl of water, which the rain had refilled, but she hadn't seen any food.

The dog sniffed the air. "You can smell that chicken, huh? Well, I bet there will be enough for you, too." It had a pointed black nose, which it turned up at her, and as she bent down it reached up and licked her face.

She recoiled from its wet tongue but couldn't help smiling. "Doggy kisses?" Then she whispered, "I think those are safer than the other kind that you rescued me from."

She looked around. It would make sense to bring all the plates and cups they might need upstairs. "What should we call him? Or is it a her?" She peeked. "He's a him."

"I suppose Lucky is too clichéd?" He pulled the

chicken out of the oven.

The dog was riveted and drooled on her arm at the smell. "I think it's perfect. You are Lucky. If you didn't bark so loud...." She shuddered at the thought of Lucky's fate and kissed his head. She managed to gather some plates and cutlery with her free hand and a bowl for Lucky.

"Let me sauté the vegetables, and we'll be ready to eat."

"I think Lucky's ready right now. I'll put him down upstairs, then I'll come back for more stuff."

Upstairs she put the plates on a dresser and set Lucky down on the soft bedding in one of the bedrooms. No sooner had she turned her back than Lucky was following her back out of the room.

"Stay!"

Lucky cocked a black-and-white ear.

"You do know what I'm saying. Stay!" She turned and left the room, but when she reached the bottom of the stairs, whining made her turn to see him up at the top. "You didn't stay. I don't think you know how to climb down stairs, though, do you?"

The poor little dog looked desperate enough to hurl himself down. "I'm coming back for you. Hold on." She climbed the stairs and picked him up again. "You'll just have to help me get the glasses and napkins."

Sandro had stuffed the chicken and put it on a big serving platter. He now spooned roast potatoes and sautéed greens around it.

"That looks so good."

"Sure you don't want your turkey roll?" He

lifted a brow.

"You might be grateful for that two days from now when we're waiting to be airlifted out of here."

"Somehow that doesn't sound so bad." He flashed a warm grin that turned her insides to liquid.

11

Sandro picked up the big platter and followed her upstairs. Somehow she managed to juggle a stack of napkins, two glasses and a carton of orange juice.

"I guess we can finish the champagne, too. Why aren't I more nervous? I should be petrified, stuck out here practically in the ocean with water rising on all sides, a storm coming from two directions and no phone contact with the outside world."

"You're calm because you know I will take care of you."

The tiny hairs on her neck prickled. Annoyance. Or arousal at his reassuringly protective words? "Who says I need to be taken care of?"

"Not you, that's for sure." He chuckled and followed her into the bedroom she'd chosen because it had a low platform bed they could spread out on.

She settled Lucky on a pillow and started to arrange the plates and make a hard surface for their drinks with a big coffee table book of sunsets, but as soon as Sandro put the plate with the chicken down, Lucky made a beeline for it.

Sandro scooped the dog up in his arms. "Not yet, buddy. We have to carve."

"He might be starving. I wonder when he last ate."

"Good point. We'll do your portion first." She took Lucky back from him, laughing at how he wiggled with excitement, attention fixed on the roast chicken. Sandro carved it into expert-looking pieces.

"Be sure to take the bones out. Dogs can choke on them. I read that somewhere."

Sandro put the chicken on the little plate she'd brought for Lucky, and the dog set upon his meal as if he hadn't seen food in weeks.

"He likes your cooking."

"He has good taste." Sandro winked at her. Again her insides shifted. How did he have this effect on her? One glance from Howard never turned her upside down. "Everything for you?"

"Please."

The food was delicious, and Lucky was such an excellent beggar that they'd fed him almost half the chicken by the time they finally put it up out of reach so he didn't vomit on the carpet.

"I am so glad I'm not here alone," she admitted. "I'd be scared to death by myself."

"It sounds terrible, but I'm rather glad my friends flaked out on me." He poured them both a glass of champagne. "Their relatives live overseas so they end up all alone while everyone else is celebrating Christmas. I got them to Altaleone two years ago, but they both had important meetings this year and couldn't go that far."

"I think it's sweet that you made the effort for them."

"Friends are important to me."

Serena sighed. "I barely keep up with my friends on social media these days. Everyone's so busy with their careers, their partners. My best college friends both moved to L.A. to work in television and I haven't made a real best friend in New York."

"But you must come into contact with people through your line of work, at least through social media."

"Well, they come into contact with my public persona. The real me is a lot more shy. I let myself get too wrapped up in Howard. I probably smothered him."

Lucky climbed into her lap and licked her chin. "Isn't he sweet? I wonder who he belongs to."

"Must be the person who owns that house. I hope they're somewhere high and dry."

"Do you think we have to give him back?" Lucky collapsed in her lap with a huff. He wasn't that big. He looked like a herding dog, but he was skin and bones under his fur—which was fluffing out as he dried. "I don't much like the idea of him being owned by someone who left him out there in this weather."

"You want to keep him, don't you?" Sandro's eyes crinkled into a smile.

Lucky looked up at her with his big blue eyes.

"Oh, I couldn't. I rent my place. I'm not sure dogs are even allowed."

"Maybe they are?" Sandro lifted his champagne glass to meet hers. "Perhaps he's a Christmas gift from the universe to you."

She laughed. "We need to at least find out who he belongs to. But maybe if they're truly not a good home...." She stroked his silky fur. A dog was a big responsibility.

Sandro moved the plates and cutlery off the bed and up onto the high dresser with the rest of the chicken.

"Now, before this dog started barking...where were we?"

Lucky had rolled onto his back and was now fast asleep.

Serena laughed. "About to do something foolish. I owe this dog a big debt of gratitude."

"I have a bone to pick with this hound." Sandro scowled at him. "But I think we can pick up where we left off."

"Really?" She lifted a brow.

"Really." He pressed his finger to his mouth, asking for silence as he took her hand and led her silently out of the room, then closed the door on snoozing Lucky. "In here," he whispered, opening the door to the bedroom they'd been in before. "It'll be easier now as our clothes are dry."

Serena stared at him. He couldn't be serious. "There's a huge storm outside. The neighborhood is flooding."

"All the more reason to act like it's our last night on earth." His wolfish grin sent a shimmy of need to her belly.

"If I only had a few hours to live, I certainly wouldn't choose to spend them—" Sandro stepped forward and slid his arms around her. Her skin sizzled through her clothing.

"You wouldn't choose to spend them how?" He

tilted his head, curious.

"Having sex."

"Having sex sounds like an excellent idea." He leaned in and captured her mouth with a steady kiss. His chest pushed against hers, stirring her breasts.

Uh-oh. Those strange feelings rushed through her again. "That's not what I meant," she rasped, tearing her mouth from his for a moment.

"Don't worry," he breathed hot in her ear. "I know exactly what you mean."

Deft fingers lifted the front of her shirt, revealing her lacy bra and the hard peaks of her nipples.

Uh-oh.

His hot mouth sucked each nipple through her bra, then lowered to her ultrasensitive belly. Where he unzipped her fly and eased her pants down over her hips…

Her core sizzled. Would it be so wrong? They were both adults. And single. Maybe she was too uptight. She'd heard that a lot in emails and comments but always prided herself on her high moral standards and— "Oh!"

Sandro's cool tongue on her hot, sensitive and super aroused flesh made her gasp. Her knees buckled, and his strong arms held her steady. He licked and sucked until her breath came in unsteady gasps and she felt almost ready to explode.

She glanced down to where his dark head moved between her thighs.

"Uh, how come you still have all your clothes on?"

"That's a problem," he murmured, pulling back

enough to look up at her, eyes dark with passion.

Fingers trembling, she plucked at his shirt, and soon they had peeled it off to reveal his ripped torso and the muscles of his arms.

Her body tingled with awareness of his hard masculinity. He unhooked her bra and slid her bikini underwear down over her hips and thighs, apparently relishing each stage of the journey and caressing her legs with his fingers.

He led her to the bed, tugged down the covers with one sharp movement and eased her into the middle of the mattress.

Then, still standing, he stopped and stared. "Your beauty takes my breath away."

His deep, rough voice—or was it that slight foreign accent?—made him sound utterly convincing. Her heart squeezed, and suddenly she was sure.

12

"We can't do this." If she made love with Sandro—if she had sex with Sandro—it would change everything. Even if this was supposed to be a casual fling, it would forge a bond of deep intimacy between them and the experience would stay with her for life.

How could it not?

Sandro didn't respond in words. Instead his lips closed over her hot flesh, his cool tongue flicking over her clitoris until her legs shuddered.

"I said—" Her words faded to a whimper as a movement of his tongue made her hips buck and her body shouted, *Yes! Yes. Yes. Yes.* She climaxed without him even entering her, as his tongue drove her beyond the point of madness.

She felt her belly quiver with the contractions, but instead of relief she had a sudden fierce urge to feel him deep inside her. She pulled him up by the shoulders, and, eyes opening just long enough to roll on a condom, he entered her swiftly but gently.

The sensation almost unhinged her. She climaxed again as he filled her, pushing gently in as she opened up to embrace him.

What was going on? She'd only had an orgasm

twice during sex with Howard. With Sandro she'd had two before he was even fully inside her.

He layered hot kisses on her neck as he started to move, filling her with hot new sensations that shivered to her fingers and toes. Already her heart filled with feelings for this strong, gentle man who'd done so much to transform her lonely Christmas into a festive occasion she'd never forget.

Who'd braved a rising flood for her. Who didn't even seem mad that she'd broken a vase over his head. He was a unique, warm and intriguing guy.

Who just happened to be a royal prince.

Her third climax swept through her, convulsing her muscles and tightening them around him. She felt him explode inside her, a deep groan peeling from his mouth. *"Oddio!"*

She wrapped her arms tight around him, holding on to his hard muscle, trying to ground herself in the sweeping sea of sensation and emotion that tossed her.

When they finally caught their breath, he cracked open his eyes. "What were you saying?"

"I have no idea." She blinked. Of course it was a terrible idea. A huge mistake. A moment she'd live to regret, possibly for the rest of her life.

"What did you say?" she asked, wondering about the strange word he'd uttered.

"I said something?"

"It sounded like Oh-dyo."

"That's Italian for I think you just blew several of my sturdier gaskets." He grinned and kissed her cheekbone.

Sizzling pleasure mingled with regret at the

realization that she'd just had the best, most exciting and satisfying sex she was ever likely to enjoy.

With a man she barely knew and whom she would probably never see again.

A recipe for disaster. Especially if you were a sensitive, romantic, wait-for-the-ring type of person whose heart was already smarting and sore from recent devastation.

But that didn't stop her from doing it again.

And again.

Until the three-pack of condoms from Sandro's shaving kit was gone and they had to put their underwear back on to act as impromptu chastity belts.

Whining from outside the door reminded her of Lucky, who must have woken from his nap. She managed to summon enough energy to stagger to the door on shaky legs and let him in, then lift him on top of the covers.

"Oh. Lucky, I'm glad you didn't see what we got up to." She could barely talk. Her whole body was wrung out and limp from her intense last release.

"Hey, Lucky, welcome in, buddy. This is the best Christmas of my entire life," rasped Sandro. "And that's saying something."

"I can't believe we haven't even checked the weather. The ocean waves could be lapping at the windowsills behind these storm shutters for all we know."

"And right now I wouldn't notice or care. What time is it, anyway?"

She hunted around for her phone, buried on the floor in a pile of their clothes. "Four-thirty a.m. It sounds like the storm is winding down. The wind isn't as loud as it was earlier."

"Either that, or we're in the eye."

Serena climbed back into bed with him. There was no sense trying to see outside until dawn. Nothing they could do. What was done was done. She crawled into his arms and rested her head on his broad biceps.

Am I in the eye of this storm? She felt so calm, like all of this was meant to happen. She was meant to be here, in this house, in this man's arms, on Christmas morning.

Which didn't make any sense at all.

"Get some sleep." His soft murmur filled her ear.

Good advice. "Okay." She needed to get some rest before the sun came up and revealed what kind of devastation had been wrought both on the landscape outside—and in her heart.

"Hey! Anyone in there?" Pounding on the front door downstairs made her sit up and clutch the bedcovers.

She prodded sleeping Sandro. "Someone's here!"

He leaped out of bed and tugged on his pants, then dived down the stairs before she could even get her pants done up. She pulled her shirt back on and followed him. Two men in florescent safety gear over damp fatigues and waders stood in the doorway. She could see through the open door that though the first few feet of lawn by the door were dry, the water lapped just beyond them.

"They're here to evacuate us." Sandro looked up

at her.

"Isn't it a bit late for that?" She didn't really want to go anywhere. The rain had stopped, though menacing gray clouds still hung low as she approached the door.

"We got everyone out of this stretch of woods two days ago. The entire island is under an evacuation order." The taller man looked stern.

"I'm sorry, I didn't arrive until late the day before yesterday. The weather was fine."

He shook his head. "The roads are under water for miles around. Only way out of here is by boat." He tipped his had back and scratched wet hair. "And they say there's snow on the way."

Can't we just stay here? She wanted to ask the question but knew better. "I'm sorry we dragged you out here on Christmas day."

"They saw the car from a surveillance helicopter."

She peered out the door. Sandro's car was on the street, submerged halfway up the doors. "Oh. The rental company won't be too happy about that." She'd put hers in the garage, where hopefully it was still high and dry.

"Why would anyone leave a car out in a storm when there's a three-car garage on this house?"

He's a prince. She wanted to explain but again wisely kept her mouth shut.

Whining at the top of the stairs tugged their attention to Lucky, who didn't know how to climb down. "And we have a dog," she said, running to get him. "He has to come with us."

The second, even surlier man sighed. "Of course he does."

As the outboard motor cut through dark flood water, past floating timbers and broken branches, Serena held on to Lucky. "But what about my car?"

"You won't be allowed back to get that until the water recedes. It could be days. Weeks."

Serena blew out. "I guess I'll just have to go with the flow."

Sandro leaned in and kissed her softly on the lips. "Literally and figuratively."

Her heart filled. Despite the chaos and devastation around her, for once she didn't feel adrift and lost. She felt safe, with Sandro.

"Merry Christmas, Sandro."

"Merry Christmas to you, too, my beautiful Serena."

THE END

1

Don't be impulsive. Be patient. Think about your dreams and goals and wait for your perfect Mr. Right.

The first line of her soon-to-be released book mocked Serena Raines as she marched into Central Park on a biting early February afternoon. *Chin up. Get through it. You'll survive.* This was the kind of advice she'd needed lately. Dreams and goals be damned.

Was he here yet? Serena pulled her wool coat about her and raised her scarf to cover her chin. Maybe she wouldn't even recognize him. They'd spent less than three days together, after all.

Three days that haunted her memory and tormented her nights. She'd rented a beach house to retreat from the world, and then Sandro turned up—followed by a big storm, a dangerous flood…and now a baby growing inside her. She glanced about, half afraid passers-by could read her mind and know her secrets.

It's him.

An electric jolt of recognition struck her, and despite her worries she knew Sandro instantly. His long strides carried him toward her, hair tossing in the cold breeze and leather jacket zipped over his muscled form. His eyes locked on hers, dark and dangerous, as he covered the tarmac between them.

The icy landscape blurred, and time slowed to an agonizing crawl as she tried to figure out the best way to tell him.

Sandro, I'm pregnant.

"Hi! I'm so glad you called. I was beginning to think you were avoiding me." He embraced her in a big bear hug that stunned her so much she didn't lift her arms from her sides.

I was.

Silence hung awkwardly between them. She couldn't begin to figure out how to make polite conversation with this harsh truth hanging over them.

Sandro looked a little confused. Then smiled. "How'd the book release go?"

"It got delayed. It's out next week." Her own voice sounded oddly distant.

"That's great. I'm sure it will be a best seller."

"That's what my publisher says, but I haven't told them my fiancé left me." How could you call yourself an expert on relationships when you couldn't even keep your own? She'd been licking her wounds from this breakup when Sandro burst into her life.

"Did you finally tell your family?"

She shook her head, as shame crept hotly up her spine. "Not yet."

To her surprise, he laughed. "You're so secretive. Seriously, you should just open up to people. You might find they like you more for it."

She stiffened, embarrassment mingling with indignation. He had no idea what she'd gone through the past few days. "I didn't come here for advice. I came because I have to tell you something."

You can do it. Just say it! She could rattle on for ages—on video—about how to apply liquid eyeliner or organize your bathroom cabinet, but when it came to the hard truths she was pathetic beyond belief.

"What? You're scaring me." He scanned her face. "Are you ill? You look ill."

"I'm pregnant."

His mouth opened, then stayed open, but no witty pleasantries flew out. Even the charming and garrulous Sandro was struck dumb by her news. "By your ex?" His voice cracked a little.

Oh, dear. Of course he hoped it was by someone else. A hot tear rolled down her half-frozen cheek. "No. We hadn't...we didn't...not for several weeks."

"Oh."

"I took the test three days ago. I've taken five of them." Tears blurred her vision.

Sandro stepped forward again and tried to take her in his arms. But she stiffened and pushed him away. "It's okay. You don't have to pretend to be happy about it." Her voice sounded distant. "I just thought I should tell you."

Sandro pulled a big white handkerchief from his coat pocket—folded and monogrammed—and handed it to her. "Should we go somewhere more private?"

"No," she said too loud and too fast. She dabbed

at her eyes with the handkerchief and tried to blow her nose. She must look so unattractive right now, on top of her unwelcome news. "Here is better. No one will hear us." She arranged to meet him in a quiet part of the park, where natural foliage blocked views of the winding paths. "I don't expect anything of you. I want to make that very clear."

She could see his chest rise and fall even through his jacket. His handsome face was uncharacteristically grim. "Have you decided what to do about it?"

"What to——?" Realization clicked into place. Was he about to offer to pay for an abortion? It wouldn't even take much money to make this problem disappear permanently. Except that wasn't an option for her. "I'm going to keep it. My dad is a pastor and I was raised to——" Tears flooded her eyes and clogged the back of her throat. What on earth was her dad going to say when he found out his baby daughter was pregnant out of wedlock?

"I'm glad to hear it," he said softly. "And no matter what you say, you can count on me for anything."

"You're very sweet, Sandro. I know this is almost as much of a shock for you as it is for me. I guess one of the condoms leaked. I never should have relied on them alone for birth control. I never did before." She sighed and swiped at her tears. Everyone knew condoms were only ninety-nine percent effective, if that. "But can you keep it a secret?"

He pulled away from her and stared at her like she'd gone mad. "Really? What is it with you and secrets?"

"My book." She blinked, wondering how red her nose was right now. "It's just about to come out. I got the advance nearly two years ago, and I spent it all. The publisher is counting on the book hitting a list so it will get picked up by more stores and make money for them. It was originally supposed to be a collection of articles about my dating misadventures, but since I thought I'd found my one and only I ended up turning it into a book about finding your own Mr. Right. If it comes out that my advice on waiting for Mr. Right is a bunch of nonsense, it won't sell, no stores will want it, and they'll feel like I cheated them."

His face softened, and one side of his mouth hitched slightly in a tiny smile. Which annoyed the hell out of her.

"It's not funny! They paid me two hundred thousand dollars. They could sue me or something."

His smile vanished. "I doubt it, but I do understand your concern."

"And it's not customary to tell people about a pregnancy until about three months in anyway, because it could end in a miscarriage. That happened to my older sister."

"Oh." He frowned and looked thoughtful. Maybe he hoped she'd have a miscarriage.

Maybe she did too.

Guilt stabbed her heart. What kind of person would have a thought like that? She really did deserve all the disaster that was raining down on her.

"Anyway, I've got to go, but I wanted to tell you as soon as possible."

"I know this must have been hard for you. I appreciate your telling me."

"It was eating me up inside," she confessed. Being vulnerable was hard for her. She was much more comfortable presenting a carefully orchestrated façade to the world.

He frowned, thinking. "Let me take you somewhere for a bite."

"No. I have to go. I have a meeting with my publicist at four."

"Later, then."

She shook her head.

"So you're going to disappear out of my life again and not answer any of my calls or texts?"

"I've been busy. I promise I won't do that again. I just didn't want you to think that I expected anything of you."

He lifted a brow. "Because I'm a prince and you're an ordinary mortal?"

"Something like that."

"Didn't I tell you enough times that I hate being treated like royalty? I'm just a guy on the inside."

Not really, she thought. You're a guy who's had everything handed to him on a silver platter—brains, looks, friends, and vast wealth. A guy with the resources to step right over any setback.

And she'd seen his picture in the paper last week with Maya Dunham, who was only twenty-one and up for an Academy Award for her heart-wrenching performance as a doomed nun. They'd had their arms around each other.

"You're a very good person, Sandro." She inhaled deeply. "I could tell that from our brief acquaintance, but you and I are from totally different worlds and there's no use pretending otherwise.

He cocked his head and looked ready to argue.

But his mouth stayed closed so apparently he thought better of it. "You promise to answer my calls?"

She hesitated. "I promise to answer them at a time when it's safe to talk. For example, if you call when I'm with my publicist, then I can't answer."

He drew in a deep breath and sighed it out. "Understood." She could almost hear his brain whirring with thoughts. What was he thinking? "Do you need money?"

"No." She spat the response so fast it sounded rude. "I'm fine. I told you I don't want that kind of help."

"I didn't mean to offend you. Just that if there's any way I can make this easier for you, I—"

"Please keep it a secret, okay? That's the only thing I need right now. In two months' time we can get together again and figure out how to deal with the rest." The taboo of revealing a pregnancy during the first trimester worked in her favor because by then her book would have faded from any lists and her news wouldn't come as an embarrassing shock to her publisher.

"Okay. Can I kiss you?" He hovered close.

Alarm bells rang inside her and she shook her head. "I don't think that's a good idea. I saw a picture of you with Maya Dunham in the papers. You're dating her, aren't you?"

"Only because you blew me off and wouldn't return my calls. I called you every day for two weeks."

"I know. I'm sorry. I just...I..." She couldn't deal with getting in deeper with Sandro—a prince who could never be her real-life Mr. Right—when her heart was still bruised and broken from her fiancé dumping her. "I'm still recovering from my ex. It's going to be a while."

"I understand." He raised her hand to his face and kissed her fingers softly. Damn—the touch of his lips to her skin sent shimmers of heat flooding through her stressed-out body.

One more reason why she needed to stay away from this man.

"I've got to go. I need to print something out before my meeting." She tugged her scarf tighter. "I'll stay in touch."

He nodded. "I miss you, Serena."

She laughed nervously. "You don't know me well enough to miss me."

"I miss you anyway." His dark gaze held hers for a moment.

That man could charm the legs off a table. Her grandmother's long-ago words rang in her ears, reminding her to keep her wits about her. "Thanks for meeting with me." Before he could say anything else, or give her another of those blistering looks, she turned and hurried back toward Central Park West.

Back in her Upper West Side apartment later that afternoon, Serena gave her dog, Lucky, a bone, which made him wiggle his little black and white body with excitement. Then she went into her bedroom and switched on her camera. *New content three times a week.* That was her mantra. She'd followed it religiously since starting her blog back in college. Until lately. When she'd barely managed to pull herself together for one item per week. Since sinking her big book advance into buying her apartment, she earned most of her weekly income from YouTube videos she made and uploaded so it was time to milk the cash cow—or get ready to go hungry. And soon she'd have another mouth to feed.

Her makeup tutorials got the most views, but her viewers had come to expect her trademark life advice on working, dating and being your best you. How was she supposed to do a makeup tutorial with tears streaming down her face? But a new sponsor had sent her a big box of shiny products to review, so she'd better get down to business.

Deep breath! At least her hair looked good. And she'd done a full face of makeup already to make herself look human. Just one more layer to add. She attempted a shaky smile for the camera and moved the mic a little closer. Action!

"Hello, my lovelies"—really? Why was she still using that greeting? She was twenty-five, for goodness sake, not eighteen. "I'm about to unbox some brand-new products from one of my newest favorite companies. They're a boutique cosmetic manufacturer based in San Diego and all of their products are—" Her voice cracked.

She was glad Sandro didn't try to convince her to get an abortion. A lot of guys in his situation would have tried. Who knows how much child support she'd be entitled to if she decided to go after him for it.

Lucky thing she'd rather die.

Deep breath. *This is why there's editing.* She picked up the pretty turquoise box, opened it and pulled out a shiny black compact. "This highlighter is the best thing that's happened to my makeup routine in weeks. Wait until you see what it does. It's like bringing a spotlight with you wherever you go." She managed a big cheesy grin as she opened the compact.

"I know you're all wondering why I've been a little quiet lately." She pulled out a small brush and applied some highlighter to her upper lids. "It's because I have very exciting news."

I'm expecting a baby!

Her viewers would go nuts if she told them that. Though some would be shocked since her wedding was supposedly still in the planning stages.

Except that her wedding wasn't at any stage anymore.

"Remember the book I've been telling you about for months? *Waiting for Mr. Right?* Well the release date is finally here. it's coming out next week and will be in bookstores everywhere."

If they knew that Mr. Right had run off, they'd probably all die laughing. Although she hadn't actually lied and said anything that would indicate the relationship was still on, she hadn't told them it was over, either. She was guilty of a sin of omission, for sure.

She switched brushes and added a subtle dust of highlighter under her eyebrows.

"So I hope you'll all go buy the book and tell me what you think." She forced a shaky smile. "Doesn't this highlighter look like natural sunlight? Watch what happens when I put some above my cheekbones."

She sucked in her cheeks and dusted some on along the top with a fat brush. "It really contrasts with the contouring I did and makes my bone structure look a lot more dramatic than it really is."

JENNIFER LEWIS

Ugh. She'd rarely even wore makeup before she'd started doing these videos. But work wasn't always supposed to be fun and she'd turned out to be good at this. Plus she got all the stuff for free from would-be sponsors.

"I know I usually talk a lot about what's going on in my life," she paused. "But lately I haven't been because it's tricky when your life isn't just about you anymore." She tried for another brave smile. Little did they know she was talking about her baby, not her used-to-be-fiancé. "I'll be sure to tell you more as soon as I can. You know how it is." She gave them a conspiratorial wink. "But right now, let's talk about this lip gloss that I just discovered…"

Somehow she made it through the six-minute video—six-minute lengths seemed to get the most views—and shut off the camera with a sigh.

What a phony. And she'd have to edit out all those awkward pauses where she was teetering on the brink of tears.

She'd have to tell them all sooner or later but first things first. She needed that damn book to sell. Her mortgage was too big, and her finances had been teetering on the brink of disaster ever since she'd taken it on.

She'd felt like such a superstar when she got that big advance that it had seemed like everything would be smooth sailing from there on out. Then she spent the advance on her condo and reality had set in. She found herself struggling to pay the high maintenance fee on top of the mortgage. She'd put the place on the market six months ago and even lowered the price twice, but so far no one was interested.

The tears she'd been holding back spewed forth

78

and made a glittery highlighter-laden trail over her carefully contoured cheek. "I need to talk to someone. Like, really talk to someone."

Most of her New York friends were all busy, successful career people whom she mostly networked with. She wouldn't even call them friends, really. Her high school and college friends were either back at home in Virginia or spread out across the country at their various jobs.

Asia had always been her shoulder to cry on. She still lived back at home and no doubt ran into Serena's mom at the supermarket from time to time. Serena's mom had no idea that her daughter's engagement had ended more than six weeks ago.

"If I don't talk to someone I'm going to lose my mind." Saying it out loud convinced her that it was true. Wasn't talking to yourself the first sign of madness?

She picked up her phone and scrolled for Asia's number, wishing she'd kept in touch more regularly.

"Hello." Asia's sweet voice soothed her. And terrified her. Was she finally about to tell someone, anyone, other than Sandro the truth?

2

"Asia, hey, it's me, Serena." There was an awkward pause. "Serena Raines."

"Serri! I don't believe it. I was beginning to think I'd never hear from you again. I do try to keep up with you on social media, but it's not easy because you're so busy. My goodness, you're everywhere. And I already have a preorder in for your new book. Maybe I'll finally manage to figure out how to snag my own Mr. Right." Serena battled the emotion rising in her chest. "Hey, Serri, are you okay?

Serena couldn't hold back the choking sobs. The sound of her oldest friend's voice—and the realization that she, like everyone else, now only knew the glossy, scented, pearl-highlighter-dusted version of her—made emotion crash through her. "I'm not okay. Not at all. Do you have time to talk?"

Asia listened patiently and mercifully without offering any banal advice, while Serena sobbed out the story of her broken engagement, her Christmas holed up in the Georgia sea islands—which led to her chance encounter with Sandro—

"A prince! He sounds yummy."

"Oh, trust me, he is. Except that it doesn't end there."

"Seriously, Serena? You break up with one gorgeous, wealthy man and start dating a prince? And you expect me to be sympathetic? You're too much, girl."

"We're not dating." She sighed. "In fact, he's very publicly dating someone else." Then she screwed up her courage. "And I'm pregnant with his baby."

The silence was deafening.

Serena wondered if the line went dead. "Did you hear me?"

"Are you sure?"

"You should see the amount of plastic sticks I've peed on. I told him this afternoon, and he was really nice about it."

"What's really nice? Did he offer to marry you?" Her friend's voice had dropped an octave to her famous scolding tone.

"No. Don't be silly. He's a prince. And like I said he's dating Maya Dunham."

"Maya Dunham! Are you kidding? I love her. She had me weeping buckets last week."

"You're not helping. So obviously there's no future for me and him, and I need to figure out how to do this on my own. If I can't even manage to tell my parents, how am I supposed to tell all my subscribers? I feel like such a fraud. But I can't afford to do anything to derail this book release."

Asia sighed. "I hear you. I can't believe Howard cut and ran. What a jerk. I never liked him anyway."

"You never met him."

"I didn't like the sound of him from your online posts. He sounded like an annoying perfectionist. I think you're much too good for him."

"Not according to him." Damn, it felt good to talk about this instead of sobbing over it in private. "He said he couldn't stand living in a social-media fishbowl."

"You're better off without him."

"Not that I have a choice."

"I'd love to see his face when you show up all over social media on the arm of a prince."

"That's not going to happen."

"Hey, you're going to be giving birth to a prince. Your child will be royal. How about that?"

Serena's gut clenched. "Don't get carried away. They might not even acknowledge the baby. They're snooty European royals, and I'm a black American."

"You can prove paternity with a DNA test."

Serena shook her head. "That's not the direction I want to go with this at all. I don't want to prove anything. I don't want to count on anyone. I just want to make sure I earn enough money to support this baby, and right now this means putting my energy into the book tour."

"What kind of tour?"

"L.A., New York and Chicago. Three morning television shows. Nine radio shows. And bookstore signings. The publisher considers it a big honor. I can't say no."

"Damn. I hope you don't get morning sickness."

"Me too."

Her first tour stop was Los Angeles, where she

was booked on a local morning magazine show. Despite the one hundred plus videos she'd uploaded to YouTube, she'd never been on a real television show. She felt like tossing her saltines and wasn't sure if it was morning sickness or stage fright.

Sandro had texted her twice to ask how she was doing and both times she'd responded, **Fine, thanks.** She wondered if Maya Dunham was lying next to him while he typed. So it came as a horrible surprise when she showed up to the studio green room—which wasn't green—and found Maya Dunham sitting there, waiting to go on the show before her.

"Hi, I'm Serena," she said bravely, working hard to keep her face expressionless.

Maya looked slowly up from her phone. "Can I help you?"

"Uh, no. Sorry. I didn't mean to interrupt you." Wow. Nice. And she always played such sweet girls in her movies.

"Oh, you're not." Maya tucked her phone away. "I'm not thrilled about being up this early. My publicist is making me be here."

"Mine too," she said conspiratorially, suddenly feeling a sense of kinship with Maya. "But I suppose I should be grateful for the publicity. I'm promoting a book."

"Oh." Maya looked disappointed.

"Congratulations on your Academy Award nomination," she said brightly. She wasn't going to be bitter.

"Thanks." Maya pulled her phone out.

Serena drew in a slow breath. She'd been dismissed. No tears, though! Pregnancy was wreaking havoc on her emotions, but she'd spent way too much time on her makeup this morning to ruin it.

I'm having your boyfriend's baby. That would be a conversation starter.

Mercifully the production assistant came for Maya and took her into the studio.

She could text Sandro right now. He clearly wasn't with Maya. The silly thought made her laugh. Not that it was any of her business whom he was with. He might have dated her if she'd given him a chance.

Which she hadn't. She was way too wary of rejection for that. If she'd known she was already pregnant it might have made sense to take the risk, but now it was already too late. He'd moved on.

"Can I get you a coffee?"

"No, thanks. I'm nervous enough already." She smiled at the young PA. "Some water would be great, though." What if her mouth dried out and she couldn't speak? What if the soles of her new shoes were so slippery that she skidded across the studio as she entered? What if her mind went completely blank and she found herself staring at them all like a moron, her mouth opening and closing like a fish?

"Serena?" A deep voice jolted her from her train wreck of thoughts.

Sandro?

A glance up confirmed that it was him. Panic surged through her on a wave of nausea. "What are you doing here?"

She'd asked the question as a reflex. She knew the answer and regretted asking as soon as the words were out of her mouth. He looked breathtakingly gorgeous, as always, in a black sweater and dark jeans. How did he manage to wear jeans and still look unmistakably like a prince?

"I'm here to pick up Maya." He looked apologetic. "We're heading straight for the airport."

"Going back to New York?" Again she asked it just to fill the air with words while her panicked brain struggled with his presence. His movements were none of her business.

"Yes." Again, he looked rueful. As if it was rude of him to go back to New York without her. Could he be any more adorable? Damn him. "Her movie is opening there tonight."

"Great."

"I am here for you, you know," he said softly.

The PA burst in with a bottle of water. Serena took it with a rushed thanks and gulped some down. But the PA didn't leave. She started gathering up a plate and coffee cup that Maya must have left there and rearranging some magazines on the coffee table.

Serena racked her brain for something genuine to say if the PA ever left, but instead she stood there, muttering to someone over her headset, then she beckoned for Serena to enter the studio.

Serena nodded stiffly at Sandro, put down her water and followed. There was no point comparing herself to Maya Dunham. Maya was a famous actress, and Serena only applied highlighter on YouTube videos and pontificated about how to find Mr. Right when she'd really only been engaged to Mr. Wrong all along.

She pinned a bright smile to her face as they headed toward the set. She could see Maya laughing, looking glamorous in her tight white jeans and white mohair sweater that perfectly set off her shiny red hair. Suddenly she felt frumpy as heck in the skirt and sweater that had looked so chic in the changing room at H&M.

Focus! Clapping surprised her, and she peered around the partition and saw the studio audience. Terrifying. And now Maya was marching toward her, looking right past her as if she weren't even there. Maya smiled her brilliant, red-lipsticked smile, and Serena turned (a huge mistake) to see Sandro standing behind her, waving to Maya from the open door of the green room.

Serena wished the floor could open up and swallow her, but instead the PA prodded her toward the set and she stepped out into the hot studio lights, blinking, prepared to make up nonsense about how to find Mr. Right for an audience of strangers who had no idea she knew less about that subject than any of them.

"How did you know when you'd found the one?" the heavily made-up female host leaned toward her.

Serena racked her brain to think of why she'd decided to marry Howard. She could no longer remember. "Something inside me just...sparkled." She smiled, recalling the fluttering feeling she'd had in her stomach when Sandro first kissed her. "Everything was different."

"Sounds like the infamous chemistry."

"That always gets me into trouble," chimed in the younger and rather sexy male host.

Me too.

"Chemistry is just the beginning." She tried to conjure her talking points. "There are more important things to consider—do you share the same goals? Will you enjoy the same lifestyle? Will your families get along?"

All reasons that things could never work out between her and Sandro.

"So instead of letting ourselves be swept away by chemistry, you're saying that you should put the brakes on until you figure out the other stuff," said the female host.

"For a lasting, long-term relationship, yes." It wasn't bad advice, was it? It hadn't worked out for her—not yet anyway—but it still made sense. She wasn't actually lying to people.

"So when is the big day?"

She froze and tried to force a shaky smile to her lips. "We haven't actually set the date yet. There's just so much to plan!" She hoped her voice didn't sound too squeaky. "When you've waited for Mr. Right, there's no harm in waiting a little longer to get everything perfect."

Okay, that sounded stupid, but luckily the male host jumped in with some platitude and held up her book.

Job done! They went to a commercial break, and she staggered off the stage, hoping she hadn't humiliated herself too badly or said anything that would come back to haunt her when she finally revealed the truth about her broken engagement.

Sandro and Maya were gone. Phew! Normally she wasn't the kind of person to go nuts and say something like, "Sandro, only seven and a half more months until our baby is due!" but with the pregnancy hormones she wasn't exactly in her right mind so she was glad not to have the temptation.

New content three times a week. Serena whipped out her phone and videotaped a vlog about her talk show appearance, glad of the opportunity to reveal genuine emotion and raw nerves and share an honest moment with her viewers. She didn't mention Sandro—or Maya Dunham, whom she might have been thrilled to meet just a week ago, before she knew about her relationship with Sandro.

She headed to a bookstore and vlogged some more while standing in front of her book on the shelves. It was kind of a thrill seeing her book there on the new releases shelf next to some of her heroes. She even stood to the side and watched someone come in and pick it up and flip through it. She was ready to offer to sign it if they took it to the register, but they put it back and picked up a book called *Decorating with Wicker.*

What would have happened if she had agreed to go for coffee or dinner with Sandro? The chemistry between them was undeniable. Maybe he'd have ditched Maya Dunham and swept her off her feet.

Until his royal family freaked out about him dating a black girl and she got unceremoniously dumped. In public.

Definitely not worth the risk.

Her phone rang. It was the publisher's publicist congratulating her on the morning's appearance and telling her she now had a radio interview early that afternoon at a studio in downtown L.A.

At least they're happy, she thought. She was unwrapping a sandwich at a table in the bookstore coffee shop when a pretty girl of about eighteen came up to her. "Excuse me, are you Serena Raines?"

"I am." She looked surprised. She rarely got recognized by fans. But then she rarely went out on the street in the kind of full makeup she did for her videos, either. "Would you like to join me?" Why not be generous and welcoming?

"Wow, thanks! I'll just get myself a coffee." The girl looked genuinely thrilled. As if she were a real celebrity like Maya Dunham. Serena was congratulating herself on having "made it" in at least one new way when her phone rang again.

Howard. Her gut clenched.

"Hello." She glanced about, hoping no one was listening.

"Serena, what's going on?"

"What do you mean?" She kept her voice very calm and level. She didn't want Howard to accuse her of being overemotional. She'd heard enough of that for one lifetime.

"I got a call from a journalist this morning asking me what it feels like to be Mr. Right."

Her blood chilled. "What did you tell them?"

3

"I told them they had the wrong number, but obviously that won't work for long. Why are you telling people we're still together?"

She inhaled a shaky breath. "It's just this book...*Waiting for Mr. Right*." She glanced about, hoping no one had overheard. "You know they gave me a big advance for it, and I spent it on the apartment." That she had once hoped to share with him. "So I really need to put everything behind this launch so it will hit a list and make them feel they got their money's worth."

"You don't need to do that. They can't get the money back."

She'd been told that before. Still...it was embarrassing to have a book called *Waiting for Mr. Right* to come out and have everyone know you were still waiting.

The pretty girl—with perfect hair and eyebrows to die for—sat down in front of her with a steaming cup of pumpkin-scented coffee.

She had to get rid of Howard. "Uh, I need to go. I'm sorry that happened."

"But what about when it happens again? Maybe then I'll just tell them the truth."

"Not yet," she breathed through a smile at the girl. "Please. Give it a couple of weeks."

"A couple of weeks." She heard one of his dramatic sighs. "Okay. I suppose I can do that. But I'm seeing someone else now, so anything longer than that would be awkward."

I'm seeing someone else. The thought fogged her brain and sent pain dancing along her nerves. How? They'd only been broken up a few weeks.

You already slept with someone else. Why wouldn't he? The girl's worried expression jerked her back to reality. "I really appreciate it."

Howard hung up in his usual brusque style.

"Is everything okay?"

"Oh, yes, just a little snag. Nothing to worry about. What lipstick is that? It's gorgeous."

"It's Cover Girl," said the girl, conspiratorially. "I can't really afford the expensive stuff."

"Oh, I used drugstore makeup all the time before companies started sending me samples."

"You're so lucky." Maybe the girl was younger, like sixteen. She still had that innocent sparkle. "I totally want to be you when I grow up. My sister got pregnant last year and now she has a baby and it's really hard for her. She didn't wait for Mr. Right."

"Oh." Guilt and embarrassment seared through Serena like a hot knife. "Sometimes these things just happen. Who's to say it's not for the best?" She attempted a smile but could feel it failing so she took a hasty bite of her sandwich.

"Maybe you're right. My mom's really mad at her, though. And I'm not allowed to even date anyone."

"No harm in waiting," she said with a wink. "I didn't date anyone until I was in college. There's no sense in racking up a lot of mileage dating different boys. It really is better to wait for someone perfect for you."

Is my nose growing? She half wanted to check it in her compact mirror.

"Howard sounds so sweet. I love that he buys little gifts for you."

Serena stiffened. He'd only bought her a gift once—a little inlaid box to keep her paper clips in. She'd just been so shocked and pleased that she'd talked about it a lot. It was the type of little detail her followers loved. "That kind of thing isn't really important."

The girl leaned in and blew the steam off her coffee. "What is the most important thing to look for in a relationship?"

"I suppose I should say that you'd better read my book and find out." Serena couldn't lie to her. "But the truth is it's probably different for everyone. Relationships are a crapshoot. I suppose you just have to jump in and hope for the best."

"Well, I'm going to download your book and read every word so I can turn out just like you."

Maybe it was nerves. Or too much stress. Or the pregnancy hormones running rampant in her system. For one horrible second Serena wasn't sure whether she was going to laugh or cry, and the next moment she burst out laughing so hard she thought she might bust a gut.

"Are you okay?"
"I have no idea."

At her radio interview, the host asked her—by name—about Howard. Had she really used his name so much in the book? That seemed like a terrible idea from where she was sitting right now. By the end of the interview she was battling tears again, and she hoped no one could hear it in her voice.

She hustled out of the studio building as fast as she could, terrified someone would kindly ask her out to dinner and she'd have to wrap herself in more lies.

If the book didn't hit the list this week, it likely wasn't going to. If it did, she could heave a sigh of relief. Either way she could finally get the truth off her chest and get on with her life.

Ping! The sound of a text arriving made her jump as she stepped out of the elevator into the lobby. It was from Sandro. She hadn't typed his name into her contacts—that felt too risky—but she recognized his number. **Call me.**

Really? He couldn't preface his demand with a hint of what he wanted? She knew he was with Maya. They must have arrived in New York. Maybe they were relaxing with some cocktails and he wanted to have a chuckle over how awkward that situation was in the green room earlier.

She couldn't call him now. She was in public. She pushed out through the revolving door and tried to remember what her rental car looked like, let alone where she had parked it.

Then her phone started ringing. She picked it up to forward the call to voice mail so she didn't have to hear it ring six times but stopped when she saw that it was her mom calling. Guilt soaking through her, she answered the call. "Hi, Mom!"

"Honey, I heard you on the radio! You sounded so calm. Just like a professional."

Whoa, the show must have gone coast to coast if her mom heard it all the way in Virginia. She didn't even know it was national. "Thanks, Mom. It was all an act. I was terrified." At least that was true.

"We haven't seen you and Howard in ages. I know you're both busy, but we miss you."

Ouch. Could she really keep lying to her mom?

The sinking feeling in her gut gave her the answer. "Mom, there's something I need to tell you." She glanced about to see if anyone was in earshot.

"What, honey?"

"Howard and I broke up." She half whispered it, afraid that someone from the radio station would overhear. Then she held her breath.

"What?" Her mom sounded poleaxed. As well she might, when her daughter was out pimping a book about her relationship with him.

Where was her damn car? It was a silver Toyota. Or maybe a Nissan. She glanced at the key. A Honda, then. She marched down a long row of cars, looking for it. Half the cars were silver sedans just like it.

"I didn't know how to tell you. I'm so embarrassed to be out promoting a book about finding true love when I'm back being single again."

Single and pregnant.

She wasn't going to mention that part. Not yet.

"Oh, no." Her mom sounded pained. Now she'd have to tell all her friends that her daughter wasn't getting married after all. "What happened?"

"He changed his mind."

"Maybe he'll change it back?"

"I wouldn't want him to. He obviously doesn't love me." Her voice sounded as flat as her spirit. "Maybe he never did and I was kidding myself all along."

"Men sometimes get cold feet. Maybe you were overdoing it with the wedding planning. That can make guys nervous, especially if it's all really expensive."

She knew her mom thought her New York lifestyle extravagant. And she hadn't told her mom how much money—an insane amount by any normal standard—she'd borrowed to buy her apartment.

"I wasn't being a bridezilla, Mom. Or at least I don't think I was." Since it was her "job" to get worked up about details and share them with her followers, maybe she had gone a bit overboard.

"Perhaps your dad could talk to him."

Her chest tightened at the thought that her mom wanted to salvage the relationship that badly. "It's too late, Mom. It's actually been a few weeks since we broke up. He's seeing someone else."

"Oh, goodness. My poor baby. Why don't you fly down here and let me pamper you for a few days?"

Emotion welled in Serena's chest, and for a moment she yearned to do just that. "I'm on this book tour. The radio show you heard was part of it. I have a few more days of interviews. Please don't tell anyone I broke up with Howard. Not just yet. I can hardly promote a book about finding Mr. Right when I'm still single."

And pregnant. The thought smacked her again.

"I see what you mean. Estelle does flap her lips a lot. And Diane too. I'll keep quiet about it until you tell me. And I'll tell your dad to do the same."

"Okay." Of course her mom would tell her dad. It crushed her that her father would know she'd struck out in the man department. Her dad was a big, strong, quiet man who probably hadn't been a huge fan of Howard's fast-talking-lawyer style but who'd done his best to befriend him in a man-to-man fashion and to welcome him into the family.

What on earth would her dad think of Sandro?

Her thoughts had run away with her, and she lost track of the conversation. "What did you say?"

"If it's been a few weeks, why didn't you tell me sooner?"

"I just needed to lick my wounds alone for a bit." Finally, she found the car and climbed in. "And it happened right before Christmas. I couldn't face that many people when I was feeling down."

"So what did you do at Christmas? I thought you spent it with Howard."

"I rented a house in the Georgia sea islands."

"That's where your great-grandpa was born. You're lucky you didn't get caught in that freak Christmas storm."

"I did get caught in the storm." And she'd been caught in another whirlwind too—Sandro. "It was more exciting than I had anticipated."

"Thank goodness you're okay."

Am I okay? She wasn't sure. "I'm glad you heard my radio interview. I've got to go. I need to drive back to my hotel."

"I understand, honey. And come visit once your book tour is done. I'll make your favorite, pot roast."

"Thanks, Mom. You're the best." She hung up the phone, feeling both better and worse. Talking to her mom had soothed her, but she felt terrible that she couldn't bring herself to mention her pregnancy. She knew her mom wouldn't be quite so understanding about the baby. She'd grown up with a million stern lectures on waiting until marriage. Par for the course when your father was a pastor.

No, she had to get through this thing one day at a time and she'd done enough for today. Now she just needed to catch her flight back to New York and crash because tomorrow she was appearing on a New York morning show, then had to head out to Chicago for a radio show that evening and another morning show the next day.

She'd call Sandro tomorrow.

4

Sandro paced back and forth in his New York apartment. There was only one woman he wanted and needed—Serena. And he couldn't have Serena with Maya still in the picture.

He took Maya out to dinner at a quiet sushi restaurant and told her he needed some space.

Her famous violet eyes flashed. "You need some space?" She leaned into the table and hissed. "What kind of garbage cliché is that? I'm in the public eye. You can't just dump me!"

"We've known each other less than a month, Maya. It's not like I'm breaking off a long relationship here." He spoke calmly and tried to sound compassionate when all he could think about was getting out of here and going to see Serena.

"You've flown on a plane with me—twice! The press got pictures both times. We're practically a one-name couple right now."

"A what?"

"You know…Mayandro. Or Sandaya."

Sandro stared for a second, then laughed. "Don't those relationships always end in an acrimonious breakup?"

To his surprise, tears filled her eyes and suddenly he felt like a cad. He hadn't thought of their relationship as anything other than an enjoyable fling, perhaps partly because she was so famous and busy. "You're going to tell the press it's over," she breathed.

"I have no intention of talking to any papers. They can believe and print what they like. I live my life without giving them a single moment of my attention."

"Easy enough when you're a prince." A solitary tear rolled down her cheek, glittering like a diamond. "I'm just another pretty girl from the Midwest, and the press are a great part of the reason I have a career at all."

"You are a very talented actress." In fact he suspected she was working her gift right now. "You have a great career ahead of you."

She gazed at him, eyes sparkling with tears. "Could you do something for me, Sandro? There's an event I really need you to come to. It's a premiere tomorrow night."

"What? Your film already premiered."

"It's not for my film. It's for Angelina Jolie's new movie. I promise I won't ask again, but it's too late for me to find another date and I can't just show up alone." Two bright tears flowed over her cheeks.

"Okay," he said grimly. "Tomorrow night. But I want to be completely clear that I am coming as your friend, not as your lover."

She let the tears fall, and they dripped onto her skimpy camisole. "Why, Sandro? Why are you breaking up with me? I thought we were good together."

He sighed. Again he felt like a jerk. They did get along well, though she was a bit too intense and demanding for his liking. "There's someone else. Someone I knew from before."

Maya's eyes narrowed. "I bet she's pregnant."

Sandro startled. "What makes you think that?"

"Why else would someone get back together with an ex?"

"Any number of reasons."

"But just from your expression I can see I hit on the right one."

"I can't say anything. It's a private matter."

"So this really has nothing to do with me." Her eyes had dried and suddenly looked very focused.

"Not really, no."

"I've got to go." She stood up suddenly and grabbed her tiny purse. "I'll pick you up at your place tomorrow night. Don't forget." Then she leaned in, and before he could think of a way to prevent it, she'd laid a cool kiss on his lips.

Her trademark fruity scent hung in his nostrils as she marched for the door.

He heaved a sigh of relief and signaled for the waiter. Now he could go see Serena with a clear conscience.

Serena had taken a taxi back from the airport, picked up Lucky from her neighbor and was now curled up with Lucky on the sofa reading *What to Expect When You're Expecting*.

She was just cringing at the part about hemorrhoids when her phone rang and made her jump. The doorman in the foyer of her building. "Mr. Leone downstairs for you."

Sandro? She didn't want to make a scene by turning him away. "Please send him up."

Heart pounding she tucked her ereader under the sofa cushion, and ran around straightening up the place.

She peered through the peephole on her door and watched the elevator doors open and Sandro step out.

He towered in the hallway, blocking the light from the ceiling. She cursed at the way her body responded to his broad, steady form on her threshold.

Serena ushered him inside, resisting the urge to yank him out of the public area. When she'd closed the door behind him, heart pounding, she turned to face him. "How did you know where I lived?"

Lucky jumped up and down at his feet, and Sandro bent to pet him. "I make it my business to know about everything that's important to me." He ruffled Lucky's ears, and her little dog wiggled with pleasure. "I see that someone remembers me."

"He's friendly to everyone." She spoke coolly, unnerved that he'd shown up with no invitation or warning. And that his presence had such an unsettling effect on her. "Why are you here?"

"You didn't return my text this afternoon so I thought I'd better come in person." His dark eyes were serious. "I just broke up with Maya. I told her I couldn't be with her anymore because there was someone else more important to me."

Serena stared in disbelief. "Did you tell her I was pregnant?"

Sandro looked a little sheepish and for a moment she got ready to be mad. "Uh...no."

Serena let out a tiny sigh of relief. "Good. It needs to be a secret. I don't want to tell anyone until at least three months are over."

"Not even your family?"

Serena crossed her arms ever her chest, which reminded her that once again she was wearing her least flattering pajamas. "I did tell my mom that I broke up with Howard."

"But you didn't tell her about me." Sandro lifted his brow.

"No. Why would I?" Serena had no idea what to say. "There is nothing happening between us."

"Except that we're having a baby together." Sandro leveled a steady gaze at her. "You can't pretend it isn't happening."

"I'm not pretending anything. I'm just trying to take it one day at a time. It's all a bit too much for me right now."

He stepped forward and took her hands in his. She could feel her hand shaking, but his fingers around hers were warm and steady. "You're not doing this alone," he said softly. His eyes were kind. "I'm here with you. We're going to do this together."

Serena blanked as emotions swirled around her. His words sounded too good to be true. She didn't trust them. "We barely know each other. The man I thought I was going to spend the rest of my life with just walked away from me without a backward glance. How can I trust you? I don't trust anyone right now. Not even myself."

"I don't blame you." Sandro tilted his head slightly. "All I know is that the universe thrust us together and I'm supposed to be here with you right now."

"Your confidence is inspiring." Serena inhaled a ragged breath. "But I'm exhausted from visiting studios and putting on a brave face and pretending to be someone who I used to think I was. I'm not even sure who I am anymore."

"Come, sit down." Sandro ushered her toward the sofa.

"Shouldn't I be saying that? This is my apartment."

Sandro laughed. "My friends do say I tend to make myself at home a little too easily." Serena sat down very slowly on the sofa as if it might suddenly be pulled out from underneath her. She really had no idea what was going to happen most of the time lately. Was Sandro—the prince—really suggesting that he wanted a romantic relationship with her? It didn't seem likely. Especially not while she was wearing these blue-and-green flannel pajamas with red-and-white-striped socks.

"Why are you laughing?" He peered at her with those captivating dark eyes that sent a jolt of electricity through her every time he glanced at her.

"I was just thinking about how you can't resist me because of my sexy clothing." She indicated her attire.

He lifted a brow slightly. "I know what's under them."

Her body heated under her baggy pj's as memories of the pleasure they'd shared rushed over her.

103

Then she remembered the baby. "I'm pregnant. I don't feel at all sexy." She was lying. Well, not entirely. She hadn't felt even a hint of desire for anything—except sleep—all week. Until Sandro showed up.

Sandro frowned. "Everything happened so fast because of the strange situation with the storm and the blackout. In a way I wish it hadn't unfolded so quickly. I would have liked to get to know you better first, then perhaps you wouldn't be so wary right now."

She sighed. "I still don't quite understand what happened between us. It was very intense and took me by surprise."

"It took me by surprise too. I thought I was just going to spend a couple of quiet days with my friends and eat some turkey." His warm grin disarmed her. "I had no idea I was going to encounter the most beautiful and intriguing woman I've ever met."

Serena's stomach quivered. She tried to remind herself that he was a seasoned charmer who always knew just the right thing to say to a girl.

"I would challenge you, but I suspect that somehow I'd only seem like I was fishing for compliments."

"I mean it." Sandro leaned in slightly. The warm, male scent of him further undermined her defenses. "I love that you've built a career out of giving people advice. That kind of confidence is very sexy."

"I miss that confidence. It seems to have gone into hiding."

"Nonsense." Sandro smiled. "Despite your recent heartbreak and the surprise news that you're carrying a child you still managed to get out in public and represent yourself well. I watched your TV interview before we left the studio this morning. No one could have any idea that you weren't on top of the world."

"Perhaps I should be up for an Academy Award myself?" She said it as a joke, but suddenly it didn't seem so funny. "Wait—I'm not comparing myself to Maya Dunham in any way."

"You don't have to." Sandro looked at her steadily. The heat of his gaze had a strange effect on her body. She was glad he couldn't see her nipples tightening under her baggy pajama top. "I find you more exciting in every way."

Anxiety flared in her gut. What did he think would happen now? "But remember everyone thinks I'm still together with Howard. Besides, we barely know each other and neither of us has any idea what is going to happen between us. I don't want to get my heart broken again, especially not in public."

"I understand. We can be very discreet." His mouth was very sensual. He had a way of twisting it that drew her attention and made her want to kiss it.

Would it be so bad to kiss him?

Yes, it would be disastrous. Look what happened last time! She needed to protect herself, and her reputation, from further potentially public disaster.

Serena steeled herself. "I think it would be better if we didn't see each other for a few weeks."

Sandro frowned. "We can see each other in secret." He rubbed her fingers gently with his broad thumb, stirring heat.

"This is New York City, nothing is secret here. My building has a doorman, for one thing, and I bet yours does too." She tried to manage a smile. "The last thing I need is to have the media thinking I'm cheating on Howard. At least until my book has a chance to hit the lists."

Sandro rubbed her hand. "Is the book selling? Or is that a rude question to ask the author?"

"It's funny, I really don't think of myself as an author. I think of myself as a blogger, even though that's actually the thing I do least of these days. It's hard to make money from blogging anymore. The book seems to be doing okay from what I've heard. I haven't seen the final numbers for this first week, but I will find out in two days if it hit a list. I would love to hit the *New York Times* best-seller list again, so my publisher won't think it was a fluke the last time." Her first book—a collection of blog posts about being a single girl in the big city and published as *Living Your Best Life*—had been a surprise hit that paved the way for the big advance on this one.

Sandro smiled. "I think you're going to blow them away."

"Until everyone discovers that I'm a total fraud."

"Or that you just found the wrong Mr. Right the first time." He grinned. "And now you found the real one."

Serena blinked. Could it really be that easy?

Her gut told her no.

What were the chances that things were going to work out with Sandro? For one thing his family likely expected him to marry some kind of princess or aristocrat, and she was anything but.

Then Sandro leaned in and—before she could summon the power to resist—he kissed her full and hard on the lips.

5

Serena felt her lips part and Sandro's tongue slid between them like a key. All her fears and inhibitions suddenly floated away. Her hands took on a life of their own, fisting into his dark sweater, roaming up into his thick hair. Even the stubble of his hard chin against her cheek seemed wonderfully soothing and reassuring.

He's here, isn't he? That said volumes. And he'd broken up with one of the hottest stars in Hollywood to be with her. That meant something.

She kissed him back, letting her tongue seek his. His arms closed around her, drawing her into a cocoon of his hard muscles. Oh, how great it would be if she really could just relax into his strength and let go of all the tension and anxiety that seemed to be the only thing keeping her going lately.

Hot sensation flared in her core and flowed through her all the way to her fingers and toes. Her entire body responded to his and she felt herself drawing closer, as if by just kissing him hard enough she could bridge the distance between them.

I had no idea I was going to encounter the most beautiful and intriguing woman I've ever met.

Did he really feel that way about her? His kiss said yes. His hands said yes. Her heart said yes.

Her fingers slid under the hem of his soft sweater and pressed into the warm skin beneath. She raked them up along his spine and felt her insides shimmy. Why was she wearing all these dumb baggy clothes? Right now she wished she looked as gorgeous as he made her feel.

When he lifted the hem of her oversize pajama top, she let him pull it off over her head. She wasn't wearing a bra, and she loved the way his eyes widened as he revealed the view. At least she was comfortable in her own body.

"You're so beautiful," he breathed, fingertips skimming her nipples. She gasped with pleasure as his mouth lowered over one breast.

"You need to take your top off too," she pleaded, amazed she could still form words.

He obliged with a smile, pulling his sweater off in one swift motion that caused such a seismic rippling of muscles that she almost lost it right there and then.

Sandro was gorgeous. By far the best-looking man she'd ever dated. And she'd thought Howard was Mr. Right? She must have been delusional. He was dull as ditchwater compared with Sandro.

Uninhibited, she let her fingers explore the hills and valleys of his chest, and his powerful upper arms.

He kissed her other breast and sucked the nipple

until a tiny moan escaped her.

Then he slid her pajama pants down over her legs and pulled them off along with her embarrassing fuzzy socks.

His rock-hard erection strained against his pants, and she suppressed a giggle at the sight of it.

"Where's the bedroom?" he rasped, as if he was now having trouble breathing.

She nodded to the door behind him. Before she had a chance to stand up, Sandro swept her up off the sofa and into his arms as if she weighed no more than Lucky.

Lucky! A quick glance showed Lucky fast asleep on his dog bed in the corner. He must be exhausted after playing with her neighbors dogs for two days solid.

Sandro carried her into the bedroom and deposited her gently on the bed utterly naked. She felt strangely unself-conscious. Being with Sandro felt oddly natural. And why wouldn't it, when she was carrying their baby inside her.

He knows about the baby, and he still wants me.

The thought sent an odd jolt of emotion to her heart. She hadn't expected that, and it floored her. And scared her. She didn't trust her emotions or her judgment anymore after what had happened with Howard.

If it seems too good to be true...

She'd heard that saying many times during her upbringing, but the sight of Sandro unzipping his pants and pushing them down over his muscled thighs drove all thoughts from her mind.

He climbed onto the bed, expression serious, and resumed kissing her as if both of their lives might depend on it. "I've been craving you," he murmured, breath hot on her neck. "Dreaming about you, longing for you."

Her mouth opened, but no words came out. Honestly she'd been too worried to think about much but surviving from day to day lately. She certainly hadn't dared to let herself fantasize about Sandro. His words shocked and energized her. Her hips lifted toward his, and she enjoyed the sensation of his hard erection between them.

"We don't need a condom," she whispered. Already she wanted him inside her. "I'm already pregnant."

"So true," he said with a smile. He laid a trail of kisses over her breasts and belly, then pushed his face between her thighs and flicked his tongue over her hot flesh.

Her hips bucked, and a shiver of arousal ran through her. She didn't remember being this overstimulated the last time with Sandro. How did he do this to her?

She writhed as he licked and sucked her, drawing tiny groans that escaped her throat. Finally, fingers woven into his hair, she couldn't stand it anymore. "Please...inside me...now...."

Sandro rose up slowly, dark eyes glittering, and moved over her body until his arousal was right over her pelvis. Her hips rose to meet him, begging him to enter. First he teased her with the tip of his penis, then he slowly slid it inside her wet folds. A wave of pleasure rushed through her as she opened to welcome him.

She wrapped her arms around him when he lowered over her, drawing him into a tight embrace.

She could feel him moving inside her, and the sensation was so intimate that for a split second she almost wanted to cry.

Too much emotion.

This was dangerous and scary. She felt way too much for Sandro when she dared to let her guard down. He'd been so kind to her, from their first meeting when she broke a vase on his head, to his quiet and warm acceptance of her shocking news. She didn't deserve someone like Sandro, even if he weren't royal and gorgeous and fabulously wealthy.

He moved over her, guiding her into a realm of pleasure she'd never experienced before. His lovemaking was gentle and thoughtful, passionate and breathless, and she could swear she felt his emotion throb in the air alongside her own.

Maybe we really can be together.... She let the thought drift through her head and fill her senses. Was it so crazy? If he liked her and she liked him, then anything was possible, right?

She felt her insides clench around him as she dared to dream something as outlandish as her and Sandro as a real couple—a real family—with all that that entailed. As she gripped him, Sandro cried out and she felt the force of his release.

As they lay together afterward, he kissed her and caressed her and told her she was the most beautiful woman he'd ever laid eyes on.

And this was without any of her carefully applied and diligently vlogged about makeup. The craziest part of all was that she actually believed him. He made her feel beautiful and desirable and irresistible. He even managed to make her feel that her accidental pregnancy was not an awkward twist of fate but a kind of miracle that happened to bring them both together.

That part was only in her mind. Sandro didn't actually say anything after the beautiful compliment, because shortly after that he eased out of her, pulled the covers up over them and fell asleep in her arms.

The whole scenario was so intimate—so darned normal—that she almost felt like they were already in a real relationship.

Lucky thing she'd already laid out her outfit for tomorrow morning's TV show appearance and packed an overnight bag for Chicago. You can never be too organized.... Her mom's familiar words rang in her head. But she couldn't even imagine how her mom would react if she could see the circumstances her daughter now found herself in.

She had to wake Sandro up and gently kick him out at an ungodly hour since her breakfast show appearance was at seven a.m. She promised to stay in touch with him during her trip. For some reason their late-night encounter had given her just the confidence boost she needed to sail through the morning talk show, even engaging in somewhat witty banter with the male cohost.

She sailed out of the studio and headed right for LaGuardia airport feeling like a million bucks. The book was selling—according to her agent—and the feedback was positive. She hadn't dared to look at any reviews herself, but her agent said they were all four and five stars so far. Her agent seemed to think she had an excellent chance of hitting at least one list and if that happened there was a good chance that Walmart would give her shelf space—which virtually guaranteed a new wave of sales.

She arrived in Chicago in plenty of time to do a drive-time radio show about dating etiquette, then retired to her hotel and ordered room service.

I hope you're having a great day, I miss you. She smiled at Sandro's text.

I miss you too, she texted back. It really did feel as if they were dating! And telling the world that she'd broken up with Howard would be way less embarrassing if she was walking right into a new relationship with a considerably more fabulous Mr. Right.

Last night was amazing. I can't wait to see you again.

She sighed. **It was wonderful,** she responded. She wanted to say more: I'm crazy about you, you bring out something wild in me, I've never enjoyed sex so much before, but she managed to restrain herself. Even though texting was theoretically private there was always the possibility that someone else could read her words over his shoulder.

Good night, sexy. I hope you have sweet dreams, preferably about me.

She smiled. **You have sweet dreams too. I'm looking forward to seeing you back in New York.**

And she really was. She couldn't wait to see him again. All her hesitation and anxiety about protecting her heart had wafted away, replaced by confidence that Sandro was truly sincere. That they might really have a future together.

Serena was in a cab on her way to the TV studio in semidarkness when her agent texted her.

Just got word. You hit NYT at 11.

Yes! If she hit the *New York Times* she'd be sure to hit the *USA Today* list as well because it was a lot longer. She texted back a smiley face and a thumbs up. She'd accomplished her main tangible goal, and now she could finally relax a bit.

She could even tell people she'd broken up with Howard.

Her stomach clenched. Okay, maybe not just yet. She might as well ride this wave of success as long as she could.

She was beginning to feel like a pro at this, sipping her water in the green room, smiling at the other guests—none of whom were famous—and touching up her lipstick. She'd just finished greeting the hosts and describing the subject matter of her book when the female host leaned in to her. She was a tall, elegant woman in a bright blue suit and perfectly penciled brows. Her smile was glossy and huge, but the look in her eyes suddenly made Serena's insides crumple.

"Serena, a little bird tells me that you and your Mr. Right are no longer together?" She asked the question with a syrupy sweetness that made Serena blink in disbelief for a moment that she'd actually said that.

How could she know?

"Uh, yes, that's true. We did decide to go our separate ways." Her voice had a ring of forced cheer. She knew she should keep going to guide the conversation out of dangerous territory, but her mind was now blank and she couldn't think of a single thing to say.

"So you realized he wasn't Mr. Right after all?"

114

She lifted a perfect brow.

"Exactly." Serena managed a shaky smile. "He's a wonderful man and I wish him all the best, but he's not my Mr. Right so I had to keep waiting."

The male host, a jovial older personality, looked surprised. "When you say waiting, does that mean you're still...." He paused, expectantly.

Serena gulped. "A virgin? Uh, no. The title of the book is more about waiting for the right person to marry, not waiting until marriage to have sex."

She felt her face heating. So far she'd managed to avoid discussing sex on air, though there had been a few veiled mentions of it. If her mom saw this she'd be mortified.

The female host teased her cohost and observed that he hadn't read the book. He went on to explain that he'd been married for thirty-seven years and was out of touch with the dating scene.

Serena was dying to ask how she'd found out about the breakup. Hardly anyone knew except a few people who knew them both personally. And possibly everyone at Howard's law firm. And his new girlfriend...and everyone she knew.

Stay focused! She struggled to drag her attention back to the present and keep her breathing steady. The female host was talking in that same syrupy tone. "It must be hard promoting a book about relationships when your relationship has just ended."

"Actually, I'm already involved with a new Mr. Right." She could hardly believe the words as she heard them coming out of her own mouth.

"Wow!" The female host looked appropriately shocked. "So you dumped your previous Mr. Right and found a new one already."

"Something like that, yes." She tried to smile. How bad was this going to sound? And what in the name of heaven had possessed her to bring up her new almost-relationship with Sandro? She must be losing her mind. "There's no shame in moving on when a relationship isn't working. It's one of the principles of the book to keep looking until you find that person who's truly right for you."

"That makes a lot of sense," said the male host, who must be trying to make up for embarrassing her earlier.

"It sure does," said the female host with a shiny lipsticked smile. "When it isn't working out, dump Mr. Right! There are plenty of fish in the sea, ladies. And with that I'd like to thank our guest Serena Raines for…"

Serena barely heard a word she said, and it was a struggle to keep her smile intact as they held up her book for the last time.

Dump Mr. Right? That had an awfully catchy ring to it. And wasn't on-message at all.

She was dying to ask the host how they got the scoop but decided there was nothing to be gained by that so she exited the studio as fast as possible and headed for her hotel to change for her book signing.

She'd dropped the news about Howard. And, without naming him, the newer news about Sandro. She could console herself with the fact that at least she'd kept the news about the baby to herself.

Back in her room she opened her laptop with trembling fingers and checked her latest video. She'd done a quick vlog while putting on her makeup this morning, and it didn't take long to see that the comments section had exploded with comments like

#dumpmrright you go gurrrl.

A handful of her most devoted followers commented on literally every video she made, and one or two of them seemed truly shocked about Howard and hurt that they'd learned the news by watching television. Chicago was a big city, and who knew how many of her followers lived here and watched that show before work.

Serena cringed at how she'd handled the situation. *Keep moving forward. Do your signing.* She changed into more casual clothing and headed out for the bookstore in a busy shopping district, again by cab. She arrived there about thirty minutes early and, suddenly starving, decided to look around for a café to grab a quick bite before she had to be there. Snowflakes were beginning to swirl in the air, so she tightened her scarf around her neck. She had just glimpsed a Starbucks and started toward it when the front of a newspaper displayed on a newsstand caught her eye.

Princess Maya? On the front page of a local Chicago newspaper was a picture of Maya Dunham and Sandro gazing into each others' eyes.

She stopped in her tracks, causing someone behind her to bump into her. What? He'd told her—last night—that he broke up with Maya?

Maybe it was an old picture. She fumbled in her purse for change to buy the paper, then shoved it under her arm and set off, almost running, for the Starbucks. In line, she whipped it open and stared at the image again. It wasn't the main story, but it was a good-sized sidebar.

She drew in a shaky breath and read the very short article beneath it. "Chicago native Maya

Dunham stepped out in fine style last night with Prince Sandro of Altaleone at the premiere for Angelina Jolie's latest production. The handsome prince appeared very attentive to our local princess—perhaps wedding bells are in their future?"

Serena glanced at the date on the paper—today. While she'd been eating a flavorless burger in her hotel room in Chicago, sighing over Sandro's romantic texts, he'd been out on the town with Maya Dunham.

He'd lied to her.

He'd come to her apartment, lied to her and had sex with her—in her own bed—under false pretenses.

She was so mad she wanted to scream. "Uh, a venti latte please," she stammered, realizing that it was her turn to order. When they asked her name she said, "Mary." Right now she wanted to be anyone but herself.

#dumpmrright
#sexwithmrwrong

She folded the paper and shoved it into her purse, wondering how on earth she was going to smile and make conversation during an hour-long book signing. And what if they wanted her to read from the book? Which passage could she read aloud without feeling like a total and utter fraud? And what if people asked probing questions about her breakup with Howard, or, worse yet, about her new relationship with the mystery Mr. Right who'd just chewed her up and spat her out?

6

It was a very long afternoon. On the one hand she was thrilled to meet her followers, most of whom were really sweet. On the other, she had to hide her sadness about Sandro's betrayal, which was terrible when people asked her probing questions about her new, mystery man. She couldn't wait to get back to New York and curl up in a ball in the relative privacy of her apartment, with the deadbolt and chain latch firmly in place.

The snow thickened and swirled outside, and Serena kept checking her phone to see if her plane back to New York was still on time. The bad weather grew into a major winter storm, and by four p.m. all planes out of O'Hare were grounded and her flight was canceled. She settled in for another night in her hotel room, knowing she should vlog something but also knowing she didn't have the strength or self-confidence to pull it off right now.

How's your day going, gorgeous? Sandro.

What nerve! She half wanted to just delete him from her phone, but he didn't deserve to have it that easy. Not when she was carrying his baby.

Were you out with Maya Dunham last night? That was all she really needed to know.

Yes, she needed an escort to a premiere. We're not together. I broke up with her just as I told you.

Could have fooled me—and everyone else in America—tutted Serena. **Why didn't you tell me?**

He must be wondering how she knew. Maybe it wasn't news in New York. He likely hadn't expected her to find out.

I didn't think it was important. It doesn't mean anything.

It does to me. I saw a picture of the two of you on the front page of the paper this morning. They suggested you might get married. Are you going to tell them you broke up with her?

Her phone started ringing. Sandro. But she didn't want to talk to him. Once he started in on her with that gruff, sexy voice and all his practiced charm she was defenseless against him.

She sent the call straight to voice mail.

Ignore the press. I don't respond to their made-up stories as that just fuels the fire. I swear to you, I'm not with her anymore. The only women I want in my life is you.

Ugh, already the charm was working.

I'm exhausted, and my plane was canceled. I'm going to bed. It was curt and to the point, but she wasn't rude enough to totally ignore him. Not that he didn't deserve it after what she'd suffered today. Did he really think it was okay to go to a movie with your ex-girlfriend after you'd broken up with her?

Even a prince couldn't have that much hubris.

I understand. I'll talk to you tomorrow.

Or will you?

The next day the snowstorm had stopped, but Serena's flight still wasn't rescheduled due to a huge backlog of flights to destinations all over the country and the world. Trucks were still clearing almost two feet of snow from the airport.

She trudged out in the snow to buy a coffee and a muffin—she'd made the mistake of buying them at the hotel the day before—and was just heading back through the lobby when she heard something that nearly made her spill her coffee.

"Serena."

A familiar deep voice stopped her in her tracks, and she spun around to see Sandro rising from a deep sofa on one side of the lobby. He looked tall, commanding and elegant as usual, in a long dark coat and a checkered scarf. She stood silent, brain working a mile a minute, as he crossed the lobby toward her, a warm smile on his face. "How are you?"

He acted as if they'd planned to meet there that morning. Which really irked her. And once again he'd caught her unprepared and underdressed and wearing no protective armor or makeup.

"What are you doing here?" She asked as quietly as possible and tried not to look as shocked as she felt. At least he didn't have to nerve to try to kiss her hello.

Had she told him what hotel should be at? No.

She was sure she hadn't told him. How did he find out?

"An old college friend is a booker for the show, so she told me where you were staying. I knew you were stuck here so I thought I would surprise you."

"You certainly surprised me. I might need a stiff drink to recover. And I can't drink." A thought struck her. "Wait. If you knew the booker, did you tell her I broke up with Howard? The host of the show knew! She asked me about it and I had to confess on live television."

Sandro blinked. "I didn't say anything. I suppose it's possible that she might have guessed." Again, that sheepish expression.

She narrowed her eyes and peered at him. "Did she ask you about whether we were a thing?"

"She might have." His expression contained a hint of mischief.

Which annoyed her. This was her career on the line, here. "And you said?"

"I told her that my lips were sealed." He made a gesture of zipping his mouth shut.

She shook her head and blew out a long, slow breath. His eyes twinkled. Damn but it was impossible to be mad at him for long. She should be furious that he'd revealed her secret—even inadvertently—but that would do no more good than being mad at the bull in the proverbial china shop.

And part of her was relieved that her guilty secret was finally out.

Sandro glanced down at her belly. Which—awkwardly—sent a flash of heat to her nether regions. "I want to congratulate you. I saw that you hit the best-seller lists."

His warm smile lit a tiny fire in her belly. "Thanks."

"And since your book tour is over for now I was hoping that you'd accompany me to Altaleone for a short vacation. I flew here in my private plane. The runway at that airport is clear and we can take off at your leisure."

She stared at him, not sure which of his outrageous statements to tackle first. "You have a private plane? I thought you prided yourself on being just an ordinary guy."

"It's a hobby of mine. I learned to fly when I was a teenager."

"You're the pilot? Then I'm definitely not coming with you."

"Why would you assume that I am a terrible pilot?" Amusement sparkled in his eyes. "I have more than 500 hours of flying experience. I fly to Europe and back quite often and have landed in all kinds of difficult conditions."

"I'm sorry, I shouldn't have said that. You just took me by surprise. As usual." She couldn't help a tiny smile sneaking across her mouth. Was there anything this guy couldn't do? "It must be pretty cool to fly anywhere you'd like to go."

"Where would you like to go?"

"Isn't that the eternal question?" This was an awkward situation. She wanted to confront him about going out with Maya, but they were in public—and really, what was the point? She'd done that already. Damn. Was his infuriating charm working on her already?

She was headed up to her room. Did she have to

invite him up there? No doubt he expected her to. She tried to remember how much of a mess she had left.

She kept walking toward the elevator. Sandro followed along confidently, which was hardly surprising.

"You should see Altaleone. Then you can decide for yourself if it's the most beautiful country in the world."

"I've barely been anywhere, so I won't have much to compare it to. I went to Mexico once on vacation, but otherwise I have never left the United States." It was hard to be mad at him now that she was in his presence.

"You've never been to Europe? We must fix that immediately." They stepped into the elevator. Being in the enclosed space with him ramped up the uncomfortable attraction she always felt for him. He was too tall, too handsome. Just standing next to him rattled her nerves and heated her blood.

The elevator arrived at her floor. She still hadn't invited him in, but apparently he was coming anyway. She walked down the hallway, conscious of his eyes on her from behind—and the effect his gaze had on her insides.

"My plane is being serviced and refueled. We can head to Altaleone this afternoon."

"What?" She reached the door and fumbled for her key card. Being around Sandro made her feel self-conscious, clumsy. "There's no way I could do that. For one thing, I don't have any clean clothes with me. And Lucky is staying with my neighbor. I miss him."

"We could stop off in New York so you could

pick up a few things from your apartment and get Lucky. There's plenty of room on the plane for him."

She blinked. "I could seriously bring Lucky with me to your country?" There was something very appealing about getting far, far away from everyone who knew her and the #dumpmrright nonsense that would take at least a few days to die down.

"Of course."

She stepped into her hotel room. Luckily it had been cleaned and looked pretty neat.

Sandro swept in after her. "You deserve a break, and I think you need one. Let me help you pack."

"That's okay." A flare of panic stirred inside her. Did he really expect her to get on the plane with him?

And why did it seem so impossible?

"Let me call the publicist and see what she has planned for me." She dialed Anita, who assured her that she didn't have anything else on deck for this week and that her editors were thrilled with her success so far. No mention of any trending hashtags. She hung up, not sure whether to be relieved or anxious. "I'm a free woman."

"Excellent. Let's head to the airport."

"You're crazy."

"Not at all. I have a house in the mountains. It's tucked away in a valley, and we'll be in perfect seclusion. You won't even have to meet any of my family."

Suddenly that made the whole prospect much more appealing. The idea of meeting his royal family scared her, even if he promised to pretend they were just friends. Sooner or later they'd be bound to find out about the pregnancy, and then things would be weird.

But if she and Sandro would be alone to get to know each other better, then maybe this could be a welcome interlude from real life. At least they'd be far away from the press and from Maya Dunham.

"So we won't have to see anyone at all?"

"Not a soul. I don't have a single servant, just a cleaner who comes twice a week and a gardener who comes twice a month."

She laughed. "I like your idea of that being no servants."

"You should see how some of my family lives. The big eighteenth-century palace where my mom and dad lived has a staff of nearly thirty at all times."

"I don't think I could handle the lack of privacy."

"It's odd you should say that when you make aspects of your life so public."

"I suppose I only invite people in to see the areas of my life that I want them to see. And they're very carefully curated. I don't show people videos of me waking up in the morning or cleaning my bathroom."

"They might enjoy some videos of your stay in Altaleone. My house is an old Roman villa I renovated. It has a courtyard and fountain."

"That does sound pretty fabulous."

"And there's an old forest of timber trees—it's full of birds and wildlife, and there are winding trails through it."

"This keeps getting more and more tempting."

"Did I mention the lake? It's large enough to take a small sailboat out on."

Goodness. This did sound like it could make for

some amazing videos. She could distract her followers from her recent drama with dramatic vistas from Altaleone.

But not show them Sandro. Since the relationship—such as it was—was likely to end in tears, she'd have to keep that under wraps. The Princess Maya episode had sandblasted the gloss off her fantasies of her own royal wedding.

And she wouldn't mention the baby.

"I do like the idea of shooting some videos there. Would you mind if I pretended that you're just my friend?"

"No pretending required." His eyes flashed something that unnerved her slightly. Was it good cheer or something more mischievous? "I promise not to kiss you on camera—unless you ask me to." His white teeth gleamed in his magnificent smile. "Would you like me to help you pack?"

She shook her head, while tucking her things neatly back into her bag. How weird to have to pack her underwear and beauty products in front of him. This felt way too intimate. She hadn't canceled her plane flight, which was bound to be rescheduled sooner or later. Was she really going to give up her ticket and get in a plane flown by an amateur?

"You promise that you're a good pilot?"

He held a hand over his heart. "On my honor as a prince of Altaleone."

Dammit. She *was* going to give up her ticket and get in a plane flown by an amateur. Butterflies stirred in her stomach, but she told them to be quiet and zipped up her bag. "Let's go before I come to my senses."

7

Serena held her breath as they taxied down the well-cleared runway of the small regional airport, on their way to New York. The skies were clear and blue. She sat next to Sandro—in the copilot seat—which was scary because she could see how many buttons and levers were involved in getting this thing into the air.

His big hands moved the throttle with confidence and a glance at his broad chest showed his breathing to be slow and steady. She wished she could say the same for hers. She couldn't help a distinct feeling that she was jumping out of the frying pan into the fire.

"You haven't told anyone about the baby, have you?" She realized her hand sat protectively on her stomach.

"Of course not."

"I want to tell my family first."

"I understand completely." He shot her a warm smile. Which made her want to snap at him to get his eyes back on the windshield. But she managed not to. They climbed above the snowy Chicago suburbs, and she could barely see the ground from this angle. "Though don't forget that my family will be excited to hear about the baby too."

Serena froze for a second. For some reason she'd almost forgotten about that. If this baby was half his, then it also belonged to Sandro's family. She was asking a lot of him to keep her pregnancy under wraps. "I'm sorry about being so secretive. It's all so unexpected." She steeled herself. "Uh, your family, might they have an issue with me being black?"

"Oh, no. They're all very sensible and kind people."

"That's good." She wasn't sure she believed him. He might be surprised to find out that they were less accepting and tolerant than he expected.

"Well, except my Aunt Liesel. She's my mother's sister, but luckily she lives in Germany most of the time. Don't take it personally, though. She's an equal opportunity hater." He smiled.

She cringed inwardly. Would she have to be nice to his Aunt Liesel even if she was rude or mean to her?

Suddenly she wanted to laugh. Was she getting ideas that she might actually become part of Sandro's family? That was the path to madness. Better to just take this trip for what it was—a chance to get away from the mess she'd made of her existence.

Like her ill-fated trip to the Georgia sea islands—where she'd been swept up in a storm and a tide of lust.

Because it was just lust. She had to keep reminding herself of that. She hadn't known Sandro long enough to develop any real feelings for him back then. She hadn't known him long enough for that now.

Lucky thing she had several hours to ask him probing questions. She turned to him—damn that striking aristocratic profile that made her heart flip—and drew in a breath. "If you could have one wish, what would it be?"

"World peace." He turned to her with an amused look.

"Everyone says that. Everyone who isn't a jerk, anyway. Something more personal. What would you really wish for?"

He turned to look out of the windshield again. They were still climbing into the clouds. "I'd like to know who killed my father and grandmother."

Her heart sank a little, and she realized she'd been hoping for something romantic like "I've always wanted a big family" or "to live happily ever after with the girl of my dreams." But he had a point. "I don't blame you. That's a situation where a lot of people might want revenge."

"I don't even know if I want revenge because I don't know who did it—or why. But they were both cruelly murdered and it was made to look as if they were engaged in bizarre sex acts. Since then my sister-in-law was kidnapped by people who wanted access to a secret Swiss bank account. We hoped we'd caught the murderers, but lie detector tests and questioning suggested that they're not behind the deaths. I just can't understand why anyone would kill them." A muscle worked in his jaw. "It's frustrating dealing with the unknown."

"Do you feel that you're at risk?" Fear trickled

through her. What exactly was she flying into?

"No. If anyone's at risk it's my brother Darias, who is now king. He's hired an ex-foreign-legion security chief to protect the family and investigate the murder. But every lead goes to a dead end. "

His phone rang. She glanced at him. He had both hands on the throttle, now guiding the plane on a curve as they climbed higher. "Do you want me to get that for you?"

"No, don't worry about it."

She glanced down at his phone, which sat on ledge near him. She could read the name Maya and a number.

So Maya was calling him. Green claws of jealousy scratched at the inside of her stomach. She didn't want to think about Maya. On the other hand, she wanted reassurance that things were really over between them. "You took Maya to the premiere as a favor?"

"Yes." He didn't even turn to look.

"She didn't try to get you back?" She hated how pushy that sounded.

"We were out in public so we didn't even have a private conversation. She did paw me like we were still together, but I couldn't really shove her off me in front of the cameras."

Why not? She kept the question to herself. But another thing was gnawing at her. "I saw a headline speculating on whether she would soon be a princess."

He laughed. "That's crazy."

"Nope. It was a Chicago paper. Because she's from there it was on the front page."

"I guess it was a slow news day. Still, I'm

131

surprised by that. Why were they even paying attention? I'm pretty anonymous most of the time. Just another Eurotrash royal." He winked at her. "I guess she's pretty big right now with the Academy Award thing."

"Yes." She wondered if Maya had fed the story to the press. It was unusual for a paper to have a big headline based on idle speculation. "I think that was she who called just now." She watched him carefully to see how he'd react.

Sandro frowned. "I wonder why. I told her I would be out of the country and busy." He turned to her, and his dark stare melted her. "I want to focus completely on you."

It was hard to catch her breath and form words the way he was looking at her. Especially since they were in a missile hurtling through space. "Shouldn't you be looking out the windshield?"

A mischievous grin crept across his mouth. "It's hard to focus on my duties when you're sitting next to me."

"Don't scare me." She wasn't really nervous. They were high enough that there were no obstacles around them, and they'd left the Chicago area so she couldn't even see another plane in the sky.

He looked forward again. "I'd never do anything to scare you."

"You mean like making me pregnant?" She lifted a brow.

"Okay, not intentionally." He smiled and shot a quick glance at her belly—which heated under his gaze. How could she be aroused by him looking at her belly? She didn't show at all yet, which was merciful under the circumstances. "See? I'm looking out the windshield and paying full attention to flying." He winked at her again before turning back.

She sighed. Sandro was hard to take. Way too sure of himself and whenever he looked at her, common sense started to fly for the nearest window. She'd definitely have to watch herself during this stay in Altaleone.

"I can't stay too long, you know." She could hardly believe she hadn't discussed the return trip with him, but that was partly because she didn't want to decide the duration until she got there. She might take one look at the place and want to leave again the same day.

"I have to be back in New York by next Thursday for a meeting with a potential new distributor for my solar technology. But we can leave earlier if you need to."

"I might get invited to do another interview." Or at least that would be a good excuse if she wanted to run. She wasn't sure how much proximity to Sandro she could take without losing her mind.

"We'll just take enough time for you to recharge and breathe—and get to know me a little better."

"You don't know me well either. How come you're not asking me probing questions?" Maybe he wasn't really interested in anything except her outward appearance?

A dimple appeared in his cheek. "I'm more subtle than that. I prefer to let you reveal yourself to me."

"Don't forget I'm used to revealing a carefully curated version of myself to the world."

"I'm not the world. You don't have to pretend to be anyone but who you are."

"Whoever that is," she quipped. "I'm so used to

putting on my game face and being the person others want me to be that I'm not even sure who's inside anymore."

"How did you get started? It seems odd for such a private person—one who won't even tell her own family she broke up with her boyfriend—to want to share her life with the public."

"At first I wrote a few blog entries just to see if I could. Then my blog started to catch on and I made some money. More money than I was making at my job at the college library. I put more time and energy into it, and it kind of snowballed from there. These days I make more money from videos. Blogging is the part I like best—maybe because it's easier to hide behind the printed word—but my audience wants videos."

"In addition to being interesting and thoughtful you have to look fabulous and be charming." He shot her a warm glance. "You've had a lot of practice for being royal."

She laughed. "I hardly think it's the same thing. If anything, being a pastor's daughter is better training. I had to be on my best behavior all the time or everyone would be talking about me."

"Are you close to your dad?"

"I used to be. It's hard to keep that closeness when you grow up and live hundreds of miles away. And it's hard to talk to him about what I do. He doesn't say much, but I can tell he things its silly to pontificate about makeup and dating. I don't think any parents would be too excited about that."

He chuckled. "My dad would have liked it if I shared details of my love live with him. He was the kind of man who liked to sit around with the guys and smoke cigars and talk about women. None of my brothers are really like that, though. I think we all have too much respect and love for our mom."

"That's sweet. It can't have been easy for her to raise ten of you."

"She devoted her life to us. Even though we had a large staff, she always read us bedtime stories and kissed our bumps and bruises better."

Serena had a flashback to putting a bandage over a cut on his forehead the night they met. The cut she'd inflicted when she smashed a vase over his head. "Speaking of which, yours healed nicely."

"There's a small scar." His dimple appeared again. "But it was worth it to meet you."

"They do say scars are masculine and sexy." She was lucky he hadn't sued her.

"What do you think?" He flashed her a glance that heated her skin.

She shrugged and tried to act cool. "I really don't have an opinion."

"That's definitely the curated version of you."

"Get your eyes back on the windshield."

He chuckled and turned back to face the front. "I think you had all kinds of ideas of what you should look for in a man, and that they were all wrong. You wanted someone nice and dull and predictable who'd live a safe and comfortable lifestyle with you. Maybe you'd have two point three children when you were both good and ready. Or maybe you'd never get around to it because the timing would never be right."

She sighed. "I wish I could argue with you, but it's true. I wanted to have my first baby when I turned thirty. I figured I'd have enough money saved by then for me to take some time off."

"How old are you now?"

"Twenty-five. And I have zero savings and took out a crazily huge mortgage on my condo, using my advance as a down payment. I've since been trying to sell the place, and no one is even looking. That's why the success of this book is so important to me. I need money coming in or I'll have to go looking for a real job, which, given my rather unusual résumé for the past couple of years, could turn out to be quite a challenge."

He laughed. "Ugh, don't get a real job. I tried that once. It was a nightmare. They expected me to show up to the same place every day, even when it was a great day for flying or skiing or taking my sailboat out on the water." He gave a mock shudder. "Never again."

"It must be nice to have the luxury to say that, but the rest of us have to hustle. I promised myself and my followers that I'll put out content three times a week."

"Content? That sounds so clinical."

"I prefer to think of it as businesslike."

"And what kind of content does your audience like best?"

She stiffened. "Makeup videos are my bread and butter, but they love hearing personal stories. Which is hard as I've shared most of them by now."

"It's not like you've stopped living. Did you tell them the story of getting stuck on the Georgia sea islands in a big storm?"

"I did." She cast a sideways glance at him. "Though I left out the part about you being there. I'm embarrassed to say it, but I recorded the whole thing as if Howard were with me. I didn't actually lie, but I didn't tell the whole truth, either."

"How did Howard feel about that?"

"I doubt he noticed. He never watched my videos. Or read my blogs." She lifted a brow. "I bet you haven't, either."

He winced. "Ouch. I admit it didn't even cross my mind."

"I'll try not to take that personally."

"Perhaps I'm only interested in the real, in-the-flesh version of you, not the well-lit video one."

"They're both me."

He turned to look at her. "Good point." He looked at her steadily for a moment. "On that note I think you should record a vlog right now. Tell your audience that you're in a plane, on your way to the most beautiful place on earth."

"Being flown by a handsome prince?"

"That's the best bit."

She laughed. "I wish I could."

"Why can't you?"

She fidgeted in her chair, fingers still grazing her belly. "I suppose I could. My book tour is over. I did reveal that I broke up with Howard." She didn't say that she'd mentioned she had a new man in her life. If she showed Sandro they'd all—correctly—assume it was him.

"Go on. Do it." He took his hand off the controls and placed it on her arm—which instantly broke out in goose bumps.

"I'm scared."

"You were scared to fly in my plane, but you're doing it anyway. What's one more thing?"

"I could do it, couldn't I?" She was asking herself

really, not him. She pulled her phone out of her pocket and switched on the video recorder.

8

"Hello, everyone." Was her makeup still okay? She couldn't believe she hadn't checked first when she was known for her makeup tutorials. For some reason Sandro had made her feel so glamorous she hadn't even thought to glance at herself. Must be the way he looked at her.

"You all know I've been busy with my book tour, and today I was rescued from snow-bound Chicago and invited to fly to Europe. Can you hear the sound of the engine? Yup, I'm in a plane right now."

This was where she should turn the camera on Sandro and introduce him. He looked at her expectantly, a half smile on his face. Once introduced him to her followers there would be no turning back. They'd be fascinated by him. Who wouldn't be?

He was good content. This was business, right?

She captured him in the frame. "This is my friend Sandro. He lives in a small country called Altaleone, and he's invited me there for a break. As you can see, Sandro is flying the plane. Sandro, without taking your eyes off the windshield, could you tell my viewers a little about yourself?"

That was much safer than introducing him herself and potentially saying something stupid or wrong.

He turned and flashed his pearly smile. "Hello, Serena's fans." She cringed. She never thought of them as fans. That made her seem too self-important. She was a nobody, really. If she stopped providing content they'd all be gone in a week or two. "I'm Sandro Leone, and I had the pleasure and privilege of spending Christmas with Serena on the Georgia coast."

She froze and felt her eyes open wide. He wasn't supposed to tell them that! Now they'd know she broke up with Howard weeks ago.

Though they'd figure out the timeline sooner or later once she made her pregnancy announcement. She tried to stay calm.

"And luckily I convinced her to join me for a week in my mountain homeland."

"Tell them what you do, Sandro." She wanted him to say he was a prince. That was good material.

"I'm an engineer by trade, and I design solar technology that powers small devices. My goal is to put solar power in the hands of every man, woman and child in the world."

"That's a big goal," she gushed, glad to be talking about something other than herself. She looked at the camera. "And Sandro is also a prince." Then she turned to him. "Right?"

Okay, that sounded dumb.

He raised a brow very slightly, as if a teeny bit

annoyed that she'd played the prince card. "Indeed I do have the privilege of being a member of the royal house of Leone, which has governed Altaleone since the time of Charlemagne."

Serena was pretty sure no one would know who Charlemagne was, especially since she had no idea herself. "How long ago was that?"

"More than twelve hundred years." He stared straight ahead, guiding the plane. "Some like to credit my ancestors' prowess in battle for our long rule. Personally I give credit to the formidable mountain ranges that surround our tiny country."

She pointed the lens at herself. "Well, I can't wait to see it, and I'll be sure to post vlogs to share with you. For now I'm going to catch some shut-eye before we get there. Thanks for joining me on this adventure."

Now she needed to post it to YouTube. "Is there an Internet connection up here?"

"Indeed there is. You know that satellite Internet is one of my passions."

"I was hoping you wouldn't say that. I can put this out there right now."

"Do it." He gave her the Wi-Fi password, and she logged in and posted the video and captioned it. Before she'd logged out again there were thirty-seven views.

"That's it? Don't you have to edit it?"

"Sometimes I do. I have a flashy graphic that a friend created for me. But I find that people like homespun-looking stuff that looks like I just recorded it on the fly.

"People want the real, authentic you."

"Yeah, shame I've been giving them something

else lately."

"You told them about your breakup, and now they've met me. You should feel good about that."

"It's still not the whole truth." She sighed and looked down at her belly. "But I'll get there in time."

He turned to her with a warm half-grin. "That's the spirit."

They flew into New York, where Sandro's Tesla was waiting at the airport. He drove her to her apartment, where they picked up Lucky and his crate and toys and food, and she shoved some clean clothes into a bag, then they grabbed takeout dinner and headed back to the airport in the dead of night.

"The timing is perfect. We'll arrive in the morning, and you'll get to see my country in all its glory."

Serena felt more relaxed this time as they taxied and took off, with Lucky sleeping in his crate nearby. *You're part of the jet-set.* The thought assaulted her and almost made her laugh.

Then she reminded herself that this was just a strange interlude. She was likely just another notch in Sandro's royal bedpost, and she wouldn't be the last.

But dammit, she needed a break and she was going to enjoy this trip.

Serena woke from a deep sleep when sunlight broke through the clouds in a bright shaft that poked into the cockpit. It took her a moment to realize where she was. Sandro smiled at her from the pilot's seat. "You said you weren't going to sleep."

He'd tried to convince her to go lie down in the cabin, which had broad recliner seats, but she'd refused, insisting that she wasn't tired. "I'm not sure what happened. I think I'm just overtired from all the interviews."

"You deserve a good rest. I bet being a celebrity is exhausting."

"You'd know."

"Not really. No one is all that interested in me." His adorable dimple showed. She knew he was lying. He got plenty of press coverage. Maybe he just wasn't interested enough to read it.

The realization that hadn't looked at her social media for many hours crept over her along with the dawn light rising above the horizon in front of them. "I guess I should check in and see how people are reacting to all the news I've dropped on them lately. I bet people are buying my book, then discovering I broke up with Howard."

"They won't be upset. If anything they'll sympathize with you."

She pulled her laptop out of her bag and flipped it open for the first time since she'd uploaded her video hours ago. She rarely read or responded to comments on her phone, preferring the bigger screen and a real keyboard. She opened her latest YouTube video—with Sandro—and scrolled down to the comments section. She wasn't surprised to see that the haters had come out of the woodwork. "Uh-oh." She glanced sideways at Sandro. "Listen to this. 'We'll see how long it lasts. I bet you're too uptight to keep a boyfriend.' Possibly true," she added ruefully.

"Anyone who takes the time to comment on a video has too much time on their hands and needs to get a life."

"Hey, those are my people. Where would I be without them?" She was starting to see the humor in the situation. "I need them watching and commenting. I have a mortgage to pay."

Instead of laughing as she'd expected, he was silent for a moment, watching the sunlit clouds ahead. "What would you really like to do, if you could do anything?"

"I love what I do."

"You love it when it's going your way. Lately, though, it's been cramping your style."

She wanted to snap back that it was none of his business, but she held her tongue. To a certain extent he was right. "I don't know. I've never really done anything else. I just kind of follow my business where it seems to be going and react to changes in the industry. That's how I made the switch from blogging to video."

"You should sit down and come up with a long-term plan."

"But how, when I don't know what's going to happen in the future?"

Now he did laugh. "No one knows what's going to happen in the future. But you'll have an edge if you plan for it anyway." He turned back to the windshield. "We're over Europe, now."

"I wish I could see it through the clouds." She peered hopelessly at the sunlit golden fluff beneath them.

"You will. We'll go down below them soon. Get ready."

He shifted the control and they swooped lower, cutting through a thick bank of clouds and emerging underneath it into blinding sunlight that bounced off the snowcapped peaks below.

"Where are we?"

"The Pyrenees. A mountain range between Spain and France."

"How come there are no people or cities? I thought Europe was crowded." When she imagined Europe, she saw the bustling streets of Paris or Berlin. The kind of scenes she'd seen in movies.

"Not all of it. Like my home, this area is too mountainous to be easily habitable."

"So it's empty and peaceful."

"Exactly."

"I bet Lucky needs to pee. Is there anywhere he can do it?"

"You don't have him toilet trained yet?" He lifted a brown, eyes twinkling. "Like, with a real toilet?"

"We'll head in there and give it a try." She rose and retrieved Lucky from his crate. He wiggled with excitement as she carried him into the bathroom. There was a stall shower in there, and she put him down on the floor. "Go pee-pee, Lucky!" She'd been working on training him to go on cue—by "capturing the behavior" and praising and treating him when he did what she wanted all by himself. She wasn't even that surprised when he lifted his leg and went against the shower wall. "Good boy!" Ha. Sandro wouldn't be laughing at her now.

She rinsed the shower and marched out. "Good boy!" She said again. "He did it."

"You're kidding?"

"Nope. I used a technique I learned in obedience class."

"You took a class with Lucky?" He looked highly amused.

"I've never owned a dog before. I needed some strategies."

"You are organized. You should post some dog-training videos."

She glowed with pride. "First I think I should master getting him to sit and stay. That's proving more challenging."

Lucky strained forward in her arms, wanting to lick and nuzzle Sandro. "No interfering with the pilot, Lucky. He needs to concentrate on getting us safely back to solid ground."

"Not long now. We'll be landing within twenty minutes."

Anxiety fluttered in Serena's stomach. They were landing in his country. Where he was a prince and a familiar face. When people saw him with a strange woman, what would they think? That she was another one in his long line of girlfriends?

She put Lucky back in the crate and took her usual morning glance at the gossip sites online. Which demonstrated that Sandro was still publicly associated with Maya Dunham. In fact there was a new picture of them together.

Maybe Maya fed it to them. Serena had a feeling she wasn't going to just let Sandro walk away.

"Is Maya still trying to get in touch with you?" She knew it was none of her business.

Sandro glanced at her. "I think she might have texted me. I haven't read it. Why?"

"Just curious."

"She knows over between us."

"I know, but there's a story about you in the *Daily News* today. Nothing substantive, just a picture of the two of you on the street."

"Weird. Never mind. I'm sure they'll lose interest." He pointed to the windshield. "See those mountains in the distance? That range is the Alps. Altaleone is tucked into the middle of them."

The whole landscape glittered like the inside of a snow globe. "You must get a lot of snow." Somehow she hadn't thought about the consequences of flying into the Alps in the dead of winter. With her New York City clothes.

"Yes. Conditions are clear at the airport, though. No worries."

Sunlight bounced off the snow, and as they drew closer to the ground the whole scene below—steep snowy mountains with the occasional village tucked into their deep crevices—looked like the kind of fake winter scene someone might create for their train set. "It's beautiful."

"Have you ever skied before?"

"No. And I don't think I should start now that I'm pregnant."

"Oh, yes." His brows lifted. "I forgot about that part."

Her heart sank a little. How could he forget something so huge and important? Would he forget that she was a real person—with feelings?

She cursed herself for being negative. "It is hard to remember. I have to remind myself to avoid coffee and certain cheeses and fish that could have listeria or toxins. Being pregnant is quite hard work."

"I wish I could be more help." He shot her a glance that sent warmth coursing through her. "It seems so unfair that women have to do everything during the pregnancy."

"Lucky thing we're tough and can handle it." She

didn't feel all that tough right now. It would be nice to collapse into Sandro's strong arms. Maybe just for a little while. Wasn't that what this trip was all about?

Out here, away from her followers—away from everything—she could gather the resources to move forward with her life.

Either that or find some cubbyhole to hide in forever.

"Look at those double peaks there." He pointed. "That's the border between Altaleone and Italy. Our culture is heavily influenced by Italy as most of the original settlers came from that direction."

"Did they bring their food? I do love Italian food."

"Luckily they did. Northern Italian food. A lot of meat and creamy sauces." He grinned. "But we can have whatever food you like. My chef was trained in L.A."

"You have a chef? I thought we were going to be all alone there." Panic flared in her gut. Who else would be there? She was already dreading the gardener and the cleaner. She didn't want anyone to know that she'd agreed to be Sandro's live-in chick-of-the-week.

"I don't need to call him. You know I love to cook."

"I'd prefer that. I could help." Anything was better than having someone else coming and going, and spreading gossip. "How do we get groceries?"

"Usually I have them delivered, but we can pick some things up when we arrive."

Gulp. They'd have to go into a grocery store? "Do people recognize you when you go into town?"

"They do." He smiled. "But they're usually

friendly. Buckle your seat belt. We're beginning our approach."

9

Serena held her breath for the landing, which involved a fairly steep descent between sharp mountain peaks toward a seemingly tiny runway. Sandro guided the plane down, while offering sightseeing information about the surrounding area, as if he were pulling his car into a parking space.

She glanced back at Lucky as the wheels bumped down on the runway, and he was standing in his crate, tail wagging, ready to go explore. She needed to learn to approach life with his boundless enthusiasm, instead of a heart full of foreboding.

Sandro pulled the plane into a large hanger, which also contained a shiny black SUV tucked into one corner. He helped her and Lucky out, then retrieved their baggage and packed everything into the SUV. After they drove out, the hangar door lowered by remote control.

"This is the way to travel," she marveled.

"Sailing is good too. Takes longer, though." He

turned to her with a grin. "And since Altaleone is landlocked it's not a very good way to get home."

Sunlight reflecting off the bright white snow almost blinded her. The roads were cleared but still sparkled with ice crystals. "How long is the drive to your place?"

"About twenty minutes. But we'll stop and pick up some supplies in the town."

"What's the local town called?"

"Casteleone. It's where my family lives. I grew up in the palace there, and my brother Darias just moved into the ancient castle right in town where my grandmother used to live."

Anxiety stirred inside her. "We're not going to meet them, though, are we?"

"Why don't you want to? They're very nice."

"I'm just…" She struggled for a polite way to say it. She didn't want to meet them and have them be rude or dismissive. She'd be hurt, Sandro would be disappointed, and the trip would be ruined, and she just couldn't take one more thing going wrong right now. "I'm kind of tired."

"Understandable. We'll save the introductions for another time. For now we'll just stop by the market and pick up some food. Casteleone's oldest bakery is still famous for its pastries."

The town was ancient, a big village with winding cobbled streets, punctuated by piles of gleaming snow. Despite the relatively early hour, market stalls were set up in the square, in front of quaint shops. Sandro parked right on the street, helped put Lucky on the leash, then led them both into a pretty café painted in navy blue with gold lettering.

"Do they allow dogs?"

"We're about to find out."

No doubt they allowed whatever the heck you wanted when you were local royalty. She hoped Lucky wouldn't pee on anything.

They sat at a tiny table spread with a white tablecloth and navy napkins, and Sandro ordered something—she couldn't understand the language, or even tell what language it was—then asked her if she wanted cream in her hot chocolate.

"Yes, please."

"I ordered you the local breakfast specialty. It's a kind of smoked fish."

Her expression must have looked appropriately doubtful.

"And I also ordered a basket of pastries."

"That sounds more promising."

Their drinks arrived and hers was steaming, with a swirl of thick cream, and looked good enough to dive into. The waiter, wearing a long white apron, brought a bowl of water and a dish of cooked chicken for Lucky.

"I guess they do allow dogs."

"Everywhere should allow dogs." Sandro smiled. Then looked up and recognized someone who'd just walked in. A woman exclaimed, and he rose to his feet and moved to embrace her. Serena was burning to look around and see who he was talking to but felt suddenly shy and didn't want to intrude.

"Serena, this is my sister Beatriz." Sandro had his arm around a slim brunette with a serious expression, who regarded Serena with a look that read as both surprise and suspicion. Serena thrust out her hand. "Nice to meet you." At least she could be polite.

"And you." His sister seemed guarded. Perhaps

Sandro had a different woman with him every time she saw him. Beatriz looked at him as if waiting for an explanation.

"Serena is visiting Europe for the first time."

"Oh. How come you didn't say you were arriving? Does Mom know you're visiting?"

"No. It was a last-minute thing. We'll come visit the palace soon. Serena needs to rest first. She just finished a big book tour."

"Not that big." She smiled and felt a bit embarrassed. It was sweet of him to brag about her tour. "But I could certainly use some time away from cameras."

Beatriz winced. "I'm not sure you've come to the best place. The paparazzi have been going nuts here lately. Apparently, Emma and Darias are the perfect royal couple and the bloodhounds want to capture their every move on camera."

Sandro winced. "How are they holding up?"

Beatriz shrugged. "Darias is a cool customer. I don't think Emma minds much, either. Mom actually likes it because she thinks all the press attention will keep them safe from killers."

"Is there any news on the murders?" He lowered his voice.

She shrugged again. "No one tells me anything. Sometimes I wonder if I'm a suspect. Let me know if you learn anything."

"All right, sis. Would you like to join us for coffee?"

"No, thanks, I've got to run." She kissed him on the cheeks and nodded stiffly to Serena, then went to the counter to order.

"Now everyone will know we're here." Sandro

sipped his coffee with a rueful expression. "Beatriz lives at the palace with my mom. We probably won't get any peace. Mom had a fit when I didn't come home for Christmas."

"I find it odd too. You seem like the kind of person who would."

"Christmas here can be a bit much. Sometimes it's nice to have a quiet celebration with a couple of friends."

"Or one rather ornery stranger."

"One very interesting and irresistible stranger." He spoke so softly that she almost had to lip-read.

His words, and the way he said them, caused an odd sensation in her belly.

She sipped her hot chocolate and tried to get the conversation back onto less dangerous ground. "Christmas can be a lot to handle at my house too. My extended family comes from all over Virginia and North Carolina. I have a lot of older relatives who still want to pinch my cheeks then ask me when I'm getting married."

"Or having a baby." He winked.

She drew in a breath. "I may never go home again." She shook her head. "I did mention that my dad is a preacher?"

"You did. But I'm sure as a man of his time he knows that things happen."

"I suppose so, but I know he'll be disappointed in me." She couldn't even imagine what her dad would think if she told him the father was a European prince. He might assume she was delusional and needed mental health counseling.

She glanced at Sandro's sister, who was now picking up her order for two coffees and some pastries. "Does your sister get endlessly pursued by men who want her because she's a princess?"

Sandro glanced over his shoulder at her. "Not that I know of." He leaned in. "Beatriz is a bit prickly. I think she scares men off. Besides, I'm not sure what my mom would do without her now that the rest of us are scattered around the world pursuing our dreams."

"Did she never leave home?"

"She talked about going to college but never actually did it. She wanted to study fashion in Milan, but my dad thought that was hilarious and would burst out laughing every time she talked about it."

"That's terrible. Was that the only thing she wanted to do?"

He shrugged. "She's a grown woman. I'm sure that if she wanted to do something badly enough, she'd be doing it. I think she quite enjoys helping to run the palace and fulfilling the more mundane duties of a princess."

"Like what?" She bit into her pastry. It was tender and delicious, with a fruity filling that made her mouth water.

"Oh, you know, snipping ribbons to open new shops and offices. Events where people want a rent-a-royal to add luster to the occasion. My grandmother found that kind of thing tiresome when she was queen so she delegated it to Beatriz since she was always available."

"Do you do those kind of events?"

"God, no." He laughed. "I'd hate it. Good thing I'm way down the royal line and in no danger of being king. Poor Darias has probably had it up to here already with royal duties. He was getting to be a pretty well-known artist internationally before he got swept back here to be king after the murders."

"Maybe he's enjoying it."

"I doubt it." Sandro ate his smoked fish with gusto.

"Is that good?"

"Absolutely delicious. Try a bite." He thrust a forkful of his fish at her.

She hesitated. Eating off a man's fork in public was tantamount to a declaration of...something. "No, thanks. I'll take your word for it. I bet Lucky would like some, though."

Lucky had already finished his chicken and sat looking adoringly up at her. Her heart swelled with pride. "Lucky is such a great dog. I can't believe he was left tied up outside that ramshackle old house."

It had turned out that Lucky's owner was an elderly man who'd bought him as a guard dog and been sorely disappointed that he wound up being so small. He'd sold him to Serena for fifty dollars after she had finally located him. He'd been evacuated to a relative's house before the storm that swept through the beachfront community she'd been staying in when she met Sandro. Rage and indignation swept through her when she thought about Lucky's narrow escape. She still couldn't believe his owner had escaped to safety, leaving his little dog behind.

"He's more proof that you were exactly where you were meant to be at Christmastime."

"I suppose that is one way of looking at it." She took another bite of her pastry. Life certainly was full of surprises in the last few months. She'd been relieved to close the book on the previous year, but this one was turning out to be just as full of dramatic upheaval.

"Do you still miss your ex-boyfriend?" Sandro watched her, and she felt as if his dark gaze could see right through her.

"Not really." Did she? It was hard to be honest even with herself. How could you not miss someone you'd planned to spend the rest of your life with? "I think what I miss most is my dreams of how things were supposed to be. I was living in a fantasy world. I suppose it serves me right. My happy little fishbowl of perfection felt like a suffocating bell jar to him."

"I think you had a lucky escape."

"Maybe." People kept glancing over at Sandro—then at her—then back at Sandro. "Your admirers are making me a bit self-conscious."

"They're curious about you." A smile played at his lips.

"I bet they are. And I don't like it." She was serious. "I thought we were going to be hidden away at your house."

"You're right, but I couldn't resist showing you my homeland's beautiful town and our delicious food." He wolfed down the last of the smoked fish. She polished off her pastry. "Let's go. We'll grab some supplies in the market."

They whisked Lucky outside, and Sandro bought an array of groceries, fresh bread, cheeses, vegetables and wrapped meat at the market stalls.

"How do they have fresh vegetables in this climate at this time of year?" she couldn't help asking as they bundled it into his SUV.

"Hydroponics. Altaleone is a leading producer of vegetables and fruits grown indoors under lights, using only water and organic nutrients. One of the farms uses equipment I developed while I was in graduate school."

"Is there anything you can't do?"

He looked thoughtful while he climbed into the driver's seat. "I'm not a very good ice skater."

"That's a relief."

He drove them out of the town on a winding road with snow piled on either side. White fields rose above them, then dropped away as they crested a hilltop and descended into a valley. Occasional farmhouses dotted the scene but no animals.

"No sheep or cows?"

"They're all kept indoors at this time of year. All the farms have big barns. The snow gets too deep for them to be outside."

"It's hard to imagine this will all be green in spring, just a few weeks from now."

"A metaphor for life, perhaps?" He glanced at her, brow lifted.

"Let's hope so. I'm glad I posted a video about breaking up with Howard. And my mom knows." Then her hand flew to her mouth. "I didn't tell my publicist. What if people call her with questions?"

"Why didn't you tell her before?"

"I didn't want to make her a liar as well. How could she book all these shows if she knew I was a fraud?"

"You're not a fraud. I'm sure your book is full of excellent advice."

"On how to end up single and alone—and pregnant—after a two-year relationship?"

"It takes two to make a relationship. Stop blaming yourself." His tone was almost stern.

"Am I?"

"You are. And he's the one who left. Try blaming him for a change." His familiar grin lifted the corner of his mouth. "I think he's a total idiot."

The road narrowed to a single lane track as they ascended into the next set of hills. She squinted at the glaring snow. "What happens if another car comes?"

"It won't."

"How do you know?"

"Because this is my estate."

She stared at the white hills around them. "You inherited it?"

"I bought it. From my grandmother. With the money I made when I sold my first company."

Serena liked that. Maybe he wasn't just a spoiled princeling waiting to have the world handed to him on a silver platter. "What did she think about that?"

"She thought it was hilarious. She offered to give it to me. It's one of the most remote properties in Altaleone and hadn't been inhabited for three hundred years. The road wasn't even passable when I first bought it."

That wasn't hard to imagine. She wasn't a hundred percent convinced it was passable right now. "What attracted you to it?"

"I think the desolate location was part of the draw. And its history. The original villa was the seat of a retired Roman general sent into exile from Rome. He built his own small empire up in the mountains and ruled it for decades. The stone villa was a great state of ruin until I modernized and extended it."

They crested another hilltop and began a breathtakingly steep descent into the pure, white wilderness. If she wanted to escape from here it would be very difficult. She wouldn't dare drive on these roads. Steep *and* icy? Sandro handled the car confidently, but he had years of experience with these conditions. "This would be a good place to keep someone prisoner."

A smile played about his sensual mouth. "Do you have anyone in mind?"

"Not at all." She crossed her arms over her chest, which didn't do anything to quell the tingling sensation in her nipples. She'd spent way too much time in close proximity with Sandro. And now they were going to be all alone in his house.

In the middle of nowhere.

"But knowing you as I do, I'm surprised you don't use a helicopter to get here."

"I do." He lifted his chin. "Just not in winter. It's too much trouble keeping the helicopter de-iced."

He drove through two big stone pillars, and the road straightened out into a broad drive—recently ploughed—that led toward a low, modern-looking house with ancient stone accents. The mountains behind it formed a breathtaking backdrop. "This is stunning."

"My sentiments exactly. I'm glad you agree."

She could feel his warmth, his pride in his home, and it touched her. "I have good taste," she teased.

"That's why your followers hang on your every word. Shouldn't you be recording this for them?"

"You wouldn't mind?"

"Not in the least. I love to share Altaleone and its beauty with people around the world. Most of them have never even heard of it."

"All right. I'm getting my camera out."

She whipped it her phone and polished the lens, then hit record and chattered away—it was surprisingly easy—as they drove up to the stunning residence, its wide stone courtyard shimmering with snow crystals. "I'll be back to give you a more detailed tour. For now my little dog and I need to unpack and settle in."

Sandro swept up all their bags, and she took Lucky out of his crate and put him on the leash. Why did this feel weirdly like a homecoming? It totally wasn't! She was staying here just a few days, then going back to her regular life in New York. If she got lucky her real estate agent would squeeze in some showings while her place was empty, and she could sell it and get out from under the big mortgage she should never have taken on.

This was just a break. Nothing serious. So she'd better not get too attached to the place—or to Sandro.

Her heart started beating harder as Sandro used his fingerprint to open a lock, and they walked through two tall glass doors and into the warm inside. Dark slate floors radiated warmth.

Then an alarming thought occurred to her. Would she have her own space? Or did he intend for her to sleep in his bedroom?

10

Serena felt a sudden need to take charge. She'd drifted down Sandro's snowy river far enough. "I am going to have my own bedroom, aren't I?"

"Yes." He didn't look at her.

She felt a tiny pinch of disappointment. Had she hoped he'd argue with her? "Great."

Maybe he didn't want to sleep with her again. Perhaps now that they were back in his country, surrounded by his people and family, he'd realized that nothing could really ever work out between them.

They'd have a quiet rather awkward few days together here, and he'd fly her politely back home.

Which would be fine. Right?

"This room is yours." He opened the door to a large bedroom dominated by a wall of windows looking onto the snowy mountains behind. "It should have everything you need." He led her in, putting her bags in front of a sleek closet. The bed was a low platform, covered in pillows. "And there's a bathroom here." He gestured inside, where she glimpsed an expanse of polished stone mosaic and a shower the size of her entire bathroom in Manhattan. Lucky ran in and ran out, tail wagging, then jumped up on the bed and rolled among the cushions.

"It's lovely."

"Thanks. I built the newer areas of the house around the views. Saved me a lot of money on pictures." His cheeky grin made her smile. They stood there for a few seconds, and she had no idea what to say. He looked gorgeously rumpled but barely tired even after staying awake for the long flight.

"You must be exhausted."

"I'm fine."

"I have a feeling you'd say that even if you'd been awake for a week straight." He was pretty tough—for a prince. She liked that.

"I might." He cocked his head. "My sisters tease me that I have FOMO."

"Fear of missing out?"

He nodded. "Sleep can be such a waste of time."

Naturally he was the type who wanted to be on the go all the time. She already knew he was a genius inventor who dated movie stars, as well as being a prince. He'd told her he was an adrenaline junkie. He'd soon grow bored with an ordinary girl.

"I happen to be a big fan of sleep."

"Then feel free to take a nap." He gestured at the bed, which looked dangerously inviting, even without the idea of Sandro in it.

"I'm not really that sleepy. I caught some z's on

the plane while you were busy flying. I guess I'd better unpack."

"Then would you like to take a tour? It's been a while since I've been here. I wouldn't mind looking the place over to see if anything needs fixing."

"Sure." The room was spotless, maintained by the cleaner in his absence. Sandro's lifestyle was pretty jaw-dropping. If she framed it right her followers would enjoy a glimpse into it.

Heck, she was enjoying her glimpse into it. But she was nervous about presenting herself and Sandro as some kind of item. She didn't want to have to break the news of two different breakups in one year.

"Text me when you're done. I'll come right back for you."

She unpacked. She could almost have come right here from Chicago, since she'd worn her fur-lined boots and down coat there. But on the stop in New York she'd sneaked some sexy lingerie into her bag. Nothing too racy, just a couple of pretty bras and some matching panties. And a slinky nightgown she'd impulse-bought to surprise Howard on their honeymoon.

That wasn't ever going to happen. Her heart still sank a little at the thought, though every day she was feeling less heartbroken and devastated about losing Howard. Clearly she was getting over him—and she might as well get some use out of the nightgown before she got too huge to put it on.

"Where are you going to sleep, Lucky?" The little dog ran around the room in excited circles. Back at home she'd kept him strictly in the living room at nights, because a friend had warned her that once you let a dog sleep in your bedroom it would always want to.

And she might want someone else in her bedroom.

Lucky suddenly ran out of the room and down the hallway. "Hey, where are you going?" She was only half-unpacked. Could he get outside and become lost in the snow?

Running to the door she caught sight of him turning right at the end of the hallway, so she hurried over the slate tiles. "Lucky!"

She turned right after him and saw him duck into a room two doors down, so she followed. And walked right into the sight of Sandro peeling off his underwear.

The vision of his muscled body, hard ridges picked out by the harsh sunlight bouncing off the mountains outside the huge window, took her breath away. He was built like an athlete, with broad shoulders narrowing to a slim waist with a flat, hard belly.

His body hair was dark, tapering to a happy trail that pointed in a direction she tried not to look at. But it was impossible because as soon as he looked up at her—surprised—he started to grow hard.

"I'm so sorry. I just...Lucky!" She couldn't even see Lucky now.

"No worries." He stepped out of his underwear, an action that used all the well-developed muscles of his powerful thighs and calves, not to mention his tight backside.

Either the room was getting very hot or she was about to pass out. "I'll just—" She wanted to turn and run, but she couldn't tear her eyes off him.

"I'll be ready in a second. Take a seat." He

gestured to a wide leather sofa. Everything was sleek and modern.

She glanced at it—then back at him. "Uh."

"I'm going to jump in the shower." He strode—stark naked and gorgeous as any statue in the Metropolitan Museum of Art—across the dark stone floor. "I won't be a minute.

Lucky darted out of the bathroom and circled his feet, bouncing with excitement.

"Lucky, give him some space," she called.

"I don't need any space from this guy." He glanced back at Lucky with a grin. "He's my buddy. I think he remembers me."

"Of course he remembers you. You rescued him."

"You rescued him. You're the one who heard him barking."

"True, but I might not have been brave enough to walk into the floodwaters all by myself." Lucky had been chained to the porch of the house next door to the one she'd rented, and they hadn't seen him until water was creeping up over the lawn.

"We're a team, then." He walked into the large open shower and turned on the water. She could see him clearly from where she stood in the bedroom. "And he knows it."

We're a team. It would be easy to read too much into those words. They had been, though, at least for a short time while the freak storm ravaged the beautiful beachfront property they were stranded in.

She couldn't even imagine what she'd have done without him. She'd have been terrified as soon as the power went out, but with him there she'd felt safe and protected. Safe enough to make passionate love while the storm raged.

She turned and busied herself studying his bedroom. It would be rude to stare at him while he washed himself. Dangerously tempting too. She might find herself rushing over to help him soap his back.

Lord knows she hadn't put up much resistance last time. Something about Sandro burned through all her defenses. It was just a superficial attraction to his flashy good looks, his bold confidence, heck, maybe even the fact that he was a prince.

The water shut off, and she braced herself not to turn around. He had a different but equally spectacular view through the wall of glass in his bedroom. A triple row of mountain peaks. His bed had a big fur throw on it—hopefully fake—and there was a minimalist clock on one wall. Other than the bed and a sofa there was no furniture in the large room.

The sound of Lucky's feet pattering back across the stone floor made her turn and crouch to pet him. "Lucky, what have we gotten ourselves into?"

As if in answer, Lucky trotted back to Sandro, who was now out of the shower and toweling himself off, once again displaying his well-toned muscles. She crossed her arms over her tightening nipples.

His phone rang. She averted her eyes as he strolled across the floor, towel tucked loosely around his waist, to answer it. "Hi, Mom.... Yes, it's true. I am here.... Not tonight. I have plans already." She wasn't looking at him, but she could feel his gaze burning into her. "I have a guest here with me."

She shifted awkwardly. How did his mom feel

about him sleeping with strange women? As a royal he would be expected to uphold the family reputation.

"We'll come see you soon, okay?"

Serena glanced at him. Was he lying to his mom right now, or had he been lying to her when he promised an escape from everything? Once again, Sandro said what he thought someone wanted to hear. A timely reminder that she could trust him about as far as she could throw him. "Love you too. Bye, Mom."

"I guess your sister told her you're here." She had to say something to avoid an awkward silence.

"Nothing stays secret for long in Altaleone. The country is too small. Even if we hadn't run into my sister, word would have got back to her from someone."

"We should have come straight here from the airport." She didn't like the idea that people would be talking about her. Wondering who that strange, dark-skinned woman was having breakfast with their handsome prince. "Do people gossip a lot in Altaleone?"

"No more than anywhere else, I suppose." He smiled. And rubbed the towel against himself, which caused an uncomfortable wave of heat to rise in her core.

"You don't mind it?"

He shrugged, creating a disturbing ripple effect in the muscles of his shoulders and chest. "I'm used to it, I suppose. Don't worry about it."

What did it matter? No one here knew who she was, anyway. Her book and her totally undeserved status as some kind of unlettered relationship expert meant nothing in Altaleone.

His phone rang again. "Do excuse me." He picked it up. "Hey, bro, yes, I was going to call you but not today." She braced herself to hear him explain that he had a *guest*—code for bedmate. "You all wonder why I didn't let you know I was coming? It's because I need some time to unwind first." He glanced up at her and smiled. "No, I can't go skiing tomorrow. I'm kind of busy now. Can I call you back later?"

She could hear a male voice talking at the other end.

"Yes, she's a friend." He glanced at her warmly. She stiffened. She didn't much like being called a *friend*, but she knew she wasn't really his girlfriend, either. "Yes, she's American. And she's standing right here next to me. Would you like to talk to her?"

Serena's heart thumped as she prayed the answer was no. Sandro finally got rid of his brother and hung up.

"It seems people are very curious about you."

"Does that surprise you?"

"Yes. My family rarely asks any questions about girls I date until I've been with them at least a few months."

"They've grown accustomed to a rapid turnover?" She tried not to sound catty, but it didn't work.

He looked sheepish. "Something like that. Maybe they can tell the situation is different this time."

"Or maybe it's because I'm black." She didn't want to say it, but her ethnicity was beginning to feel like the elephant in the room.

"Nonsense. People in Altaleone aren't racist."

She inhaled. "Perhaps there's no overt racism

169

here because everyone is white." That's how it looked in the town, anyway. "That doesn't mean they're totally open-minded. You might be too optimistic about people's attitudes."

He didn't respond immediately but seemed to digest what she had to say. "Perhaps you're right."

She felt a sense of relief that he took her concerns seriously.

"I like to give people the benefit of the doubt." He stood there in his towel, serious. "But if anyone—and I mean anyone—displays even a trace of racism toward you, or toward us, I will deal with them very severely."

His words sent a frisson through her. He sounded protective, like a bear. "Pistols at dawn?" She suddenly felt the need to lighten the atmosphere.

"Something like that." Warmth sparkled in his eyes.

Her heart swelled. She felt like they'd had a moment of genuine communication about something that had been silently nagging at the back of her mind. It was good to know his thoughts.

Now she liked him all the more.

And he still looked damned delicious in that towel...

"Would you please get dressed!"

"Why?" He lifted a teasing brow.

"Pregnancy has a strange effect on the mind as well as the body. Watching you walk around almost in the buff is having a dangerous effect on my sanity." It was a relief to joke about it, because seriously, heat was building up inside her at an alarming rate.

Sandro was so gorgeous she couldn't seem to tear

her eyes off him. Lucky, crouched adoringly at Sandro's feet, was clearly having the same problem.

"What's the point of these wonderful radiant heat floors if I can't feel them through my bare feet." He wriggled his toes.

She had to laugh. "Perhaps you can keep your feet bare, but put some pants on."

"If it will make you happy."

"It would be a huge relief." She had her hands crossed over her chest and hated the way her nipples kept tingling against the inside of her bra.

Sandro's broad back flexed as he pulled a long-sleeved gray T-shirt and a pair of army-green pants from his closet. His biceps rippled as he pulled the pants on over his strong legs. She still couldn't look away, and if she closed her eyes she might just fall over.

Looking at Howard's body never had anything like this effect on her. In a way it was therapeutic to see how much more attracted she was to someone else.

Even if that someone was far less likely to fulfill her criteria—outlined in chapter three of *Waiting for Mr. Right*—for choosing a successful husband. A guffaw escaped her at her own hubris in presuming to tell other people how to live their life and especially how to make relationship decisions.

"What's so funny?"

"You're exactly the kind of man I told my readers to stay away from."

"What?" He wheeled around. "Why?"

"I told them to hold out for someone who shares your lifestyle goals."

"You don't believe in energy access for everyone

on the planet?"

She laughed again. "Okay, that I am onboard with. But having your own jet aircraft and living in an ancient Roman villa were never on my to-do list."

"Ah, but that's simply because they hadn't occurred to you. Can you see how handy it is to have your own jet? And the Romans knew how to construct a wall that stands the test of time. My lifestyle choices are simply practical."

"For someone with vast sums of money at their disposal." That was the bottom line, really. He lived in a world where very few could even breathe the air.

"Money is simply a resource, like water. There's no point in hoarding it, as there are ways to find more when you need it."

She stared at him. "There are so many things wrong with that statement that I don't even know where to start. Don't you believe in conserving water?"

They both cracked up. How could Sandro get away with saying such outrageous things and still be adorable? On most people it would be obnoxious and unbearable. "My resources have been strained by buying an apartment that's way too expensive for my actual income. I had one amazing year—when I got the book advance—and for some dumb reason I thought that was just one step on the ladder to riches. I sure wish I could turn on a tap and watch more money flow out."

"Do you love your apartment?"

"No. I don't even like it anymore. The best thing about it is the neighbor who looks after Lucky while I'm working."

"So sell it."

"It's been on the market for months. There's a lot of competition, and apparently my view is considered subpar."

"Perhaps we can convince my friend Zadir to buy it. He's a real estate investor. He owns several apartments in New York."

He was the guy who owned the Georgia beach house she'd rented—only to find out that he'd simultaneously loaned it to Sandro. "I don't trust Zadir. Look what happened last time I made a deal with him."

Sandro's face creased into a smile. "Yeah. I owe him big time." He'd pulled the T-shirt on over his head, giving her another breath-stealing view of his six-pack in action. "I should buy your apartment and give it to him as a present."

"Oh, my goodness." Serena blew out. "You're illustrating exactly why an ordinary mortal like me needs to stay far, far away from guys like you and Zadir."

"We're ordinary mortals too. We're just successful in our chosen business. As you are in yours. I think it's quite arrogant of you to suggest that we're different."

"You crack me up."

"Good." He took a step toward her. *Uh-oh.* Her skin jumped as he grew nearer. How did he get her so overheated? It wasn't just his good looks. His infectious good humor had a way of undermining her tendency to be too serious—which loosened up her body in an alarming way. "A crack is where the light gets in."

"Says who?" Her belly shimmered as he took another step closer.

"Leonard Cohen."

"Who?"

"He was a brilliant poet and philosopher and singer. You'd like him."

"Oh, would I? You presume to know quite a lot about me."

His gaze rested on her face, his dark eyes—as usual—seeming to peer past the surface to something deeper. No doubt her powerful attraction to him was written in her dilated pupils, swollen lips and alert nipples.

It was hard to hide anything from this guy.

Sandro's gaze shifted to her mouth, which quivered slightly. *He's going to kiss me.*

11

I want him to kiss me.

She felt her body move toward his, as if drawn by unseen forces. And she took the final step, tilted her chin to raise her face to his. Her eyes slid closed and—

His phone rang.

Her eyes snapped open. Sandro's arms closed around her waist, stopping her sudden attempt to step back. He held her firm. "Where are you going?" he asked softly.

"You should answer it."

"I can call back."

"What if it's important?"

"Nothing could be more important right now than kissing you." He said it slowly, and from the look in his eyes she could tell he was deadly serious. She felt herself melting under the heat of his desire—and her own.

Their lips met and their tongues tangled. Her

body leaned into his as heat raced through her. Kissing Sandro, tucked away in his secluded house, even Lucky being here—as he was when they made love at Christmas—felt perfect.

The kiss deepened, and his warm arms closed around her. She found herself wanting to peel off the clothes he'd just put on. Her heart filled as she thought of his words—that she was the most important thing to him right now. Maybe the idea of them being together wasn't so crazy after all.

Her heart squeezed as she thought of the way he'd pursued her—respectful but insistent—even following her to Chicago. He seemed serious. Maybe she should take him seriously.

His hands roamed up and down her back, stirring hot waves of pleasure that coursed through her.

Then his phone started ringing again.

They ignored it, but just as he slid his hand under her top to touch her agonizingly aroused breasts—it rang again.

A sigh shook him. "Who on earth could be calling me right now?"

"You really should check." Her heart sank as she said it. For a few moments there she'd been so sure, so confident, in her desire and affection for Sandro. But now their peace and seclusion were shattered.

Sandro pulled his arms from her with considerable reluctance, at least that was how it seemed from how agonizingly slowly he tore himself away. Then he strode across the room to where his phone vibrated on a ledge. He frowned. "It's from the palace."

Odd. Why wouldn't he say, "It's my mom," or whatever other relative it was.

He answered the call with a gruff, "What's going on?"

There was a long pause. Then Sandro dropped an uncharacteristic curse. "Is my mom okay?" He shook his head. "Damn. I'll be there as soon as I can. Thank you for calling me."

Still holding the phone he turned to her, expression now dark with fury. "Someone dug up the bodies. My dad's and my grandma's." He squeezed his eyes shut for a second. "They cut off my dad's finger and sent it to my mom in a box."

She shuddered. What a horrible image.

Before she even had a chance to respond, he was calling someone else on his phone.

"Gibran, what the hell is going on? Weren't the bodies under guard?" He paced, shaking his head. "It's got to be an inside job." He bent to pet Lucky. "What kind of drugs? How did they administer them?" He rose and strode around the room. She could feel the frustration and anger rolling off him.

Their lovely interlude was over. Her heart ached for the sweet sense of confidence that she'd enjoyed, even for a few fleeting seconds. Clearly she was not the most important thing on his agenda now—and with good reason. As a member of the royal family he had responsibilities and duties beyond his own desires and wishes, and she admired that he took them seriously.

Sandro hopped into a pair of socks and grabbed a jacket from the closet. "We need to head to the palace."

But you promised I wouldn't have to meet your family. She couldn't whine about it now in the middle of a crisis. Still, she dreaded the thought of being thrown into his royal milieu. What if they hated her? At the very least they wouldn't think her worthy of Sandro. "Could I stay here until you get back?"

"I'm afraid it's not safe. The old family graveyard where the bodies were buried was under guard, and someone managed to drug the guards and dig up the bodies in the night. It's right on the palace grounds, and the very expensive and highly recommended security chief we hired doesn't seem sure how it happened. Under those circumstances we really can't consider anywhere to be safe."

She suddenly felt cold. She wasn't any safer with him at the palace than she was here all by herself if there was some kind of crazy person out there who would dig up a dead body and cut off the finger. An involuntary shiver shook her again, and a wave of nausea rose inside her.

"Are you okay?" He rushed toward her. "You look like you might pass out."

"I overheard the part about the finger." She wasn't sure if it was that or the prospect of being introduced to his mom that had her the most freaked out. "It's so horrible."

"It is, and my mom is having such a hard time dealing with the deaths already. I don't imagine that she saw the severed finger herself, though. All of her mail is opened by her assistant. I'm not even sure what they've told her. Let's get over there fast. Where's your coat?"

He knew where her coat was since he'd taken it from her and hung it in the closet in the foyer. She straightened her clothing. "Should we bring Lucky?"

"Definitely. We might be there for a few days."

"Days! Then we need clothes too. And his crate

and bowls."

"Don't worry about that. We can send someone for those. Let's go."

He scooped Lucky up in his arms and headed for the front door so fast that she could barely keep up. Every time something in her life seemed like it was about to start going right, something else exploded in her face.

Don't be so selfish. At least no one in your family is dead. This was Sandro's own father who'd been desecrated in this cruel way. She'd better take a page from Sandro's royal notebook and learn how to put other people's concerns before her own for a change.

Sandro drove so fast over the icy roads that they skidded a few times—despite the tire chains. She bit her tongue although she wanted to tell him to slow down. This was not a situation where she felt qualified to give advice or warnings. Once again she was out of her depth and in over her head.

"Is there anything I should know before we meet your family?" she asked tentatively. They were waiting while the scrolled black-and-gold wrought iron gates were rolled open by uniformed guards.

"That we're a family." He turned to look her in the face. "Just like any other family in a lot of ways. A conglomeration of different personalities and interests yoked together by blood. Don't get too hung up on the royal thing. It's just a distraction."

"I'll keep that in mind." It must be hard to know that every person meeting you showed up with a set of expectations that had nothing to do with you as a person. For all she could fault her too-perfect online persona, it was her own creation and she had no one but herself to blame.

They pulled up in front of a grand neoclassical building wrapped around a wide courtyard. Staffers rushed forward to open their doors, and two tall men rushed down the steps and up to the car.

"Does Mom know what happened?"

The taller man, regally handsome and dressed in a black shirt and pants, nodded. "She hates when we keep things from her. She hasn't seen the package, but I described the contents." They removed their coats and handed them to waiting staff.

"Serena, this is my brother Darias."

The king. "Very pleased to meet you." She followed his lead in extending her hand. For an awkward moment she wondered if she should curtsey, but he continued talking to Sandro.

"Gibran wants to replace our entire security staff with his own hired men."

"It's the only way to assure neutrality." The second man, also with bold features and dark hair but with a more Middle Eastern look about him, cut in. "I know it causes upset to remove people from long-held positions, which is why we've avoided it up till now, but I can't guarantee anyone's safety when it appears we have dangerous elements here on royal property."

"Serena, this is Gibran, the chief of security." Gibran didn't offer his hand but simply nodded. "Can we give all of the staff lie detector tests?" Sandro started to walk with them back to the palace.

"We've administered quite a few," said Gibran. "But the problem is that a sociopath—the kind of person who plots and murders without a qualm of conscience—doesn't react to this kind of test, which ultimately measures emotional response to the question, so they slide under the radar. It's just not effective at catching that one bad apple in the barrel."

"I see." Sandro climbed the steps, carrying Lucky in his arms. Serena thought it odd that no one had commented on the dog, but of course they had bigger things to worry about.

As did she. She was about to meet Sandro's mother.

"Sandro, darling!" A blonde woman of about fifty rushed out of a gilded archway at the sound of their voices. "I had no idea you were coming to Altaleone until Beatriz told me she saw you in the village! No one tells me anything anymore."

He kissed her on both cheeks. "I'm sorry, Mama. My trip wasn't planned. I hadn't even unpacked yet when I heard the grim news."

"Can you believe it?" His mom's pretty face creased with distress. "Whoever they are, I feel like they're taunting us."

"We'll find them. Don't upset yourself." Darias put his arm around his mother.

"But why now? The murders, all of it… Things have been peaceful for decades. For centuries, even."

Darias pulled back and raked a hand through his dark hair. "Gibran thinks that money is the root of most evils. And we know there's keen interest in that Swiss bank account maintained by the Cross of Blood."

Gibran cleared his throat loudly.

"Oh, am I not supposed to talk about that openly?" Darias looked around. Even Serena could see that several members of the palace staff were in earshot. And she knew some might be under suspicion based on the conversation outside.

"Mama, I'd like you to meet Serena."

Serena felt a wave of relief. She'd begun to worry that they were just going to ignore her presence.

Serena shook the older woman's hand. Sandro hadn't told her what to call his mom. He hadn't even said her name. "I'm very pleased to meet you."

"Are you visiting Altaleone on business or pleasure?" His mom's question might be an innocent conversational gambit, but Serena froze. What kind of business could she have in Altaleone? But to say she was here for pleasure was tantamount to being Sandro's royal concubine.

"A bit of both," cut in Sandro. "She's never seen Europe before, and I insisted that she start with the most beautiful country of all. She's a well-known presence on social media and will be making videos and writing blogs about our country. I convinced her to come as I know it will be good publicity for us."

She found herself smiling. Sandro was obviously much better at thinking on his feet than she.

"And who is this adorable little fellow?" Sandro's mom petted Lucky, who licked her hand then strained up trying to lick her face.

"This is Lucky, Serena's dog," explained Sandro.

"Wonderful. We could all use some good luck right now." She turned to Serena. "I'm sorry you're here under such trying circumstances, but I do hope you'll feel welcome and make yourself at home during your stay. Oh, and do call me Lina."

"Thank you." Even though Lina's words were typical pleasantries, they drew some of the tension from Serena's shoulders. She truly did seem warm and had shown no signs of shock or dismay at Serena's arrival.

"We'll need our bags and Lucky's things from my house." Sandro lowered Lucky gently to the floor.

Lina gestured to a blonde male staffer in a pinstriped shirt and gray slacks. "Wilhelm, could you please arrange for everything they need to be brought here today?"

"Certainly, Madam." He nodded and rushed off.

Serena wondered how the staff felt at having to obey the beck and call of these privileged royals. Though it was really no different than any other job and probably paid a lot better than some.

"Come in and sit down." Lina smiled warmly at Serena. "I'm sorry you've arrived in the midst of a crisis. I'm sure Sandro will still have plenty of time to show you around."

"No worries," she said. Then cursed herself for sounding too offhand. She should cultivate an air of respectful formality. She wondered how wrinkled her clothes were from the long plane flight but didn't dare look down.

Lina led them into a sitting room the size of a basketball court, with brocade sofas and delicate carved wood tables that looked like they belonged in a museum. Ancestors in powdered wigs glared down from the pale yellow walls. A quick glance up at the ceiling revealed that it was painted to look like the sky and populated by plump winged cherubs.

Her family would die of laughter—or of shock— if they could see her right now.

"Serena, would you like some tea?"

"Yes, please." It seemed polite to accept even though she didn't really like tea. A girl in a neat uniform appeared with a silver teapot and a delicate cup and saucer on a tray, then filled the tea and added milk and sugar after glancing at her to see if she wanted each one.

Serena took the cup and saucer with trembling hands, hoping she wasn't about to spill tea on the antique silk rug that must be almost half an acre in size. She glanced nervously around for Lucky and hoped he wasn't peeing on the leg of a priceless table.

She was just lifting the teacup gingerly to her lips when Lina leaned toward Sandro and whispered— loudly—"You can sleep in your old room. Will Serena be joining you there?"

12

Serena's teeth clinked against the cup, and tea sloshed dangerously against the rim. She looked anywhere but at Sandro. If they hadn't been interrupted by his phone they would have made love already this afternoon.

But she didn't want everyone here in this room to know that.

"Is the room next to mine open?"

"The moonlight room? We hardly ever use that one. Are you sure?"

"Yes. It's not really haunted. That's just a rumor." He turned to Serena and winked. "You're not afraid of imaginary ghosts are you?"

Yes.

"No. At least I don't think so." Were they seriously going to put her in a haunted bedroom? Maybe this was Sandro's way of making sure she didn't want to sleep alone. "I'm sure it will be fine."

"Great." Lina turned to another staffer—there

seemed to be an inexhaustible supply—"Ava, please get the room ready." Then she looked back at Serena with a warm smile. "It has a connecting door to Sandro's room if you need anything in the night."

Serena blinked. This was really awkward! Her parents would be glaring and frowning if she attempted to sleep with a man she wasn't married to under their roof. Howard had slept on the sofa in the basement when they visited, even after they were engaged.

"I suppose we should get back to more dismal matters," said Lina with a sigh. "Tell me the truth. Was there a note inside the box with the..." She swallowed hard. "If so, what did it say? Don't lie to me!"

"There was no note, I'm afraid." Gibran spoke softly. "We are dusting the box and its contents for fingerprints and other forensic evidence, including DNA, to see if we can determine the sender."

"What do they want?" Sandro peered up at Gibran. "Why would anyone do this?"

"To rattle us," growled Darias. "They want us on edge, worrying, wondering what's going to happen next."

"Well, that's certainly working," said Lina. Her smooth forehead creased. "I don't think any of us are safe traveling without a security guard, even just to walk to the castle in the village. Is Emma there now?" She glanced at Darias.

"She's at the local primary school reading to the pupils. You know how much she loves to. I didn't have the heart to stop her."

"Emma used to be a teacher before she became queen here," Lina explained. "I don't know how we'll ever go back to feeling normal again. What about that creepy secret society—the Cross of Blood? Could they have something to do with this?" She looked at Darias.

"We can't rule them out, but from everything they've told me—and everything I've learned about them—they exist to protect us."

"Then they're doing a horrible job of it." Tears filled her eyes. "I know they're all important personages, but I don't see why they can't all be called onto the carpet to reveal what they know."

"Gibran thinks," said Darias, "and I agree, that could be more dangerous than using more subtle methods to investigate them. We've managed to figure out the identity of all but two of them."

"And who are they?"

Darias glanced at Gibran. "We can't reveal that. Don't take it personally. There are just too many people around."

Lina let out a long sigh. "Sometimes I almost feel like a suspect here."

"You're not, Mama," said Darias. "I promise. But in some ways you're safer the less that you know. Emma was taken because the kidnappers wanted a secret bank account number and passcode from me. If you knew it, you could have been taken and who knows what could have happened."

"Do you even know the numbers?" Lina peered at him.

Darias mouth settled into a line. He clearly wasn't willing to answer the question. She turned to Sandro. "Do you know it?"

"No, Mama." He rubbed her upper arm with his hand. "I'm not in the Cross of Blood. Only members of the society know the details of the ancient trust."

"Well, that's a relief. This makes me not want to let Darias out of my sight."

"I can handle myself, Mama." Darias lifted his chin. Truth be told, Darias was built much like Sandro and looked as if he could handle an MMA fight more easily than a palace tea party.

"I understand money as a motive, but why would someone kill my husband and his mother?"

Gibran's brows lowered. "Possibly because they wanted Darias to be king—"

"But why?"

"I ask myself the same question all the time," said Darias. "It doesn't make sense."

Gibran cleared his throat. "Or they want to extinguish the House of Leone completely."

Lina gasped. "Who would want to do that?"

"Who would stand to gain from it?" asked Gibran.

"No one. Well, unless there was someone who didn't want Altaleone to have a monarchy anymore. But given how many descendants there are I think they would be on a fool's errand."

She sounded brave, but Serena watched her face grow pale as she contemplated the prospect of each of her ten children being picked off, one by one. Serena's heart squeezed with distress. She couldn't imagine losing Sandro—and they were still barely more than acquaintances.

"Of course there are antimonarchist dissidents here," said Darias. "As there are anywhere. But they are usually just people with too much time on their hands who need something to complain about. Our citizens enjoy the highest standard of living in the world, and they know it. There's no serious groundswell of resistance. Lord knows we're not interested in ruling anyone with an iron fist."

"What about business rivals?" asked Gibran. "Perhaps in the diamond industry. That's a cutthroat field that's no stranger to international intrigue."

Darias sighed. "True. We haven't really considered that angle. We don't mine the diamonds here. Our gem merchants buy them wholesale and cut them for all of the European markets. We're second only to Antwerp as the diamond capital of Europe."

"Is the royal family involved in the diamond business?"

"Absolutely." Darias looked surprised at Gibran's question. "It's our main income producer, even ahead of the vineyards."

"This angle demands further investigation. I'm going to put one of my team members to work on it immediately. The diamond trade has historically been no stranger to murder and extortion unfortunately. Is there any link between the Cross of Blood trust and the diamond industry?"

They looked at each other in silence. Then Lina spoke. "I'd imagine so. The Cross of Blood dates back to the Middle Ages. The diamond industry goes back even further, to the Roman Empire. It's likely that the wealth of one filled the coffers of the other."

"In my homeland, Ubar, ancient grudges may be set aside like a favorite sword, but they are never truly forgotten. We learned that the hard way. We must dust off the history books and search for connections."

"Beatriz would be good at that," offered Lina.

"She's always been a history buff. She wrote an illustrated history of the village of Casteleone when she was nine."

"Where is Beatriz?" asked Sandro. "She's usually right here with you."

"I'm not sure." Lina pulled out her phone and pushed a button. "I called her as soon as the news of the package arrived, and she hasn't called me back."

Serena watched Sandro, Darias and Gibran all stiffen and seem to grow a couple of inches taller. "We must find her." Sandro's voice cut the air like a knife. "Where did she say she was going?"

Lina frowned. "She took her car out early this morning. I heard her asking one of the staff to tighten the tire chains. She called me to tell me that Sandro was in town but I haven't heard from her since."

"So she must have been planning more than a quick trip into the village."

"Yes." Lina bit her lip. "And why isn't she answering? She always answers my calls."

"I'm sending men out right away to search for her." Gibran strode from the room, dialing and speaking fast into his phone in a language Serena had never heard before. "I'll keep you updated. Let me know the instant you hear *anything*."

"Oh, dear." Lina's voice shook.

"Mama, come sit down." Sandro put his arm around her and walked her toward a sofa. "No one has died since Gibran came here to help us. Rest assured that he'll find Beatriz just like he found Emma when she was kidnapped."

"But why can't we figure out who's behind this? It's even more alarming to think that they could be right under our nose. In this room, even!" She glanced around. The staffers present—Ava removing an abandoned teacup from a table, an older man standing in the doorway and a young girl fluffing a brocade cushion—all seemed to halt in their tracks for a split second. Or maybe she just imagined it.

She couldn't imagine living her life with this many eavesdroppers. It was a whole different level of exposure than putting a few carefully framed minutes of her life up on YouTube for people to watch.

"When we saw Beatriz this morning." Sandro sat next to his mom. Serena sat down in an adjacent chair, careful not to spill her tea. "She was in the old village café."

"How odd." Lina peered into the distance. "We had breakfast together this morning. Why would she go to the café?"

Serena remembered seeing Beatriz pick up two coffees and a bag of pastries. She must have been buying for herself and someone else. Would she be stepping out of bounds to bring that up? Since it might be a matter of life and death she decided to throw caution to the wind. "When she left the café she had two coffees in take-out containers."

Lina stared at her. "Two? She didn't say she was meeting anyone."

Serena swallowed. "We didn't see anyone with her, but I suppose she must have been meeting someone." Why else would you want two coffees? Unless it was finals week in college…but Sandro had said that Beatriz never went to college and her job was basically being a princess.

"Who has she been spending time with lately?" asked Sandro. He looked from his mom to Darias.

Darias shrugged. "Emma might know. She's spent time with Beatriz."

"Goodness, I hope it isn't that dreadful Lorenzo Aldobrando. I almost had a heart attack when he came to the coronation."

"He was invited, Mama. I was rather wary, given that his family has that ridiculous claim to our lake, but he behaved like a gentleman. Besides, that was months ago. I'm surprised you even remember it."

"He was flirting with Beatriz, though, wasn't he? I saw them talking more than once."

Darias laughed. "I dare anyone to flirt with Beatriz. They'd get their head bitten off."

"True," said Sandro. "Could she be with a girlfriend?"

"I don't think so." Lina looked up, as if searching her mind. "Her girlfriends from school have all moved off to Vienna or Zurich or Paris for work. You know how it is here." She wrung her hands. "I'm worried, but I'm reassured by the two coffees. I'm sure she's just busy with someone."

"Perhaps a secret lover?" Darias lifted a brow. "I always said Beatriz was a dark horse."

"Nonsense. Beatriz is an open book," protested Lina.

"Oh, my goodness." Serena put her teacup down with a clatter at the sight of Lucky peeing against the curved leg of an ornate chair. "Lucky!"

"Poor thing! We forgot to take him outside for a pee after the drive." Sandro rose too. "Let's do it now."

"I think that might be locking the barn door after the horse has bolted," said Darias with a wink.

Serena swept Lucky up in her arms and ignored

his playful attempts to lick her face. "Where can I find a cloth to wipe it up?" She'd been afraid something like this would happen. At least it wasn't on a rug, but the elaborate parquet floor might be ruined if the pee sat there too long.

Sandro laughed. "Are you trying to put our staff out of a job?"

Already a young woman hurried over with a folded towel, and she could see another arriving behind her with a bucket and mop.

Must be nice…

"We'll just take him out for a breath of air," explained Sandro to his mom. "We'll be right back."

Instead of heading back down the front steps into the grand courtyard, Sandro led her out of the living room by a different door, and across a marble-floored hallway and out into an interior courtyard. The courtyard was larger than most yards in her parents' suburban neighborhood, with grass—scraped of snow but glittering with ice crystals in the pale late-afternoon sun—and big bronze urns filled with evergreens. She put Lucky down on the crisp frozen grass. The palace rose up around them, all white limestone walls with tall, elegantly proportioned windows.

"This place is huge."

"It dates back to an era when the royal family had way more servants than we do now, though we rival any eighteenth- or nineteenth-century brood of royal children. Mom jokes that she unconsciously felt the need to have so many kids because of all the bedrooms just begging to be filled."

"It's very beautiful."

"It's the house that champagne built. One of my

ancestors planted acres of vineyards on the hillsides nearby, and just happened to catch a huge wave of champagne becoming popular among the well-to-do across Europe. Our champagne is still considered to be among the finest in the world. The high altitude of our mountains gives it a unique flavor."

"That's interesting." She shivered violently. Would she be a wuss to complain that it was absolutely freezing out here? They hadn't stopped to put their coats back on. Lucky had wandered off across the grass, following some scent trail.

"You're cold! I'm sorry. Let's go inside again. Sometimes we Altaleonians joke that our blood is so hot it never freezes. I think we're just used to our frigid winters. C'mon, Lucky!"

To her surprise Lucky stopped his sniffing and ran right back to them. She felt a tiny burst of pride for her rescued baby. "He doesn't seem to mind the cold."

"He has a warm black-and-white fur coat." Sandro slid his arm around Serena. Despite the warmth of his body, she stiffened. What if someone happened to look out of one of the windows? There must be fifty windows looking down at them. She could almost feel curious eyes burning a hole in her.

She was trying to think of a polite way to pull back, when a door to the house burst open and Darias leaned out. "Sandro, come quick!"

13

Sandro tugged his arms from her with obvious reluctance, swept Lucky up off the icy grass and headed for the door. "What's going on?"

"Beatriz was spotted leaving Casteleone late this morning in the passenger seat of a dark blue Audi sedan."

"That's not her car." Sandro ushered Serena in. She'd never been so grateful for indoor warmth. "Who saw her?"

"Iris, one of the cooks. She was buying groceries at the market and saw Beatriz climb into the car."

"Did she look like she was under duress?"

"No. Apparently she was smiling. She was with a man, but Iris didn't recognize him."

"Let me try calling her." Sandro pulled out his phone and dialed her number.

She answered immediately. "Hi, Sandro. What's going on?"

"Beatriz!" He gestured excitedly to the others.

"We're all frantic about you. Mom's been trying to call you."

"Why?" Serena could hear Beatriz's voice at the other end quite clearly.

He glanced at his mom. "There's been a…development. Something awful arrived in the mail. Why didn't you answer?"

There was a moment of silence. "I was busy"

"Who are you with?"

"Is it really any of your business? I don't question your every movement and quiz you about your companions."

Serena watched Sandro frown. Clearly he held his sister to a different standard of behavior from his own. "Can you come home now? It was some kind of threat. Gibran is investigating, but he wants us all safely under guard here at the palace. I'm here myself now, with Serena."

"Oh." Another long silence. "I'll be back soon. Bye."

Serena heard her hang up. "That was odd." Sandro looked at his brother. "It's not like her to be so mysterious."

Darius had a twinkle in his eye. "I think we need to keep an eye out for someone driving a blue Audi."

Lina still looked worried. "I just don't understand why she didn't answer my calls.

"Every girl needs a little privacy sometimes, Mama," said Sandro. He glanced silently at Serena. Lord knows she'd claimed enough privacy lately. Hiding her breakup and her pregnancy from her mom and everyone else she knew.

Lina sighed. "I suppose you're right. It's just that we're so close. We tell each other everything."

"I'm sure she'll tell you when she's ready."

Serena wondered if Sandro's mom would ever embark on a new relationship. She'd only been widowed a few months, so might not be ready yet, but she was very beautiful and Serena suspected that a wealthy widow living in a palace would have no shortage of suitors.

"I suppose I depend on her too much because she's here with me all the time. I've been suffocating her." Lina refused an offered cup of tea. "On the other hand, I've been so focused on the deaths and on getting Darias and Emma settled into their new roles and their new home at the castle that I haven't paid enough attention to her needs."

"She understands, Mama, trust me. You've all been under a lot of pressure lately."

"And now there's this new drama. You won't show it to her, will you? She loved her father so much."

"Don't worry, Mama. No one will see it except those closely tied to the investigation."

"Thank goodness." She leaned in and whispered. "I have nightmares of the sordid details of the murders leaking to the press."

"And they haven't," replied Darias. "Try not to fret over things you can't control. We need to focus on the important things, like identifying and catching the killers."

"You're right, sweetheart. I wonder if Beatriz will be home in time for dinner. I do hope so. I'm going to shower and change and come down with a fresh attitude."

"That's a great idea, Mama." Sandro rubbed her hand affectionately. "I'll take Serena to her room and settle into mine, and we can meet back down here."

Sandro had been holding Lucky—who could be a squirmer—in the crook of his arm this whole time. Lucky gazed up at him with unabashed adoration. "Let's go upstairs. I'll show you your room."

Serena pushed a polite smile to her lips and glanced at the others. She really wished she had her travel bag here. She'd been wearing this outfit since last night, and she'd feel very out of place if they were all going to get dressed up for dinner the way royals did in movies. At the very least she'd like to put on her trusty little black dress and a sparkly pair of earrings.

Sandro gestured for her to climb the stairs ahead of him. They were wide enough for about eight people to walk abreast. More grim ancestors stared down at her, along with their horses and hounds and even a kind of pigeon perched on one young woman's finger.

"Your family is very nice," she said softly when they were out of earshot.

"See? I told you they were. You should believe me more often."

She shot him a challenging glance. "I really want to believe you about my room not being haunted."

"Only one way to find out, right? If anything scary happens just call for me and I'll rush right in." He caught up with her at the top of the stairs and leaned in close. "Come to think of it, don't wait for something scary to happen."

Her skin sizzled as he touched her. Surely he didn't expect her to fool around with him under his mother's roof? With about fifty people within possible earshot.... The idea made her shudder.

"Don't look so nervous. You'll be fine."

She lifted a brow. "Maybe it's not the ghost I'm worried about." They walked along a wide hallway lined with polished wood doors encased in ornate white plaster casing. More cherubs gazed down at them from the ceiling, and the rug felt very soft and expensive under foot.

"Here's your room." He pushed open the door.

"Wow, it's stunning." She stopped and stared. The walls were covered in ornate blue-and-silver fabric. The tall four-poster bed had dark blue velvet curtains gathered at the corners with tasseled ties. The floor-length curtains were blue velvet edged with silver.

"It's been known as the moonlight room since the palace was built. Traditions don't die quickly in Altaleone. I think you'll find the bed comfortable, though.

"I suppose that's a relief." She walked over to the bed. Definitely fit for a queen, and most likely more than one queen had slept in it. "But why moonlight?"

Sandro hesitated for a moment. "It was originally intended for the king's chief mistress."

Her hand froze just above the luxurious covers. "*Chief* mistress? He had more than one?"

Amusement sparkled in Sandro's eyes. "They didn't have the Internet to entertain themselves with back then.

"What did his wife think?"

"She was accused of poisoning her."

"So she's the ghost? The poisoned mistress?" A chill ran down her spine.

"There isn't any ghost. I don't even know if she

was poisoned. She probably just got sick and died. That was hardly a rare occurrence in the old days before antibiotics."

Serena drew in a shaky breath. "So what happened to the wife? Who was accused of the poisoning?"

"The king divorced her, and she went to live in a nunnery in the mountains."

"Poor her."

"Indeed. And she was his third wife. She had the best fate of all of them."

"I thought you said your family was nice!"

He laughed. "I was talking about the current generation. I make no such promises about my forbears." He walked over to a tall wardrobe that could easily double as a portal to another world and opened the door to reveal hangers already filled with the items from her suitcase. "They've delivered our luggage."

"How did they do it so fast?" She felt like they'd only just got here.

He shrugged. "It's not a long drive. And they work as a team. One person ironing while the other folds. You know."

"They ironed my clothes?" Eyes wide, she walked to the closet. Sure enough each item was smooth as a lake in a summer. "How am I going to go back to normal life after this?"

"Who says you should?"

She instantly regretted her comment. She still had no idea what Sandro really wanted with her. She couldn't imagine that he actually intended to propose marriage—baby or no.

Just the fact that she was assigned the room of

some long-dead royal mistress should give her very serious pause. "Am I supposed to get dressed up for dinner or something?"

"My mom always changes for dinner. I suppose it's one of those traditions she loves. My dad used to put on a fancy smoking jacket. Us kids rarely do. You can wear whatever you like."

She resolved to go with the little black dress, which was reassuringly unwrinkled. She'd always rather be overdressed than underdressed, regardless of the occasion. She chose a pair of pretty moonstone earrings and a matching necklace with a single stone on a delicate chain. By the time she'd finished her makeup routine—using a new tinted lip gloss that one of her sponsors had sent—she felt almost glamorous enough to attend a royal dinner.

Sandro had told her he'd come to get her on his way down, so she decided to kill time checking her social media. She was cheered to see that most of the posts about her breakup were compassionate, not critical, and she took the time to thank people for supporting her. She ignored the few snarkier comments. It didn't make any logical sense, but the physical distance—tucked away in the mountains of Altaleone—from her normal life gave her a sense of insulation.

And then there were the questions about Sandro. Those made her heart trip. "OMG so fine! Is he your new boo?" and questions to that effect. They made her smile—then panic. She could hardly write, "I don't know," even if it was the truth.

And she couldn't honestly write, "He's just a friend," when she was carrying his baby inside her.

"Sandro's a pretty amazing guy," she wrote in

response to one comment. Enthusiastic but noncommittal! "I'm really enjoying my visit to his country."

How long was he going to be? Did she have time to record a quick video? It seemed a shame to waste her flawless makeup. She looked around for the best backdrop—the four-poster bed—and propped her camera on its stand on a tall chest of drawers.

She used a remote to hit record.

"Hi, everyone, I thought I'd record a quick video before I head to dinner. I'm here in the royal palace at Altaleone"—she almost had to pinch herself as it sounded so grand when she said it—"and I wanted to show you the bedroom I'm sleeping in."

She launched into the story about the mistress and the ghost and how excited she was to be here. As always she kept her eye on the timer, intending to bubble away for her usual six minutes. She had just thanked them for their support and said she was slowly but surely getting over her breakup when a knock on the door made her jump.

14

Serena froze for a second unsure of whether to quickly sign off or to say, "Come in."

The door opened anyway. It was Sandro, tall and regal in a fresh black shirt and dark gray pants. He walked in, bold eyes appraising her in her fitted dress. His gaze heated her skin and made her thoughts dissolve into vapors. Before she could gather her senses he said, "You look radiant."

She blinked, feeling radiant. And also like she'd been caught in the act of something. "Hi, Sandro, I'm just wrapping up a video." She beckoned him into the shot—like it was no big deal that she had a prince coming to find her in her bedroom. "I was just telling them the story of the moonlight room."

Sandro came up to her—into the shot—and to her distress he put his arm around her waist. He spoke directly to the camera. "Do you not all agree that Serena is the most beautiful woman you've ever seen?"

She felt her face heat. "Oh, don't be silly! Besides, they know all my secrets. I'd have no cheekbones at all without contour." She heard a goofy giggle escape her. "Can you see what a charmer he is? Anyway, I'd better go. I'll keep you posted on my trip here in Altaleone." She pushed the stop button and widened her eyes at him. "Now they'll think we're...up to something."

"And they'll be right." His eyes glittered. He moved in as if he was going to kiss her.

Panic fluttered in her chest. "I really should post my video. So it's fresh."

"Go for it." His posture relaxed. So did hers. She loved how respectful Sandro was and how he didn't push or try to interfere with her professional activities. Not many people—including Howard— would be so understanding. Howard had found it rude and disturbing that she'd have to hold them up for five minutes to post her videos or respond to a comment. Though he had no trouble taking phone calls from his clients in the middle of dinner or even when they were in bed together.

She uploaded the video and titled it "In the Moonlight Room at the Palace." That should draw some views.

She wasn't sure exactly where this series of videos was going. But since she had no idea where her life was going either, that seemed appropriate. For once she didn't feel the need to control every aspect of her life. Maybe she was finally starting to relax?

And damn if it didn't feel good to be on camera with the very gorgeous—and intriguingly royal— Sandro. It certainly took the sting out of being jilted by her fiancé and made getting dumped seem way less depressing and embarrassing.

She watched the first comments pop up before anyone had even had time to watch the whole video. "Wow! Lucky you XXoXX," and similar gushing from some of her lovely regulars who got notifications as soon as she posted a video. "I'll be ready in a sec!" she said. Sandro stood, looking relaxed and unhurried, drinking her in with his eyes in a way that made her feel unbelievably glamorous.

Then her phone pinged. She checked her texts—there was a new one from an unknown number. **I see you are inside the palace. Good for you.**

She frowned. Who was this? Her heart started bumping. She never, EVER posted her personal number on social media. She hadn't told a single friend or family member that she was coming here and none of them would have watched her video so fast.. So who was it from?

"We really should go," said Sandro. "My mom is a stickler for punctuality.

"I just got a weird text." She showed him.

Sandro peered at it, then frowned. "I think we should show it to Gibran."

Visions of Gibran going through her phone and reading the humiliating trail of messages between her and Howard—that she wasn't quite ready to delete—made her cringe. "Oh, I don't think it's anything serious. Just odd, that's all. It must be someone who knows me who saw the video. I lost all my contacts when my last phone died. I'll text them back and ask who it is." She didn't want to annoy his mom. She put Lucky into his crate, which was set up in the corner of the room, complete with his favorite squeaky toy. "Let's go."

She resolved to text the mystery person later, so she wouldn't get into a texting convo in the middle of a royal dinner. She hadn't gone to etiquette school, but everyone knew that would be rude. As they walked downstairs she tried to rack her mind for who it could be. It might be quite innocent. Maybe it was her friend Asia, texting from an unfamiliar number?

Yes. It could be something like that.

"My goodness, you look beautiful." Lina's greeting made her wonder how terrible she'd looked before.

"Thank you." She wanted to return the compliment but somehow that seemed inappropriate. Instead she went with, "That's a beautiful necklace you're wearing." It was deep yellow gold and looked like a series of vines weaving in and out of each other.

Lina's hand rose to touch it. "Thank you. It's been in the Leone family for centuries."

"We had a jeweler appraise it three years ago, and he said it likely dates back to the Byzantine era, and may even have belonged to Empress Theodora." A female voice rang out. Serena turned to see Beatriz, dressed in black pants and a black turtleneck, with her hair in a neat bun. She wore no jewelry of any kind.

"Fascinating, Beatriz," said Darias, who'd appeared in the doorway. "But stop trying to distract us with trivia and tell us where you were all day."

Serena watched her chest rise and fall. "I simply went for a drive."

"Taking two coffees and a bag of pastries with you," said Sandro.

"Exactly." Her mouth narrowed into a line. "It takes a lot of caffeine and calories to keep me going when it's this cold."

"I can relate to that," said Serena. Everyone in the room turned to stare at her. Had she said something wrong? Or was she not supposed to just chime in on the conversation without being spoken to first?

She didn't know the first thing about royal etiquette. Heat rose to her cheeks, and she hoped it wasn't visible.

"See?" Beatriz's solemn face cracked into a smile. "Finally someone else here understands. It's nice to see you again, Serena. I hope they didn't put you in the moonlight room."

"Why?"

"Oh, stop it, Beatriz," said Lina. "You know there's nothing wrong with that room. It's one of the nicest. And it's right next to Sandro's."

"Oh, yes. I'd forgotten about that." She lifted a brow very slightly. "But no one can argue that strange things happen in that room. I swear a voice told me to look on top of the big armoire one afternoon, so I pulled up a chair, and found the strangest thing up there."

"What were you doing in there in the first place?" asked Darias gruffly.

Beatriz shrugged. "Oh, it was right before the coronation. I think I was just making sure it was set up to receive guests after Emma moved out."

"Surely the servants could have taken care of that," continued Darias.

Serena noticed a willowy blonde woman next to him, eyes growing wider with every word in the exchange between Darias and Beatriz. Was she

Darias's wife, Emma?

"Aren't you going to ask what I found up there?" Beatriz stood, arms coolly crossed over her chest.

"I think I know what you found," said the tall blonde, her voice quiet.

"I bet you do. And since it's common knowledge now that my brother paid you to marry him—for one year—it will come as no surprise to anyone here that there was a contract detailing the particulars of the arrangement. That's what I found on top of the armoire."

The blonde woman turned pale.

"The year isn't up yet." Beatriz looked at Emma and Darius.

Darias put his arm around Emma's waist. "Emma and I have long since moved past that. My urgent need to find a wife in time for the coronation proved to be the best thing that ever happened to me." He turned and kissed her on the cheek. Not a quick peck intended to show fake affection, but a slow, tender, gentle kiss, that caused a blush to spread over Emma's cheek and a tiny smile to lift her mouth. Suddenly they both seemed to glow.

Serena's heart squeezed. *That's what love looks like.* Beatriz had just lobbed a thunderbolt at them, and they stood and quietly weathered the storm together.

"It was my fault it was up there." Emma no longer looked pale. "I should never have brought it here with me. I'm not even sure why I did. And when I moved into Darias's bedroom after the wedding I forgot it was up there. Then a coronation guest moved into the room and I wasn't able to retrieve it. When I finally found the time to sneak back in there, it was gone." She blinked. "I'm glad it was you who found it, Beatriz. I was worried it might get leaked to the press."

"I'm the very soul of discretion." Beatriz smiled coolly. Serena couldn't figure out what was going on with her. Why had she just brought this up?

Then it dawned on her. *She's trying to deflect attention from herself.*

What was Beatriz up to? Serena resolved to be very wary around her. And not leave any contracts lying around. Or, in her case, any copies of *What to Expect When You're Expecting* or her phone with its text exchanges with Sandro.

Her hand flew to her pocket, and she heaved a silent sigh that her phone was right there at her hip, not left in the bedroom where anyone might find it.

"All right, everyone," Lina spoke in a commanding voice. "Let's go in to dinner." She led the way from the sitting room into a grand dining room, where the long, oval table was set as if for a royal banquet.

Each setting had three delicate crystal glasses, three knives, three forks and two different spoons.

Uh-oh. Once again she wished she'd taken that etiquette course her dad had suggested when she was in high school. She'd laughed and said that no one cared about that kind of thing anymore. Clearly she was wrong.

She resolved to quietly observe and follow someone else's lead.

Lina pointed out a place for her to sit, and she lowered herself gingerly onto the delicate, upholstered chair. Sandro sat next to her on one side, Emma on the other. Emma leaned in and introduced herself quietly. Serena smiled and did the same, since no one had thought to introduce them. For an instant Serena was tempted to joke about following her lead with the confusing place setting—since she knew that Emma had been an ordinary American girl like herself just a few months ago—then she remembered that Emma was now queen here in Altaleone and decided to err on the side of caution.

"White or red?" asked a waiter, brandishing two bottles of wine. "Uh, neither, thanks," Serena blustered. "I'll stick with water." She hoped that wouldn't make anyone suspicious. If pressed she'd just say she didn't drink. Hopefully they wouldn't find her video series on wine tastings from two years ago.

They started with a hot dark red soup that soon revealed itself to be beetroot. It was surprisingly delicious and perfect for the winter weather. That took care of the soup spoon. Then a tiny pastry thing arrived with a curl of mystery vegetables on it. She followed Emma's lead and ate it with a small fork. The main course was some kind of bird—not chicken or turkey, so maybe duck?—served with au gratin potatoes and a diced root vegetable that she didn't recognize.

Lina guided the conversation carefully, making sure everyone was included and steering clear of the pressing question of what had happened to the bodies of her husband and his mother, recently excised from the royal graveyard.

"Serena, what do you do?" asked Lina.

This was never a terribly easy question to answer. People over fifty or so—which she guessed Lina must be—didn't always know what a blogger was, and almost none of them—at least in her parents' circles—had heard of vlogging. "I'm a writer." At least everyone knew what that was. "I was just on a tour promoting my book." She smiled. That even sounded pleasantly respectable.

But she regretted it an instant later when Beatriz lifted her glass and peered at her. "What is your book about?"

She'd forgotten that part. Serena gulped. "It's about dating, sort of."

"You do a lot of that, do you?" Beatriz regarded her coolly.

"Oh, no. It's really about waiting for the right person to come along." She hoped and prayed she wouldn't have to go into detail about her failed relationship—whose few highlights were described in great detail in the book.

"The right person..." Beatriz cocked her head. "Someone like a prince, for example?"

"Beatriz!" Lina scolded her. "What's gotten into you?"

Beatriz sipped her water. "Just asking, that's all."

Serena's face was blazing. Once again she hoped it didn't show.

"I'm sure it's a book about waiting for a man who will love you in the way you deserve," said Lina warmly. "Not someone who has a certain title or bank account."

"Exactly," exclaimed Serena with relief. "It's really about not settling for someone for the wrong reasons and about being patient enough to figure out who is right for you. We're all in such a rush to do everything these days." She was no exception. Looking back she could see she'd rushed Howard into things he wasn't ready for.

"Serena has an audience of devoted followers who hang on her every word," said Sandro proudly. "She posted a video from her room before she came down."

Lina looked surprised. "From inside the palace?"

"Is there a problem?" asked Sandro.

Lina hesitated for a second. "I suppose not. We're just usually so paranoid about keeping the media out of our private lives."

"She's not the media." Sandro turned to her. "Are you?"

He seemed to need some reassurance. Was she? Probably the answer was yes, in a lot of ways. *Oh, dear.* "I respect your privacy completely." The words sounded stiff and formal. Maybe it would be better if she didn't make more videos here. The sinister text she'd received popped into her head.

I see you are inside the palace. Good for you.

No doubt it would be better if people didn't know exactly where she was and who she was with.

A uniformed older man entered the room. Serena recognized him as the one who'd greeted them at the front door. "Madam, we have a visitor."

"Now? Who is it?"

"Your sister."

Lina's face went pale. "Oh. Wonderful. Do show her in." Her words sounded flat. As soon as he'd turned, she made a face at Darias. "As if things weren't bad enough."

"You don't have to invite her in, Mama," he said, very low.

"But I do. Imagine the scandal if I didn't," she whispered. "The paparazzi would eat it up." Darias and Sandro nodded slowly in rueful agreement.

Serena was surprised by how much they'd already revealed about their private lives in front of a virtual stranger—her. Maybe they trusted her implicitly because Sandro did. Or maybe they simply didn't consider her important enough to worry about.

Sandro leaned into Serena and whispered, "Brace yourself."

15

All heads turned to the doorway, where a tall, thin blonde woman made her appearance. "Darling!" She zeroed in on Lina and rushed toward her. "I came as soon as I heard."

Lina frowned. "Heard what?"

"About the bodies being dug up! Why would anyone do such a terrible thing?" She rushed to Lina's side and threw her arms awkwardly around her sister, who stood there stiffly, looking confused and alarmed.

"But I don't understand. The story hasn't been in the press."

Liesel seemed to freeze for a moment, arms around her sister. "A little bird told me."

"Who?" The question shot from Lina's mouth.

Liesel pulled back, a fake smile plastered to her chiseled aristocratic features. "I'd never tell my sources. I'm only looking out for you."

Lina blinked, obviously thinking. Darias and

Sandro exchanged glances. Serena busied herself with a sip of water.

"Well, I'm fine, under the circumstances," Lina said stiffly. "But since you seem to know more than you should I think you should speak to Gibran immediately."

Liesel blinked. "I'd be delighted to speak to Gibran. I'm rather surprised he's allowed this to happen under his watch."

"Perhaps he's offering the perpetrators an opportunity to incriminate themselves," said Darias slowly.

"That hardly seems appropriate where my dear brother-in-law's body is concerned." Liesel finally noticed Serena. She stopped speaking and stared for a moment, then turned back to Lina. "Am I too late for dinner?"

"Yes, I'm afraid so. Allow me to introduced Serena Raines. It's her first visit to Altaleone."

Liesel barely acknowledged her before launching into a litany of complaints about her airline journey. Serena decided that Liesel was just as awful as Sandro had described her. But no one's family was perfect. His mom and his brother Darias seemed very nice.

"I think we should get out while the getting is good and take Lucky outside," murmured Sandro in her ear.

"Good idea. But this time I'm wearing a coat." She rose from the table with relief, glad to be out of the pressure cooker environment.

"You handled that very well," said Sandro quietly, as they climbed the stairs.

"Handled what?" Did he think she'd never eaten

a formal dinner before? She was ready to be offended.

"My crazy family. I don't know what's eating my sister Beatriz. She's not usually like that. Something's got her back up."

"I can imagine that everyone is pretty tense under the circumstances. Your mom is lovely."

"Yes, she is." He smiled. "I knew you'd like her. And that she'd like you."

They retrieved Lucky from his crate, and Sandro put his leash on and picked him up. It touched her to see how sweet he was with Lucky, even letting him lick his face enthusiastically.

They donned their coats and boots downstairs, and instead of going into the courtyard again, this time they went out another door onto a large lawn. The air was cold and crisp and a huge silver moon illuminated the snowy landscape. The palace loomed behind them, big windows glowing golden in the darkness. Tall evergreen trees stood around them like giant sentries.

"I'm sorry you've been plunged into the midst of all this drama. I was truly hoping we'd have a few days of peace and quiet." The moon illuminated his contrite expression.

"Don't worry about it." She watched Lucky nose around in the snow. "I just hope I'm not in the way."

"Absolutely not. I want you to get to know my family."

His words touched her. Was he still thinking that he might pursue a relationship with her? If so his persistence was endearing. She couldn't imagine how the royal crew would react to the news that she was already pregnant with his baby. Beatriz would

216

suspect she'd done it on purpose to trap Sandro into marriage.

"I'm glad I've met them. I don't know what I was expecting, really, but they seem like any other family—just more...royal."

"My dad was the fun one. He always got everyone laughing. It's strange and different since he's been gone. My mom is holding up well, considering, but I'm sure she misses him terribly. At least she has Beatriz here to keep her company."

"And a small staff of fifty or so," teased Serena.

"True." He chuckled. "But employees are never the same as family or friends." He frowned. "Maybe Beatriz is feeling hemmed in by being needed so much."

"Could be."

"Perhaps I should encourage her and my mom to take a trip somewhere. They could visit my sister Callista in Paris or my sister Cosima in Los Angeles."

"She might not be ready for that yet. People need time to grieve. My grandmother took nearly five years after my grandfather's death before she would even agree to have a birthday party for herself."

"I'm not that great at being patient. I always want to fix things."

"I can tell." Lucky had done his business on the sparkling white ground. "We forgot to bring a bag to clean up after him."

"Don't worry about that. We don't want to put anyone out of a job. It's not easy keeping such a large staff busy now the palace isn't filled with Dad's hunting parties. They're all worried about layoffs, especially since Darias went to live in the castle in town, which is a lot smaller and doesn't need a full staff."

They started to walk back inside. She was impressed and maybe even a little surprised that Sandro hadn't tried to pull any moves on her out in the darkness. Maybe the situation with the bodies had banished thoughts of romance from his mind.

A tiny pinch of sadness plucked at her heart. It would have been so nice to spend two or three days in his beautiful, remote Roman villa in the mountains. But nothing in her life was going smoothly lately, so she just had to keep rolling with the punches.

Back inside the palace the others were gathered around a piano in a big drawing room. Beatriz played a complicated classical piece while Liesel exclaimed over her talent. Sandro guided Serena over to Emma, then, much to her consternation, nodded for Darias to follow him out of the room and disappeared, taking Lucky with him.

Serena smiled nervously at Emma. Emma smiled warmly and beckoned her through an alcove into an adjoining room. "It's all a bit overwhelming at first, isn't it?" she said, after they sat down on a plush sofa.

"I've never seen that many spoons and forks on a table in my life."

"I had no idea what to do when I first got here. Beatriz took me through everything step by step. She's a bit prickly at first—she's naturally quite shy and doesn't have the best social skills—but she was a great help to me."

Serena was burning to ask how she came to sign a contract to marry Darias but didn't dare.

"I had a second job as a gallery assistant at the

New York gallery that represents Darias's painting. It was all Sandro's idea for him to ask me to be his wife for a year. I'd never even spoken to him before."

Serena laughed with relief—Emma had answered her question without her even asking it. "That sounds like something Sandro might come up with."

"He must care a lot about you if he brought you here to meet his family."

Serena paused. "I wasn't really supposed to come here. We were headed for a quiet interlude at his house in the country. He knew he had to come here when he heard what happened."

"Oh." Emma's smooth brow wrinkled a little. "Well, I can tell he cares about you from the way he looks at you."

"He's a very nice guy." Maybe he looked at everyone that way. Emma might not even know him that well since she'd only been in the family a few months and Sandro lived in New York most of the time. "I suspect he's a bit of a ladies' man."

"I suppose these handsome princes always are, aren't they?" Emma smiled. "But I think they get tired of women flocking around them for the wrong reasons. They can tell when someone cares about who they are as a person rather than how big their castle is."

Serena felt like a fraud. Emma had no idea that she and Sandro had only spent a couple of days together in total. She probably assumed they were in a real relationship. Emma must have felt that way herself once. "It's intimidating, having so many people around. How long did it take you to get used to it?"

Emma laughed. "I'm still not used to it.

Thankfully, we don't need a big staff at the castle. It weirds me out that so many people need to know about everything I do. Right now I can't even go out for a pastry without alerting security. I can't wait until they catch the murderers and we can settle into some semblance of normality. Darias said it was never like this when he was a kid. He and his brothers and sisters used to run around the village like ordinary kids. I want our children to grow up like that."

Serena could almost feel the baby in her belly. Her child would be a member of this family—Emma's niece or nephew. "This does seem like it would be a nice place to grow up. Very sheltered."

"And totally different from my upbringing." Emma sighed. "My dad was a rocker with a drug problem, and my parents never married. It's kind of scary that my idea of what a normal family is supposed to be like comes from TV."

Serena laughed. "I come from a very traditional family—my dad is a pastor and my mom stayed home while we were little except for teaching piano and organ lessons."

"You're a lot better prepared than me, then. Sometimes people ask me if we're going to start trying for a baby, and I want to laugh. I'm not sure anyone in my family has ever gotten pregnant on purpose."

Like me, thought Serena. She never thought this would happen to her. Hers was the kind of family that planned everything. Her parents had probably waited until marriage to French-kiss. "Are you and Darias talking about having kids?"

"Not yet. We want to settle into marriage and our

new roles first. If it happens that's perfectly fine too. I think Lina is dying to be a grandmother. She's such a loving and supportive mother. I want to be just like her when I grow up."

Serena smiled. "She does seem lovely. You've lucked out in the mother-in-law department."

"Yeah. Shame about her sister, though." Emma rolled her eyes. "She's a nightmare, and Lina's too nice to tell her to get lost."

"She does seem…challenging. Do you think there's any chance she's involved in the murders?"

"I doubt it. She's awful, but I think she's just lonely and bitter and jealous of her sister's royal husband and beautiful family."

"That could be motive for some people." She could hardly believe she was talking this boldly to a member of the family. But the thought had been bugging her since dinner. "Though she couldn't have done it alone."

"There's definitely some kind of conspiracy going on. Darias thought it might be related to this creepy secret society that all the monarchs get inducted into. It has a huge trust held in a Swiss bank, so there's a possible money motive. I was kidnapped by two people who wanted the secret code—one of them was an old girlfriend of Darias's—but as far as we can tell they had nothing to do with the murders." Emma pushed back her long, blonde hair. She was ridiculously pretty. She really did look like a fairy-tale princess. It was kind of weird—and reassuring—that she came across as so unpretentious and normal.

"And then there's this ancient land feud over a lake on one of the borders. This guy Lorenzo Aldobrando—who's young and hot, just to confuse matters—made some overtures about buying it back so he could develop the land on his side, and he was upset that Darias's grandmother wouldn't consider it. Everyone seems to hate him, so I suppose he's a suspect, but they can't pin anything on him...yet. Darias says it's a waiting game. We have a lot of evidence, but it's like a puzzle where none of the pieces fit together. We need to stay safe until they play their hand and we get more pieces to figure it out."

"That sounds scary."

Emma laughed. "I suppose it does, but honestly, day to day life is so full and busy I don't have time to worry about whether someone is watching me through crosshairs. I've been visiting every class in all of the local schools and reading to the kids, then discussing the books with them—in English, thank goodness. I wanted to be a teacher since I was little so it's about the most fun I can imagine."

"It's great that you're so happy."

"I know, right! Who'd have thunk it?" They laughed, then Serena noticed Beatriz staring at them from across the room. Beatriz looked away quickly when Serena glanced up. "Do you suspect Beatriz of anything?" Once more she felt like she was overstepping her bounds, since Emma had said Beatriz taught her everything when she'd arrived. But again, she couldn't resist speaking her mind. As the newcomer here, she might be a more clear-eyed observer than the others.

Emma's smooth brow wrinkled slightly. "I did wonder about her when I first arrived. She is rather cagey, but I can't think what her motive would be. And she's super close to her mom. I don't know what Lina would have done without here over these last few, tough months since the murders. She's been a rock to her."

Serena glanced up at Beatriz. Maybe, since she had no real life or interests of her own, she felt a need to make herself indispensable. At that moment Beatriz glanced up again and looked right at her.

Serena glanced away so fast she could only look guilty of something. This whole socializing-with-royals thing was exhausting. Luckily Sandro was walking toward her so she turned her attention to him. "I'm really tired," she said quietly when he drew close. "Would it be okay if I go up to bed?"

"Of course." His expression brightened. "That's a great idea."

And the light in his eyes suggested that sleep was the very last thing on his mind.

16

Sandro offered to take Lucky out, and Serena was only too happy to let him since it was so cold. Her heart filled with affection for him. He would be the kind of dad who'd go comfort the baby in the middle of the night rather than just bumping her awake and telling her it was crying.

Stop it, Serena! Letting herself think about Sandro as a loving dad was one sure route to madness. He was a prince. He had servants to get babies in the middle of the night. And most likely even if the impossible happened and this did turn into an actual relationship, he'd be busy traveling to bring solar power to the world and wouldn't even be aware of any midnight disturbances back at home.

And she'd better hurry up and shower before he came back so he didn't catch her naked.

What if he expected to make love with her? She'd been hesitant enough about that in the privacy of his mountain retreat. Here, under his mom's roof, with about a million people within earshot, having steamy sex was about the last thing she wanted to do.

She rushed through her shower and donned her plain blue pj's, then plugged in her phone to charge and climbed under the heavy covers of her dramatic four-poster bed.

It was only then that she remembered the ghost. What did ghosts do again? In movies they mostly fluttered around trying to scare people but didn't cause any actual harm—unlike whoever was out to kill key members of the Leone family. She had more to fear from living, breathing humans than from spooky beings.

Which reminded her of the text she'd received. She'd turned off the sound on her phone for dinner as she didn't want the meal interrupted by her social media notifications. She should check up on her video and comments before bedtime, so she reached for her phone.

There was a text from Asia. **How was Chi-town? Call me!**

Serena sighed. It was almost impossible to believe that she'd been in Chicago yesterday. It felt like at least a week ago! And she felt like she'd gone a week without sleep. Pregnancy was really sapping her energy. She had way less get-up-and-go and already wanted to sleep one or two more hours most nights.

She texted back. **I'm in Europe with Sandro. Long story. Will update soon!** She didn't have the energy to go into detail right now. Her body was ready to sink into the thick feather mattress.

There was another text from a number she didn't recognize, and when she clicked on the thread she could see it was from the same mystery texter as before. **Boo! I am the ghost in your room.**

She sat bolt upright in bed and suppressed the urge to scream. She glanced around, knowing that of course it wasn't the ghost, just someone trying to scare her.

Another, longer text came in. **Did I frighten you? Good. Your stay in Altaleone will be short, and you have important work to do. You must convince Sandro to join the Cross of Blood Society. If you tell him about this message or my communications, he will die just like his father and grandmother. His life is quite literally in your hands.**

She frowned, unable to stop herself searching the room with her eyes. **Who is this?** She texted back, trying to stay calm. Sandro should be back with Lucky any second. For all she knew he was in immediate danger. She, however, would mean nothing to the person texting her except as a means to their end.

She jumped when her phone pinged. *The ghost.* **History is a part of the present in Altaleone. Don't ever forget that. I'm watching you RIGHT NOW.**

She swallowed and pulled the covers up over her. Was someone watching her with a hidden camera? Or even possibly the camera on her phone?

She slid out of bed, crossed the room and rifled through her bag for the box of tiny Band-Aids she kept in case she got a blister walking around New York City. She unwrapped two and stuck one over the front camera and one over the rear camera.

At that moment she heard a knock on the door. Heart pounding, she hesitated.

"Serena, it's me, Sandro. May I come in?"

"Yes." The word sounded forced, panicky. Part of her wanted to tell Sandro about the text so they could both go to Gibran immediately, but what if that meant he would be killed—perhaps shot right now in front of her by some hidden assailant? It would be safer to wait for morning and at least tell him somewhere outside the palace, while they were walking Lucky and out of earshot.

If she could just get through this night and keep this crazy person on the hook thinking she might help them, she and Sandro could figure out a strategy together in the morning.

"Sorry we were gone so long, he wanted to smell everything in the garden." Sandro held Lucky in his arms, and Lucky licked his face affectionately. He put the dog gently down on the floor. "What's the matter? You look like you just saw the ghost."

"Maybe I did." She forced a laugh. She wanted Sandro to get out of here fast. Every moment he stayed she risked telling him and possibly causing his death. "No, really, I'm fine. Just very tired."

He smiled and moved toward her. Oh, no. He was still thinking they might.... Her whole body was rigid and almost shaking with fear. She really didn't want him to touch her and find out. "I'm way too tired for...anything." Another forced laugh. "Being pregnant really takes it out of you."

His eyes glimmered with disappointment. "A kiss?"

She swallowed. "I don't think that's a good idea right now. Our kisses have a way of getting out of hand."

A teeny smile tugged at his mouth. "That is true. I

suppose I'll have to be uncharacteristically patient and wait for a better time."

"Yes," she said quickly. "I'm sure tomorrow will be better." She wanted to make plans to meet with him and head outside but didn't want to tip off whoever might be watching her. "Come get me in the morning. I'm an early riser, as you know!" Her words sounded so weird and unnatural. He frowned slightly, like he knew something was up and wondered what, exactly, it was.

"Are you sure you won't be nervous? I could sleep in here with you. I could even promise to keep my hands to myself.

Yes! Her body ached to be close to him. She even kind of believed him about keeping his hands to himself. He'd been very good about respecting her wishes.

But there was no way she could get through the night without telling him about the menacing text. "I'm sure. You're right next door. If I need anything, I'll yell. And you do the same!"

"I might well take you up on that." He looked amused. He had no idea she was truly afraid for him.

The idea of someone killing Sandro sent a chill right through her. Why would anyone want to do that? He didn't even live in Altaleone most of the time, he wasn't close to being in line for the throne, and he was a nice person doing important work for the world.

It made her damned angry that someone could even think about killing him. "Are you going right to bed?"

"I'm going to go chat with Darias for a bit first. We need to come up with some ideas."

Be careful! She ached to warn him. And Darias too. Did they have any idea that someone was in their midst, wishing them ill?

Of course they did. Their dead father's severed finger had arrived in the mail today. She shivered at the thought.

"Are you sure you're okay? You look quite strange."

"Just exhausted. I really must sleep!"

"Okay." He looked doubtful, like he really didn't want to leave her. "If you need anything, don't hesitate, okay?"

"I promise." She watched Sandro as he walked to the door, Lucky hard on his heels, then turned and gave her a wistful look before he closed it behind him.

"Lucky, come up here!" She patted the bed. Lucky looked up at her. Maybe he was shocked because she wouldn't let him on her bed at home. Right now she wanted all the protection and comfort she could get. Also, Lucky would be sure to bark if anyone tried to get into the room.

She had to get off the bed to lift him up, and he kissed her enthusiastically. She ignored the pang of guilt at breaking her own self-imposed rule about dogs on beds. Desperate times called for desperate measures.

I'm watching you right now. The creepy message gave her goose bumps. Where was he—or she—watching from? The windows were covered with heavy curtains, but there could be a hidden camera anywhere. Maybe even somewhere in the carvings of her elaborate bed.

She refused to look at her phone to see if there

were any new missives. "Come here, Lucky." She pulled him into her arms and rested her head on the pillow. How on earth she was supposed to sleep tonight, she had no idea. Between the menacing "ghost," a potential real ghost, the baby in her belly, her feelings for Sandro, Sandro's intimidating family—not to mention her newly revealed status as a professional phony for writing a book about waiting for Mr. Right and then getting dumped by him....

Sandro walked back downstairs, cursing the desire that stormed through him. It was almost unbearable to be so close to Serena and unable to touch her. He felt guilty at bringing her here to the palace when she'd clearly stated that she wanted peace, but he was also thrilled at the opportunity for her to meet his family. How could she not like them?

"Hey, Darias." He called to his brother, who was sitting in the living room chatting with the others. "I want to show you something I got in New York."

"Can't we all see?" screeched Liesel.

"Sorry." Sandro shrugged. "It's in Dad's office, and it would bore you to death anyway. Some new tech." He barely even flinched at the lie. He was desperate to get Darias alone.

Darias rose and followed him, and together they climbed the stairs up to their father's old study on the third floor. Sandro ushered him in and closed the door. "Are we being tapped?"

"Probably," answered Darias. "Gibran has the whole place bugged to protect us. He claims they're not actually listening to conversations, but I don't know whether to believe him. That's one of the reasons Emma and I moved out to the castle."

"What the hell is going on here? How can the bodies be dug up and defaced under our eyes? It's got to be an inside job."

"Yep. And with a staff this size there are too many possibilities. Everyone is under scrutiny."

"Including members of the family?"

"You mean Liesel?" Darias's face creased into a wry smile.

"I'm not kidding. She's nasty enough."

"She has no motive."

Sandro sat down in a leather chair. "We don't have any idea what the killer's motive was. That's what makes this so alarming. You can't predict someone's actions when you don't know what they want."

Darias sat down nearby. "The motive has to be something to do with either money or power."

"Or both. They are usually inseparable."

"Agreed. Whoever is behind this is doing their best to destroy us, but they've underestimated the Leone family. I've heard that some people didn't think I'd move back from New York to be king, and I'll admit I wasn't thrilled by the idea myself, but now I'm determined to fulfill my role to the best of my abilities."

"We're all grateful. And I want to do everything I can to help you. What do you need from me right now?"

Darias frowned. "You've always been more of an outgoing charmer than me. Could you move back here and do some socializing with the local aristos?"

Sandro recoiled. He could hardly move back to Altaleone and expect Serena to stay here with him.

And he knew all the caveats about trying to maintain a long-distance relationship. He'd tried—and failed—at them before. "You're hardly the reclusive artist."

"I'm no Van Gogh, but everyone knows I don't really love parties the way you do." Darias cocked his head. "Papa and Grandmama were very social, and we need to figure out exactly who they were associating with."

"Aren't there records of that? Invitation lists, that kind of thing."

"Yes, but it's the unofficial contacts I'm more interested in."

Sandro hesitated. "Like the Cross of Blood."

"Exactly."

"Aren't they a sort of…sex society?"

He watched Darias pause like he was choosing his words carefully. "They do exist to, uh, satisfy the less socially acceptable desires of the royal family. And as you know I am now married and have no desire to engage in activities with anyone other than my wife. You're still single and—" Darias stopped. "Or are you? You've never bought a girl to the palace before. Are you serious about her?"

"I am." Sandro said it without hesitation. "So there is no question of me participating in any activities of that sort." He shuddered at the idea that a bunch of masked aristocratic weirdos were ready to get naked with any member of the Leone family.

"Damn. I can't see Rigo doing it either. He's way too serious. And the others are—"

"Too young. Leo's not even twenty-one." Sandro shoved a hand through his hair. "Perhaps I can join. I wouldn't have to do anything. I could just pretend I might want to while I feel them out."

Darias looked pleased. "I think they'd open up to you more than to me. As the king—and something of an unknown quantity due to my years abroad—I'm suddenly treated with a rather respectful distance that keeps information at bay."

"Okay. I'll join. What do I have to do?" He didn't need to tell Serena about this. It wouldn't mean anything to her anyway. She knew nothing about the Cross of Blood.

"I'll let my contact know you're ready. They'll plan an initiation. Mine at least was painless. Once you're in try to befriend them and figure out what makes them tick. Go hunting with them, invite them for dinner—all the kind of stuff Papa would have done."

"Except for getting murdered," he said grimly.

"Exactly. Forewarned is forearmed. Gibran has wireless audio equipment to wear any time you want someone listening in."

Sandro shook his head. "This is all so hard to believe. We had such a quiet and normal life here before." He sighed. "I wanted to show Serena our country and have her fall in love with it, not get scared out of her mind by gruesome events."

Darias's mouth pulled into a smile. "I can't believe you're serious about someone. I thought you'd be the last of us to settle down."

"Some events have a way of making you mature quicker."

Darias lifted a brow slightly. "She's pregnant?"

Sandro cursed his loose lips. How did he manage to inadvertently reveal Serena's secret to almost everyone? But he could hardly lie to his own brother.

"Yes. But don't tell anyone. It's too early yet, and she wants to keep it quiet."

Darias rose and hugged him. "Well, congrats anyway. I'll keep mum until you make it public."

"Please. She's still very hesitant about having a relationship with me. She doesn't like me being a prince, for one thing."

"That's a turnabout." Darias laughed. "Usually that's the biggest draw."

"Tell me about it. She's not like that. Which is one of the reasons I like her so much. There's something very old-world about her but not in the stodgy, fussy, snobbish way we're used to."

"She has values."

"Exactly. And they've been under siege lately, partly due to me," he said ruefully, "and partly because of other events beyond her control. So I don't want her getting further freaked out by anything if I can help it."

"So we won't tell her about the Cross of Blood." Darias's eyes twinkled with mischief.

"Absolutely not. I'm sure that would scare her right off me."

"If recent events and Aunt Liesel haven't already done the job."

"I know I didn't exactly pick the perfect time to bring her here. I should get her back to New York before anything else goes down."

Darias leaned forward. "Don't leave yet. I need you here. And we need to get Rigo's sharp legal mind here too. We're missing something, and I bet he's the one to find it."

"Call him and command him—as his king." Sandro was only half kidding.

"I already tried that, but he's in the middle of a big civil rights case. He says it could go all the way to the Supreme Court."

"Altaleone always was too small for Rigo. But I know he'd do anything for Mom. Maybe you just haven't tried the right angle. I'll talk to him tonight and see if I can work my famous charm on him."

"Good luck. You'll need it."

He didn't have any luck. Rigo promised to come as soon as he was able, which in Sandro's experience with him could be any time in the next two decades.

He slept passably well in his bed—considering that Serena was lying in a different bed without him only a few yards away—and in the morning he went down for breakfast.

Where his luck took a considerable turn for the worse.

17

"Uh, Sandro." Beatriz called to him from across the dining room. She was eating the usual boiled egg with toast fingers that she'd eaten every morning—in that same spot—since she was about two.

"Just a mo. Let me get some eggs." He grabbed a plate from the sideboard and piled eggs, fresh local ham and sausage and hot baked pastries onto it, then poured himself a coffee. "I do miss these royal breakfasts when I'm not here."

"Really? I thought we were too dull for you here. I bet you're missing your fiancée right now."

Sandro stopped in his tracks on his way to the table. "Fiancée?" He hadn't planned a proposal to Serena, let alone popped the question and told his family about it.

"Yes. Your fiancée. I was just reading about her in *Hello*."

Sandro put his plate down with a clatter and reached over to grab the paper from his sister. It took him a moment to find the short article declaring that he and Maya Dunham had announced their engagement and that they were planning their wedding.

"What the—?" He threw the rag down on the table. "I'm not engaged to her. Not even close. I broke up with her."

"I suppose that explains why you're here with someone else."

He glanced around. "Has Serena come down yet?" He hadn't wanted to text her when he got up in case she needed to catch up on sleep. He was an early riser, like most people in his family.

"Not yet."

"Don't let her see this." He shoved it back at Beatriz. "I'm serious. She means a lot to me, and this might upset her. Why are you reading this rag anyway?"

"Um, did it occur to you that it might be better to show it to her and explain the situation rather than have her find it out from someone else? We women don't really enjoy being lied to, despite what you men think."

"It's not lying. I just don't want her getting her feelings hurt over nonsense. She has enough on her plate."

"Well, don't say I didn't warn you."

"You won't tell her, will you?"

Beatriz shook her head—with exasperation rather than disagreement—and rose, taking her plate and *Hello* with her. She was gone before he could even ask her where she was the day before when everyone was worried about her.

Beatriz could be annoyingly mysterious and he

had to admit that until now he'd never put a great deal of effort into trying to investigate her mysteries. She was always there, like the antique furniture and the freshly cooked breakfasts. It occurred to him that he should stop taking her for granted. "Beatriz, wait!"

But she was gone.

What the hell was going on with Maya Dunham? He wanted to text her and ask, but he had a feeling that would open a whole can of worms that he really didn't want to unleash.

He decided to text Serena.

The sound of Serena's text alert woke her from a deep sleep. She groped for the phone on the bedside table and quickly realized that the bedside table wasn't there because she wasn't in her bed at home. The horrible realizations flooded back—she was in a strange royal palace and possibly under the gaze of a murderer.

She groped around and found her phone where she'd left it on the other pillow, already dreading what the new text might say.

8:03 a.m. She must have been so exhausted she could have slept through the end of the world. Poor Lucky must be desperate to go out by now. Though it was still the middle of the night in New York, so maybe he didn't care.

And the text was from Sandro. Heaving a huge sigh of relief she opened it. **I'm downstairs having breakfast. Would you like me to come get Lucky?**

I'll bring him down in a minute, she replied.

Relieved to have made it through the night, she

eased herself out of bed, switched on a light, since the curtains left the room in almost total darkness, and tugged some clothes on. She spent more time than usual on her hair and makeup for first thing in the morning, because she might well come face-to-face with the whole royal clan downstairs.

Lucky was still sleepy, and she picked him up in her arms and carried him before tucking her phone in her pocket and leaving the room. Hopefully she could get Sandro to come outside, out of earshot of the palace, where she could warn him about the threatening texts she'd received last night.

She could hear voices coming from the dining room—on the far side of a long hall—so she braced herself to face the group.

"Good morning." Sandro's deep voice startled her. She spun around to face him. Dressed in dark jeans and a navy sweater, he looked good enough to drink instead of coffee.

"You made me jump."

"I was waiting for you. I wanted to get a moment alone with you before you went in for breakfast."

"Why?" Alarms rang inside her despite his calm expression. "Is something wrong."

"Why is it wrong for me to want some privacy with you?" His eyes twinkled with amusement. "Isn't that why you came to Altaleone?"

"I don't even remember why I came here." Everything had spiraled out of control so fast. "But I really should take Lucky out."

Sandro pulled her coat from the big hall closet, took Lucky from her and helped her into it, then ushered her down yet another wide hallway toward a side door. Together they stepped out onto about an inch of new snow coating the big lawn on that side of the house.

"Goodness, it is beautiful." The lawn rolled away into fields, then rose up again in the distance toward snowcapped mountains.

Lucky yelped at being put down on the snow but soon made use of the opportunity.

She wasn't going to waste her opportunity either. She reached into her pocket and switched her phone completely off. "Something weird happened last night," she whispered.

"The ghost?" Sandro didn't look like he was taking her seriously.

Who are you?

The ghost, of course.

The text—designed to creep her out—sprang into her mind. "A human. Someone texted me." She kept her whisper as quiet as possible. "And they said they would kill you if I told you." She couldn't hide the fear in her voice.

Sandro peered at her. "Told me what?"

She frowned. She wanted to look at her phone to check the message but didn't want to draw attention to it in case someone was watching from the palace's many windows. "They want you to join the Cross of Blood."

Sandro looked shocked. "Can I see the message?"

"I don't think it's safe for me to show you my phone right now. They could have a gun trained on you." She fought the urge to look behind her at the house. "Isn't the Cross of Blood the society you guys were talking about last night?"

"Yes." He frowned. "And I was planning on joining it anyway. Darias wants me to infiltrate it and get to know the other members."

"Why would this person want you to join?"

"I have no idea." He spoke slowly, scanning the snowy landscape as if for clues. "I need to tell Darias. And Gibran."

"But they told me not to tell you. What if they find out and—" She swallowed, assaulted by the awful thought of Sandro being shot dead in front of her. "Why don't we go back to New York today?"

She hadn't planned to say the last part. She knew he was royal and had a duty to his country. But it just flew out. She wanted to get out of here more than anything—and take Sandro with her for his own protection.

"I can't. I have important work to do and I can't abandon my family at a time like this. But I understand why you would want to go." His expression grew grim. "If you feel that you can't stay here, I can have someone drive you to the airport as soon as the roads are clear."

Yes! Her heart soared at the prospect of escaping this intimidating royal milieu complete with ghosts and death threats.

No. Something in her gut—something sharp and powerful—told her not to leave Sandro. Told her that he was safer with her here. That if she left she might never see him again.

"I don't think I should leave yet."

"I don't want you to leave." He said it softly. He took her hands in his—his were warm—and looked into her eyes. "With so much going on I want you and our baby close. I swear I'll protect you both."

Her insides stirred at his powerful words. Was it the baby inside her? She felt such a powerful connection to Sandro.

That was bad. His family had no idea that she was carrying his baby, and even having met them she still had no idea how they would react.

And how could he promise anything with an unknown killer right in their midst? "We shouldn't stay out here too long. I don't want the killer to know that I told you."

"What makes you think it's the killer?"

"Because they said they'd kill you the way they killed your father and grandmother."

"That's a confession. We have to get the source of the text analyzed."

"But what if—?" She held her tongue. "I shouldn't have told you."

"If I do what you supposedly really told me and join the Cross of Blood, then you can tell them you did your part."

"True. And we mustn't talk about it unless we're away from the house and any recording devices. I turned my phone off, just in case someone can listen to me through it." She glanced around. "I'm getting paranoid."

"With good reason, apparently." He sighed. "Damn I want to take you in my arms right now."

"I don't think that's a good idea." Danger aside, she didn't want anyone ogling them from the house. Anything that happened between her and Sandro was their private business.

"Then I guess I'll continue to exercise my impressive self-control."

She smiled. "I appreciate that. "

"And today, in between signing up for the Cross of Blood and whatever other madness is coming my way, I intend to spend some private time touring Altaleone with you."

"And a small entourage of security guards?" She lifted a brow.

"And them, too."

Before she could protest he leaned in and pressed a swift kiss to her lips. He pulled back just as fast, leaving her lips humming with sensation.

He gathered up Lucky, and she tried to collect her thoughts. Sandro's kisses had a way of scattering them to the four winds. "I'll tell the texter that you will join the Cross of Blood," she whispered. "Should I say anything else?" They started to walk back to the house.

"Ask them what they really want." Sandro spoke low. "I don't want you to be alone, though. Not even for a second."

"What about in the bathroom?"

He hesitated. "Hmm, maybe Lucky can guard you in there. But I don't think you should sleep alone."

"No?" She lifted a brow. This was an interesting pretext to get into her bed with him. And truth be told she'd feel a lot more protected with him there, even if she wasn't actually safer at all.

"Are you hungry?"

"A little," she admitted. "I slept like the dead." She instantly regretted her choice of words. "Sorry."

"Don't be. I'm glad you slept well. Our three-hundred-year-old beds are more comfortable than they look."

Back inside, they hung up their coats and let Lucky run off to wherever he wanted. Then they headed back to the dining room, where Sandro's mom, Lina, his sister Beatriz and his Aunt Liesel were eating or drinking coffee at the long table.

"Good morning, Serena," called Lina as they entered.

"Good morning. I'm sorry I slept so late. I had a very good night."

"No disturbances from the ghost?" inquired Liesel, peering over the rim of a gold-edged coffee cup.

Serena shook her head and managed a smile. Was Liesel somehow behind this? She hadn't dared mention her conspiracy theories to Sandro. She wasn't sure he'd appreciate hearing his family members accused of treason. "Do I help myself?"

"Yes, dear. Plates are on the sideboard. Do let us know if you need more of anything." Sandro's mom smiled with what appeared to be genuine warmth. Then again, royals got a lot of practice being polite.

Serena would have preferred a bagel with cream cheese, but since that wasn't an option she helped herself to scrambled eggs, a piece of ham and something that looked like brioche, and was heading for the table when Liesel spoke.

"Sandro, when were you going to tell us about your engagement?" Her words—delivered in a syrupy sweet toll of delight—stopped Serena in her tracks. She glanced at Sandro. Did his aunt think they were engaged?

Sandro glanced at Beatriz, who shrugged and said, "I didn't say a word."

Serena's stomach clenched. *What's going on?*

18

"It's nonsense," said Sandro gruffly. "Made-up nonsense."

Serena felt chastened. Clearly he hated any rumors of him being engaged to her. Ouch.

"Serena thinks you mean to her," said Beatriz coolly.

"What? No! I..." Serena stammered. "What's going on?"

Sandro had the decency to look mortified. "It's some stupid story in the papers about me and Maya Dunham." He turned to the others. "Serena knows I broke up with Maya. I don't know where they got the idea that we're suddenly engaged."

Sandro knew about this story and hadn't warned her? That reliable sinking feeling returned. She couldn't trust him to be straight with her.

"There are some lovely pictures of the two of you together." Liesel gazed at them as if riveted.

"It was a brief thing."

"It always is with you." Liesel shot him an icy smile. "So you're not engaged at all?"

Serena still hadn't managed to move. She attempted to lower herself into a chair while wishing the floor could swallow her up. None of these people likely thought she was just a friend to Sandro—originally here to stay overnight at his remote home—so this open speculation about his love life with someone else was beyond humiliating.

"No. Not to her." He looked directly at Serena. But didn't say anything. Which was merciful. She might have just died on the spot if he'd said he was in a relationship with her—because she'd made it clear that she wasn't ready for that.

"You should make them issue a retraction," murmured Liesel through a sip of coffee. "She apparently says you're planning a June wedding."

"She's insane. Besides, she probably didn't even say that. Who knows where these papers get their stories from?"

Serena burned with curiosity to see the article. Had Maya Dunham been desperate enough over losing Sandro to plant a false story? That seemed crazy, especially when her personal star was burning so bright right now.

"Did I upset you...?" Liesel appeared to struggle to remember Serena's name.

"Not at all." She managed a cool smile. "This ham is delicious," she said to Lina. "Is it local?"

"Why, yes. It's from the palace estates. Our farm raises heritage breeds that are in danger of extinction."

"Then we kill them and eat them for breakfast," said Sandro with a wink.

"It's a sustainable practice," protested Lina.

"I know. I'm teasing." Sandro shot Serena a conspiratorial smile. "Serena knows I have a wicked sense of humor."

Serena attempted to smile. Sandro didn't even seem bothered that there was a newspaper story about him marrying someone else. It bothered her, partly because she'd featured him in her videos and some people were bound to recognize him as the same guy now engaged to Maya Dunham.

Would she have to explicitly address it? And if so, what could she say? "Actually he's mine. Well, not really. I'm having his baby, though."

And the worse part was that Sandro had known and hadn't told her. Like it wasn't any of her business. Her heart constricted and she tried to gather some food on her fork, but her stomach had shrunk to the size of a peanut. Then she realized Lina was talking to her—and she hadn't heard a word of it.

"Sorry, what did you say?" She felt her face heating. It was embarrassing for them to see how upset she was about getting blindsided by the news story.

"Just that we're used to being the subject of constant rumor and speculation so we've learned to ignore it." Lina shone a warm smile at her. "It doesn't mean that we don't sometimes get hurt by the stories. I haven't looked at the papers myself in years. I certainly didn't want to read anything published after my husband's death. People can be so cruel."

"I can imagine."

"It'll blow over," Sandro said. "Stories evaporate

fast when there's really nothing there. Denying it sometimes just fuels the fire. As soon as you're done we can head out on our tour." He looked at her cheerfully, obviously hoping she'd already stopped caring about the story. "I need to talk to Darias before we go." He glanced at Lina. "He and I have resolved to discuss important matters only in person. It's too risky using our phones. And our privacy in the palace is an illusion."

Serena became all too aware of the five or six staffers currently within earshot, refilling the coffeepot, bringing in mail, sweeping crumbs off the table, etc.

"Very sensible, my love. Do be careful, the two of you. I know your daring sometimes exceeds your common sense."

"Mama!" Sandro did his best to look scandalized, but the amusement in his eyes showed that he knew it was the truth. "We're being very careful. And we're going to meet with Gibran this morning, so rest easy."

"Impossible, with enemies in our midst." Lina glanced around, not looking at the staffers, but Serena knew she must be thinking that anyone here could be involved in the murders and the subsequent gruesome exhumation and delivery.

"Indeed. You be careful too."

"You know I am. But please do tell me anything you find out. I don't like being kept in the dark like a child."

"Me either," said Beatriz. They turned to her in surprise, as if they'd forgotten she was there. "No one tells me anything. I call sexism."

"I promise to update you if we learn anything at

all," said Sandro.

Serena could tell Beatriz didn't believe him. She didn't either. He had no problem keeping secrets from her so why not his sister too? She sighed, then realized it was audible and tried to cover it with a fake cough. She wasn't sure how much longer she could keep her cool in this royal fishbowl. She wanted to go on their tour, if only to get out of there. "I'm ready." Did she clear her plate or would someone come get it?

"Let's go find Darias. He said he'd come here this morning so perhaps he's on his way." Sandro rose, texting into his phone. "Where's Lucky got to?"

Serena realized with a start that she hadn't seen him since before breakfast. Hopefully he wasn't chewing the gold leaf off the leg of a precious table. "Lucky! Lucky?" She rose. "I'd better go look for him."

"I'll come too," said Sandro. He abandoned his plate on the table—presumably for staff to clear—so she did the same. "Let's check the back hallways." They exited the dining room and hurried down the hallway, past a young staffer with an armful of manila envelopes.

"Lucky!" she called. She strained her ears to hear the tinkling of his tag against his collar. As they hurried along the hallway, she couldn't help asking, "If you knew about the engagement story with Maya Dunham, why didn't you warn me?"

"It's just rubbish." He stopped and turned, looking rather shocked. "Not worth paying attention to. I didn't think it would be relevant."

Because we're not an item.

She heard the words, even though he didn't say

them. In his mind it was her fault that they weren't an item. He'd been clear that he wanted to give a relationship a try. But this kind of behavior was exactly why she didn't dare risk her heart on him.

"I do care." *I'm having your baby.* She didn't dare say that aloud in the palace. "What happens to you affects me. I need you to be open and honest with me."

"I know it affects you." He hurried to her and took her hands in his. "I'm very sorry that you were blindsided by the thoughtless story. If anything similar happens, I'll tell you about it right away." His eyes shone with sincerity.

Her heart warmed. "Thanks. I'd appreciate that." She wanted to ask if there were any other secrets he'd been keeping from her, but she didn't want to risk sounding like a harpy.

"I wasn't going to tell you about joining the Cross of Blood."

"Why?"

He leaned in until his lips were almost at her ear. "Darias tells me it exists to provide for the monarchy's more salacious sexual needs and desires."

Her eyes widened. "Are you going to have to…?" Words failed her.

"I'm not planning to *do* anything with them." Mischief glimmered in his eyes. "But I'm telling you that in the interest of full disclosure." He squeezed her hands.

"Okay." Her horror at the idea of him being in a sexual situation with someone else warred with her delight that he'd risked telling her the unsavory news. "I do appreciate your being honest."

"Now, aren't we supposed to be looking for Lucky?"

She blinked. "Oh yes." Lucky had gone right out of her head. Maybe she wasn't a fit dog owner. She didn't deserve a sweet dog like Lucky. "Lucky!"

The tinkling of his collar preceded his appearance bounding through a doorway, black and white fur flying. "Oh, thank goodness." She knelt down and rubbed his ears. "I'm putting you back on a leash." She slid her slim belt from the belt loops of her pants and slipped the non-buckle end through his collar.

"Now that's sorted, I need to find Darias."

"You're not going to tell him about the text, are you?" she whispered. She didn't want to bear any responsibility for him being hurt.

"Not yet. I'm going to move full speed ahead with joining the Cross of Blood and take it from there. And since honesty is our new policy, I'd like you to tell me immediately if you get any new messages."

She glanced around. Even though he'd kept his voice low, someone nearby could overhear. "I'll try. If I ask to go outside with you to walk Lucky you'll know why."

Sandro checked his phone. "Darias wants me to come to the castle. Let's go together, and we can begin our tour. You can blog about it."

"I don't know if that's a good idea." Her gut recoiled from the idea. For one thing she didn't want to put him in danger. For another she didn't want to end up the subject of rumor and speculation now that Sandro was in the news with someone else.

"Of course it is. You told the news about your

breakup. Now show your followers how much fun you're having."

"With Maya Dunham's fiancé," she said ruefully.

He laughed. "Why the hell not?"

19

Sandro kept glancing in the rearview mirror at the black van of security officers driving behind them on the way to the castle. Normally he'd have walked the relatively short distance through the village from the palace to the castle, but Gibran had made it clear that was not a good idea right now. Why did Altaleone have to be in an uproar when he wanted to show Serena how peaceful and beautiful it was here?

He'd survived an entire night knowing she was just on the other side of the wall from him, and it had required a very cold shower this morning to get himself ready to face her. She would barely let him touch her, and he'd had to steal a kiss. Desire was rising to dangerous levels inside him. Hopefully he'd get some quiet—and intimate—time alone with Serena soon before he blew like a volcano.

Darias and Emma welcomed them at the door, Emma leading Serena off to show her their newly decorated bedroom and Darias leading him into his study, where he plopped Lucky down on the floor. He'd grown used to having the sweet little dog as his shadow. "It's all arranged." His older brother seemed far more grim and serious than usual. "The Cross of Blood will hold the initiation tonight."

Sandro stiffened. Tonight? He hadn't thought it would happen that quickly. "Where?"

Darias hesitated. "The lake house."

"What? Where Dad and Grandma were murdered? It's in the middle of nowhere."

"I know, but I was told it's safer than meeting here in town. They say there's an enemy right in our midst. Possibly in the castle or the palace, they're not yet sure which."

"Here? Are Emma and Serena safe?" Adrenaline flashed through Sandro's veins.

"Yes. There's no one here and this castle has been defending royals against marauders since it was built." Darias's eyes twinkled. "So Serena and your baby are fine."

Sandro sighed. "I can't believe you know about the baby. I suck at keeping a secret. She'd kill me if she thought I'd told you."

Darias grinned. "No, she wouldn't."

"Trust me, she's not that crazy about me. She thinks I'm an arrogant, entitled royal."

"So? You are."

"You're not helping."

"I'm just stating a fact. That said, I'm hugely appreciative that you are joining the Cross of Blood. The whole organization has me stumped, and because I'm king they all stand at a respectful distance and won't tell me anything useful."

Sandro's gut flared with a warning. "Something

weird happened." He glanced around. "Is this room bugged?"

"Yes. Gibran has the whole castle bugged for our protection. Everywhere except the bedroom." He winked.

Sandro looked around for some pen and a paper. Then he wrote, "Serena got a text telling her to convince me to join the Cross of Blood." He wrote it in a close, scrolling hand so it would be hard to read if anyone was watching via camera. "So our enemy wants me in it."

He watched Darias frown. "We should tell Gibran," he murmured. He pulled some music up on his phone and set it playing.

Sandro shook his head. "I'm doing what they want, which should force their hand. If we learn what they want we're ahead." He spoke low, his words barely audible over the jazzy trumpets coming from Darias's phone. "Don't worry about me. I can handle myself."

"And I'll be there." Darias ran a hand through his hair. "But why do they want you to join?"

"The most obvious answer is that they want me to learn the bank code so they can try extract it from me. Who else knows the code?"

"Only the initiates, so, yes, that is a risk. But that's not why our father and grandmother were murdered. There's something more going on. A conspiracy that lies outside the Cross of Blood. And the Cross of Blood is there to protect us. So perhaps the person texting Serena is a friend, not an enemy."

Sandro stared. Was it possible? "I didn't see the text, but she seemed to think the tone was threatening. She was warned that I would die if she told anyone."

"Apparently she told you and you're still alive."

"For now," he lifted a brow. Then rubbed his hands together. "Damn, I'm ready to get on with it. I want to solve this mystery so I can get back to enjoying my life."

"With Serena."

"Hell, yes, with Serena."

"All right, bro. I'll do my best to stop you from screwing everything up with her."

"I don't need your help. I know what I'm doing. I told you to marry Emma, remember?"

"Before we knew anything about her. I could say your choice was just dumb luck."

"Nonsense. I prefer to think of my excellent instincts as a gift." Sandro grinned. "Now tell me more about these kinky aristos in the Cross of Blood."

Serena followed Emma upstairs into her bedroom, which was beautifully decorated in chalky white, bleached wood and old-gold accents. It managed to be both masculine and feminine at the same time.

"It's beautiful," she said.

"It's also the only room in the whole castle that isn't bugged," said Emma with a wink. "How are things going between you and Sandro?"

"There's really nothing going on." She smiled. The smile was fake, but the words were true.

"I bet you two haven't had a moment alone."

"Nope! Which is fine, really. He's a nice guy and everything but…" Luckily Emma didn't know about the pregnancy.

"He's a prince. Trust me, I felt exactly the same way. It never occurred to me that a man raised to be a royal could be the kind of giving, caring, truly loving man I could trust and count on. But that's exactly what Darias turned out to be."

"I'm sure he's lovely, but just being here around all the servants and antiques and everything—"

She was interrupted by her phone ringing. It was her agent, Barbara Clay, whom she'd called to give the heads up about the breakup revelation. She was very hard to get hold of. Always "on the other line," according to her assistant. "I'm sorry, do you mind if I take this call?"

"Go ahead." Emma moved off to the far side of the room.

Serena answered the call, heart pounding. She wasn't even sure if her agent knew she'd revealed the breakup. "Hello." She glanced up. Emma was looking at a scarf she'd pulled out of a drawer.

"Uh, Serena, rumor has it that you broke up with Mr. Right."

She swallowed. "Yes. It happened a while ago and I kept it secret until after the book was launched, but I had to let the truth out."

"You do realize that it makes your book seem like fiction." Barbara sounded almost incredulous. "Why didn't you tell me this?"

"I didn't think you needed to know."

A long pause throbbed in the air. "I'm your agent. I need to know *everything*."

"What difference does it really make?" She heard her voice rise. She felt defensive. "I didn't want to break up with him. It was his idea. I didn't want to ruin the book's release since I already spent the advance."

"I suppose that was the sensible choice. Still, I don't like to be blindsided by this kind of news. I need to know. Is there anything else you're keeping from me?"

I'm pregnant.

"No." She could always pretend that she didn't know yet. She couldn't bear the thought of that news getting out into the world. She hadn't even told her mom yet.

"Uh, are you sure you don't have any news about something going on between you and a certain European prince?"

Serena chewed her lip. "I'm in Altaleone right now. With Sandro." It felt like a fairly safe confession, being the honest truth.

"Wonderful." Her agent's voice brightened. "I love it. I'm pretty sure I could pitch a book about dating—and even better marrying—a prince to your publisher."

"No!" Serena panicked. Could Barbara do that without them even working up a proposal? Her first two books had been completely written—as blogs—before they were even shopped around. Only then had she been talked into adding all the stuff about her relationship with her supposed Mr. Right.

"It's the perfect time to strike. You're a hot property, on the best-seller lists. This will quickly eclipse the news that you broke up with an ordinary dude."

"I...I...everything's in a very early stage." She glanced at Emma, who was at least pretending to be preoccupied with something else. "I'll keep you posted." Might as well keep her enthusiastic. Because she had another issue to ask about. "How long do you think it will be before I start to see royalties from the book?"

There was another intense pause. Then laughter. "You are kidding, right? I mean, you got a two hundred thousand dollar advance. You're not ever going to see royalties on that book. It's fallen off the lists already."

Serena's heart sank. She could hardly tell her agent about her cash crunch. She hadn't heard a word from her Realtor about the apartment, which meant that yet another week had gone by where no one had wanted to see it. And where she hadn't had time to make the kind of videos that generated her income. Which meant her audience was on the brink of deserting her in droves for more active and engaged content providers. Which meant that soon she wouldn't be able to pay her mortgage and monthly maintenance fees and—

"I guess that wedding book idea we'd discussed is a no-go area." Barbara had a snarky New York attitude that Serena had previously enjoyed. Right now it just hurt.

"I'm afraid so." She been wracking her brain to come up with book ideas for weeks, but nothing made sense any more. Every time she started writing, her enthusiasm just fizzled out.

"I can see that your makeup videos are your money makers, but I can't sell a makeup book."

"I know. I'm sorry." She wished she had some other hot potential idea to float, but the reality was that she didn't. "At least the book hit the lists," she said brightly.

"Yeah. Thank god for that. Now the publisher

won't freak out too badly. Next time anything happens, let me know right away, okay? We're on the same team."

"I know, Barbara. I really appreciate everything you've done." Ouch, that sounded so final. She wanted to get off the phone. Emma had already overheard too much. "I'll let you know if I have any new ideas."

"You do that," said Barbara snarkily, as if pigs might fly first. Then she rung off.

Serena put her phone away, embarrassment surging in her veins. "My agent. Kind of awkward."

"It's so great that you're a writer." Emma beamed. "That's the kind of job you can take with you wherever you move to. All you need is a computer and an Internet connection."

"I'm not really a writer." Serena shrugged. "I've never sat down to write a book." She'd never felt that more fully than this moment. She just tried to keep some balls in the air in the hope that some of them would find somewhere to land. But soon her face would puff up or something—that happened to the women in her family during pregnancy—and she'd have to put a bag over her head to make a video.

Or, more likely, get a real job. Except how could she do that if she told people she was pregnant?

And it was ironic that her agent was upset by the kind of secret keeping she'd accused Sandro of.

"Are you okay? You look like you've seen a ghost."

"I *am* sleeping in the haunted bedroom," Serena said with a wry smile. "I'm a bit overwhelmed right now. I came here for a brief escape from everything."

"And got plunged into a murder mystery with an intimidating royal cast."

"Exactly." Serena smiled. Emma was warm and easy to talk to.

"I know it's hard to believe, but you get used to it. The palaces, the staff, the excess. I didn't think I would, but it starts to seem normal."

"I don't think I'll have to worry about that." She tried to smile again, but it wobbled on her mouth. "I'll be going home soon."

"Are you dying to get out of here?" Emma cocked her head and looked sympathetic.

No. Her gut clenched. She didn't want to leave Sandro. Which alarmed her. "Not just yet. I suppose I'll be leaving when Sandro has time to fly me back."

"Good. Because it would be a shame if you left before you had time to fall in love with Altaleone and its people."

Serena and Sandro ate lunch at a quaint restaurant in the village—under the watchful gaze of the security staff. For some reason she didn't feel all that bothered by people looking at them. The villagers were polite and didn't stare, and now that she'd been in the palace and met everyone she actually didn't feel like a total outsider anymore.

The food was delicious, a rich soup followed by crusty bread with cheeses and pâté and a warm "salad" of root vegetables.

After lunch he drove her around the village, then out toward the ski slopes, where they watched the long ski lifts carrying people up to the high peaks.

"Come on, you have to do a video." Sandro had

goaded her several times.

"What about?"

"About Altaleone, of course. Don't you care about our tourism industry?" It was hard to tell when he was joking. Maybe Sandro was always joking. He didn't seem to take anything very seriously.

"I'm not really in the right mood. I'm nervous. When are you joining this creepy society?"

"Tonight. Darias and I are driving out to the lake house."

She inhaled sharply. "I want to come too."

"What?" He looked stunned. "Why?"

To keep you safe. Though she had no idea how she'd go about it. She was hardly a black belt in anything. "It seems interesting."

"You can't videotape the meeting. It's a secret society."

"I know." She wanted to laugh. "I wasn't going to vlog the experience." *I don't want to let you out of my sight—and into danger.* "I just think everything will be smoother with…a stranger like me there."

"I'm not so sure. They'd keep you out of the secret parts anyway. And I swear I won't have kinky sex with anyone."

She blinked. "You can do whatever you like."

"Do you really think I'd want to?" They sat in the car, the heater blowing warm air, as they watched the skiers winding their way down the slopes."

"I don't know." She looked at him. She really didn't know him well at all. They'd been thrust together by a real estate mix-up and a storm…and now a baby.

"There's only one person I want to make love with." He spoke softly, looking directly out the windshield.

Serena's insides almost burst into flames. She forced herself not to look at Sandro. That would be the end of her. Already the car crackled with the electric energy they accidentally created. "I think we both know that wouldn't be a good idea."

"Speak for yourself." Now he turned and she could feel his gaze on her, burning her cheek. "And for the record, I think you're wrong."

"Look at the trouble that's already got us into." Now she turned to confront him. Damn his handsome, arrogant face.

His gaze met hers. "We're having a baby together." He paused for a moment, and she could feel her heart beating. "It's a miracle, not a problem."

Her insides melted. Could he really be so naïve? It was rather adorable. Still— "We're from completely different worlds. Your family and everyone else expects you to date a celebrity or a princess or someone like that, not a commoner like me."

He laughed. "You are a celebrity. You have followers hanging on your every word."

"Hardly! Some of them are really upset that I broke up with Howard. You should see the comments."

"What did they say?" He looked shocked.

"There are people who think I must have done something wrong to lose such a good man. I guess I made him sound too perfect. But heck, maybe I did do something. I was too controlling and concerned about what other people think."

Sandro's eyes glittered. "There might be some truth to that. When something so obviously wonderful is happening between us and all you can think about is whether we're *appropriate* together."

She swallowed. Was he right? She did like Sandro a lot—as a person, not just a prince. He was warm and energetic and caring. He loved his family, and he'd been endlessly patient with her. Okay, not endlessly patient but somewhat patient. What was she so afraid of?

Humiliation. Getting dumped—again. Being rejected.

"I'm wary and with good reason," she protested. "I don't mind living my life in the public eye in a small way..."

"A very controlled—by you—way." He lifted an arrogant brow.

"Yes. And what's wrong with that? Do you enjoy tabloids speculating about your business?"

"I've learned not to pay any attention to it. If I'd done all the things the tabloids reported I'd have at least eight wives and fifteen children by now." He turned his shoulders toward her and reached for her hands. She braced as he took them and the warmth of his skin heated hers. "I've been getting requests for information about my engagement to Maya Dunham all day. Am I really supposed to respond to such nonsense? What strangers say about me doesn't affect who I am."

She blinked as his words struck her with force. She drew in a shaky breath. "I'm not sure who I am right now. I've put so much effort into creating a persona that I don't know what *I* want. I thought I wanted to marry Howard and live happily ever after with him in some expensive suburb, but part of me is really glad I escaped." It was a strange admission and liberating to get it off her chest. "My followers would have a heart attack if they knew that."

"I bet some of them would feel cheered by the truth." He squeezed her hands gently. Her skin sizzled under his touch. "You're unique and vibrant and daring. Most people would crack under the pressure of your book tour while hiding a secret breakup and an even more secret pregnancy—"

"Who says I haven't cracked?" She felt half crazy most of the time lately.

He laughed—and leaned closer. So close she could smell the scent of his skin. "Me. You have a core of steel under that beautiful exterior. It's one of the many things about you that I find absolutely irresistible."

Her insides turned molten. Which probably wasn't safe when there was a baby in there. "You're not helping. I think I'm getting crazier by the second. And we need to have our wits about us at the Cross of Blood do tonight."

"You really can't come." He looked apologetic. "It's a secret society. By invitation only."

"Are there any black people in it?"

He stared at her for a moment. "I don't think so."

"Then they might appreciate some diversity." She smiled sweetly.

Sandro's face creased into a smile. "When you put it like that, how can they resist? But seriously, you need to be safe back at the palace with my mom.

"Would you promise to come back safe if you get to come and give me a good night kiss?"

His eyes widened. "Absolutely. Is that a promise?"

"It's a promise."

The grin on his face spread contagiously to hers

and she wanted to kiss him right now, but she knew the security crew in the car behind them was watching their every move.

Really, she had nerve, offering him the honor of coming to kiss her! But the way Sandro spoke to her and looked at her did make her feel special, as if she deserved to be treated like a princess.

He started the engine. "Damn, I can't wait to get this evening over with."

She bit her lip. Would he expect her to make love to him?

And if he did, would she be able to resist?

Her body throbbed with excitement at the prospect of him visiting her late at night.

You really are losing it. But maybe that wasn't such a bad thing after all?

The snowy drive back to the palace went by too fast, and soon they were back in the warm gilded interior being fussed over by staff and licked to death by Lucky, who'd spent the afternoon there being fussed over by everyone.

"Darling." His mom rushed up to him with a worried look on her face. "There's someone here."

"Who?"

She whispered and gave a weird look to the side, as if warning him not to say anything untoward. "Maya Dunham."

"What?" Sandro hissed the word.

"She arrived this afternoon. I didn't know what to do so I invited her in."

Sandro looked uncharacteristically lost for words.

"She's in the blue sitting room. What should we do?" She shot an anxious glance at Serena. Did she think a catfight might break out between them?

"Perhaps I should go up to my room," said Serena, as calmly as possible.

"No," said Sandro firmly. "I want you to come with me."

"Uh…" She hated the idea. "I don't think so."

"Please come. I broke up with her and she knows about you, so by coming here it's like she's pretending you don't exist." He stroked her back. "Don't worry, you won't have to say anything."

But we're not even dating, Serena wanted to protest. But she knew better than to say it aloud in front of family and staff. Already she was learning to behave like a royal. "Okay," she murmured. "Just for a moment."

"Trust me, it won't be more than a moment."

Sandro thrust his arm through hers, which gave her a weird thrill of pride as well as a flutter of misgiving, and together they marched over the polished parquet floors toward yet another of the many elegant sitting rooms.

Maya sprang to her feet—she was much smaller in person than she looked on screen—but froze when she saw Serena. "What's she doing here?"

"I'm honored to have her as my guest here. The pressing question is what are you doing here?" Sandro spoke far more formally than Serena had ever heard him before.

Maya's eyes darted around the room for a moment as if she was plucking up the courage to speak. Then two fat tears rolled simultaneously from her big, famous blue-green eyes. "I'm pregnant."

Serena felt her mouth drop open.

"I don't believe you." Sandro spat back his answer at lightning speed.

"Sandro! How can you say that. We shared such special times."

"We shared a few nights in bed. Why did you tell the press we're engaged? I broke up with you."

Serena felt like he was saying that for her benefit. He didn't want her to think he'd lied about breaking up with Maya.

"I don't know where they got that idea. They sure seem to love it." She looked up at him with those big eyes.

Serena felt Sandro's body stiffen. "I don't believe you're pregnant."

"She's pregnant." She shot a withering look at Serena. "Why can't I be pregnant too?"

Serena felt her knees grow weak. How did Maya Dunham know she was pregnant? Sandro must have told her. She pulled her arm from his like it was a snake that might bite.

"Oh, did I spill your little secret?" Maya looked right at her, eyes flashing fire. "Well, step aside, honey, you're not the only one here who's having Sandro's baby."

Sandro turned to Serena. "I didn't tell her."

How could she believe him? What other way could Maya have possibly know about the baby? Serena hadn't told anyone at all except Asia and Sandro. And Asia certainly wasn't spilling tea with Maya Dunham. "I'm going upstairs." She turned and fled.

"Wait!" She heard Sandro's footsteps coming after her. She wasn't sure whether to be relieved that he followed her or annoyed that he wouldn't let her get away. "Serena, she's probably lying. About everything."

"How could she possibly guess that I'm pregnant?" She whispered it, but it came out as a super obvious stage whisper. Not that everyone in the palace hadn't already heard Maya's pronouncement.

"I don't know, but I'm going to send her away immediately."

"How can you do that?" Her heart ached at a very real possibility. "What if she really is pregnant? I would have been devastated if you'd been cold and cruel to me when I told you."

"I don't trust her as far as I can throw her."

"Still…" Serena resisted his attempt to stroke her arm. "You need to get to the bottom of this. Go talk to her."

Sandro heaved a sigh, then nodded. "For you I will."

Serena blinked. Again, she wasn't sure whether to be flattered or furious. But either way she wanted to be behind closed doors right now. She hurried down the hall and up the stairs to her bedroom as fast as she could walk without actually breaking into a run—Lucky at her heels—but not fast enough to avoid overhearing Maya's wail of distress, "It's true! I swear it!"

Behind the door of the infamous moonlight room, Serena collapsed on the bed. Typical that this had to happen! Just when things were beginning to feel the teeniest bit hunky-dory with Sandro, when she was starting to think that something real might actually happen between them, another new explosion of madness erupted in her life. She didn't think he was going to rush off and marry Maya, but at the very least she was sure that the secret of her own pregnancy was no longer a secret.

And she was going to have to reveal the truth and deal with the fallout—in her family and among her followers—fast before someone else did it for her.

Who should she tell first? Her mom or her sisters? It was the kind of news that was supposed to be happy—"Guess what? I'm having a baby!"—but under the circumstances she knew no one would really be happy for her.

She decided to get the worst over with first and tell her mom. But as she picked up her phone, a text came in. A text from the "ghost."

20

Sandro arranged for Maya Dunham to be driven to a hotel in Zurich. He wanted her out of Altaleone. Although there was no way to prove or disprove paternity at this early stage, he did not intend to acknowledge anything. But Serena was right to call him onto the carpet—he had to be a gentleman about the whole thing. Even though in his gut he felt it was all a sham and that Maya was a lot crazier than most people realized.

As soon as Maya was escorted from the palace, he went into an empty room and called Darias. "I need to bring Serena tonight."

"Are you crazy? It might be dangerous."

"I don't like leaving her here. Some stranger has already been in contact with her. And she wants to come. Was Emma there for your initiation?"

"Um, well, yes. Not for the ceremony itself, but she met them and was there in the castle while it happened."

"See? It's important to me that Serena be a part of this. She thinks I don't consider her important enough to come. And now Maya has her thinking I betrayed her. I need to prove to her how much she matters to me."

"You're totally smitten, aren't you?"

"I'm just being practical," Sandro protested. "She's having my baby, and I need to keep her close." Very close. Preferably in his bed.

"You're madly in love with her." He could hear the laughter in Darias's voice. "I never thought I'd see the day."

"Would you focus on what's important?"

"I thought I was. I want to keep us all safe."

"Gibran and his men will be coming with us. They'll wait right outside. We can summon them at the touch of a button."

"True." Darias paused. "I suppose there isn't too much that can go wrong. Except that I've thought that before...."

"Relax. My goal is to join, pay close attention to everyone there, memorize that damn top secret bank information, and see if I can offer more insight into who is out to get us and why."

"You realize that by learning the number you're putting yourself at risk."

"Hardly." Sandro paced impatiently. He couldn't wait to get on with tonight's events. "I'm only any use to someone who wants it if I'm alive."

"You have a point. Get dressed. I'll be at the palace for dinner and we can ride to the lake house together."

Serena braced herself as she checked the text.

Tonight's the night. Your lover will learn the secret bank code and you will ask him to tell you as a proof of his trust in you. When you relay that information to me your financial problems are over.

Serena froze, heart pounding. This was the bank account they'd spoken of. Two people had abducted Emma in a failed attempt to extract the information from Darias.

And how did this person know about her financial problems?

She glanced around, sure she could feel eyes on her right now.

Fish for information. The family had no idea what this person really wanted. She needed to stay calm and help their effort.

How will my financial problems be solved?

Three million dollars will be deposited to your account 480097451 immediately following successful capture of the funds.

A chill slide down her spine. That was the number of her Citibank savings account. The one that had been rattling empty for months now. This person had done their research.

Except that they hadn't researched her character. If they'd done that they'd know she'd never in a million years agree to their scheme. **I'm interested. How do I convey the information?**

Text it to me then destroy your phone. Destroy it completely, with fire.

She managed to keep a serious expression. How did she subtly catch her phone on fire? The idea, and the terror streaking through her veins, made her want to burst into a panicked laugh. **Okay. I'll do**

273

my best. He might not trust me enough to tell me.

That's a chance I'm willing to take.

Ugh. How could she impart this information to Sandro? She glanced at Lucky. He'd need to go out for one more pee before they left for the night. She clipped his leash on and headed downstairs but didn't dare text Sandro in case the person texting her was somehow tapping her phone.

They must be. They had her bank account information.

Sandro didn't answer her knock on his bedroom door so she put on her coat and took Lucky outside. The palace was quiet, and there weren't many staff in evidence tonight. Lina and Beatriz would be changing for dinner. She'd have to get through dinner, knowing that she kept a terrible secret from them all. At least Sandro hadn't agreed to bring her along tonight. She didn't know what she'd been thinking. She'd had a crazy idea of keeping him safe, but in fact he'd be anything but with her there. If he had to get home to give her the number he'd be a lot safer.

Lucky did his business while she glanced over her shoulder repeatedly in the darkness. It was safe to assume that she was under constant surveillance by the mysterious "ghost." They could be watching her right now from an unlit window in the palace.

She hurried back inside and went upstairs to change for dinner herself. No new messages on her phone. How would she get time alone with Sandro before he left tonight?

She'd only just got back to her room and was stripping off her sweater when a knock on the door made her jump half out of her skin. "Who is it?" She tugged her sweater back on, panic flaring through her.

"It's me, Sandro."

"Come in." Damn. She couldn't talk freely to him in here. She attempted a shaky smile. "Are you nervous about tonight?"

"Not at all. And it's fine for you to come with me. Darias has obtained their consent."

"What?" The word fell from her lips too fast. "Are you sure?" If she brought her phone she could be putting them all in danger. "I don't know if me coming is a good idea."

Sandro looked confused. "I thought you wanted to come."

"Uh, I did."

"It's settled then." A smiled tugged at one side of his mouth. Warmth burned in her chest. He'd gone up against tradition to fulfill her wishes. That touched her—even as it scared the heck out of her. It made her think that if she did ask him for the bank account number he might actually give it to her as proof that he trusted her.

If only she could get him alone—away from surveillance devices—to warn him that someone wanted the number from him—tonight.

Sandro must have mistaken her confused hesitation for something else because he took a step toward her. "Please may I kiss you?" He asked with such tender hesitation that her heart contracted.

"Yes." She couldn't say no.

His lips met hers softly, and a tide of emotion swept through her. This whole trip wasn't going like she expected. Sandro wasn't turning out to be what she'd expected. In spite of herself she knew feelings for him were growing deep inside her, along with their baby.

He didn't try to deepen the kiss or grope her or anything that she might have anticipated from an arrogant prince finding the woman he wanted alone in her bedroom. He pulled back and looked directly into her eyes. "I want you by my side tonight." He blinked, his gaze tender. "I want you by my side always."

Her chest threatened to explode as emotions roamed assaulted her. *I've got to warn him.* Hopefully she'd get a chance in the car. Her foolish ideas about keeping him safe tonight mocked her. How could she keep any member of this family safe where professional security forces had failed?

But so long as the "ghost" thought she was going along with his plan—if it was a man—she'd be safe, and so would Sandro. They wouldn't risk harming him until she got the number.

"I'm excited about our baby." Sandro's soft words, spoken in a voice husky with emotion, reminded her that he knew nothing about the texts she'd received today.

"I am too," she admitted honestly. "At first I was terrified, but now I've had time to get used to the idea I'm more excited than nervous." She was still very nervous about the future for her and Sandro, but she'd come to peace with being a mother. An unpleasant thought interrupted her. "Is Maya Dunham okay? If she really is pregnant, she's very scared right now."

"Don't ever forget that Maya Dunham is a very talented actress. I'm fast learning that you should take everything she says with a grain of salt."

"But why would she do it?"

"Because she wants to be a princess or something stupid like that. She couldn't get me to return her calls so now she's grasping at straws. She must think you did the same."

"You don't think that, do you?"

Sandro frowned. "You know me better than that by now."

She drew in a breath. "But you don't know me all that well. Maybe I orchestrated the whole thing to boost my social media rankings."

He stared at her, and she heard the blood pound in her ears for a moment. What was wrong with her? Why had she said that just now? Did she want him to distrust her?

A guffaw burst from Sandro's mouth. "I'm a much better judge of character than people give me credit for. You'd no more fake a pregnancy than sell your mother."

"True." She bit her lip. "I was about to finally tell my mom about the pregnancy then—" She stopped short. She couldn't tell him about the texts. That would be disastrous.

"Tell her! Go on. Call her now. I'll stay here for moral support if you like."

She blinked. "I'm not sure you'd like what my mom might have to say about the situation. She's a very religious woman."

"I'm tougher than I look."

She chuckled. How did Sandro manage to relax her no matter how dire the situation seemed? "I'm not. But I will tell her. First I need to get dressed for dinner."

"I can help." His gaze drifted to her torso—where her nipples instantly tightened.

"I need to shower."

"All the better." His low voice only stoked the fires burning in her.

But who was watching? She remembered the "ghost" who might be studying her through a camera or a hole in the wall or ceiling...or floor. "I think it would be quicker if I was alone. I don't want to be late for dinner."

"I suppose you have a point. Knock on my door when you're ready." He ruffled Lucky's fur on his way out of the room.

Serena exhaled as the door closed. How on earth was she going to get through tonight? I will keep him safe, she reasoned. While he was busy with the ceremony or trying to figure out the identity of masked aristocrats, she'd be watching everyone, ready to alert security if needed.

She'd forgotten to ask what one wore to a secret society initiation, so she decided on her faithful little black dress, with a black blazer and tiny silver earrings. The more she blended into the background tonight, the better.

She knocked on Sandro's door and they went down to dinner together, looking every inch like a real couple. The part of her that wasn't in a total panic managed to enjoy entering the dining room together, and Sandro's warm appraising gaze of her simple outfit as he announced to his mom, Beatriz and Liesel that Serena would be joining him that night.

"But surely such a thing is unheard of," muttered Liesel. "The society is for titled aristocrats."

"If all goes according to plan, Serena will soon be a titled aristocrat," said Sandro, coolly, pulling out her chair for her.

Serena froze for a moment before gingerly lowering herself onto the seat. Had he just announced his intention to marry her? Without even asking her... He had blown her mind earlier when he said he wanted her by his side always. Was he serious? Her brain was spinning so fast she missed Beatriz's question to her.

"Sorry, what did you say?"

"Just that I'm envious. I've always been curious about the Cross of Blood. Grandmama was always very mysterious about it and Papa always shushed me when I asked him about it." She turned to Darias, who'd just entered with Emma. "Can I come too?"

"Not this time," he replied. "With Serena and Emma attending we'll be quite a crowd. I don't want to unsettle them."

"Typical," said Beatriz with a pout. "You don't want me there because you don't trust me."

"Nonsense," said Darias. "There's just no reason for you to be there tonight."

"What reason does Serena have to be there?" She stared at Darias, then at Sandro.

Serena felt her face heat. *She's having my baby.* Did they know? Maybe they hadn't overheard Maya's rantings. Or chose to ignore them as the ravings of a madwoman.

"Because she's my guest of honor." Sandro sipped his wine, nonchalant.

None of them had any idea that she was the supposed envoy of their enemy.

They ate an elaborate meal of several different fish dishes and caramelized vegetables, while Lina quizzed them on family history. Serena wondered if this was for her benefit. Surely they'd all heard the family history stuff before. Perhaps Lina wanted to remind her that they were of ancient, aristocratic lineage while she was just an American nobody.

"But wasn't our founding ancestor an *illegitimate* son of Charlemagne?" asked Darias after a long description of the founding of Altaleone from a land grant to him.

"Almost everyone was illegitimate back then, brother dearest," explained Beatriz. "If you were a man it meant that your daddy gave you great estates and wealth rather than the actual crown."

"What happened if you were a woman?" asked Serena, curious.

Beatriz took a bite of her fish. "Nunnery."

"Oh."

"I have little interest in things that happened nearly a thousand years ago," said Darias, breaking off a piece of bread. "I'm far more invested in the present."

"But don't forget, the past is always with you." Liesel said brightly. "Whether you want it or not."

Serena paused with her water glass halfway to her mouth—she was avoiding the wine like it was poisoned—since Liesel's words were so similar to those of the "ghost."

"You've inherited a great legacy," continued Liesel, staring at Darias, "and it is your job to carry it to the next generation." She glanced rudely at Emma. "If there is one."

"Liesel!" Lina scolded her sister. "They only just

got married. There's no pressure whatsoever to have children. They can enjoy each other for years if they like."

"I suppose that given the family history any illegitimate children could inherit as well," said Liesel sweetly. "Like Maya Dunham's baby." Her words dropped in the air like shattered glass. She must have overheard some of the drama of earlier.

Which meant she had could have also overheard the part about her being pregnant with Sandro's baby. Serena froze, waiting for the other shoe to drop.

"Liesel, if you can't behave yourself I'll have to ask you to leave." Lina spoke sternly. Darias and Sandro stared at her, as did Beatriz.

"Excuse me," said Liesel, dabbing her mouth with a napkin. "I suppose I'm just trying to make you aware of the things that others are saying at their dinner tables all over Europe." She shot a cold glance at Serena. "Sometimes this family seems utterly oblivious to things going on right under their noses."

Serena felt her breathing grow shallow.

"I think people have more relevant things to discuss over dinner," said Sandro gruffly. Then he looked at Darias. "We should get going."

"Don't you have time for dessert? It's a chocolate mousse that Beatriz and I made ourselves."

"We can have some when we get back," said Darias softly. "Sandro's right. We need time to get the security in place before the ceremony begins."

"Sandro, can we take Lucky out?" Serena desperately wanted to get away from the table before Liesel said anything else, and she needed a moment alone with him before things got under way. She could leave her phone in her bedroom when she picked up Lucky.

"We really should get going," said Darias. "The roads are still snowy."

Sandro looked at Serena apologetically. "One of the staff can walk Lucky. Wilhelm perhaps." Obviously he didn't catch the hint that she needed to talk to him privately.

Darias stood up. "Wilhelm's driving us tonight."

"Why?" Sandro stared.

"So we can drink." Darias lifted a brow. "The usual driver is home sick with a stomach bug."

They moved into the hallway to get their coats. Emma donned hers as well. "I'm coming too," she explained to Serena. "We can keep each other company during the secret parts."

Serena was momentarily cheered before realizing that now yet another person was potentially in danger. Her phone pinged and she checked it.

Your services are no longer needed tonight. *The ghost.* **If you tell anyone about our communications you will die first.**

Serena had a violent urge to beg off this trip.

"Who was that?" asked Sandro.

"My mom," she lied. But if she let Sandro go without her and something happened, she would never forgive herself.

Sandro smiled at her. He must be thinking that she'd told her mom about the baby, but she hadn't had time yet. Or wasn't brave enough. She was almost more scared of that than encountering whatever villain was watching them all.

So, for whatever reason, the villain no longer

wanted her to extract information from Sandro. Could it be because they were planning on doing it themselves?

"You're shaking." Sandro stroked her back through her coat.

"I'm fine," she managed a weak smile. "Just getting ready for the cold night air. Let's go."

21

Sandro opened the car door for Serena. Two rows of seats faced each other. He sat next to her and shot her what he hoped was a reassuring smile.

"What am I to expect?" Sandro looked at Darias. "Cloaks and daggers?"

"Cloaks but no daggers."

"And we're sure these people didn't kill our father and grandmother."

"The current theory is that Dad and Grandma went to the lake house expecting a Cross of Blood meeting and were ambushed. It wasn't a real meeting because none of the others knew about it. But whoever killed them must have intimate details of the society because they engaged in…uh…"

"Sexual acts," said Sandro. He'd heard the salacious details of how their father was found naked, stabbed with a thousand-year-old blade, and their grandmother was dressed in black leather and appeared to have been asphyxiated during some sort of edge-play sex game.

"Yes. Or at least that's how the scene was laid out to appear. That they were engaged in sexual acts when they were murdered."

"I never knew any of them be into the kind of scenario that was described."

"Does any kid know that their dad or grandma does BDSM?"

"I suppose not, but I'm still not convinced." Sandro frowned. "Have the members tried to do anything like that with you? It seems like it would provide good material for blackmail."

Darias shook his head. "They did make it clear that their role is to provide a safe space and protection for the monarch and their desires, but when I told them I wasn't interested no one pressured me. They didn't seem to think the acts that Dad and Grandma were engaged in were out of the ordinary for them, so it seems they did use the society to fulfill their private needs."

He glanced sideways at Serena, who looked appropriately shocked. She might be wondering why he was letting her hear all this. She was a grown-up, and he didn't need to hide anything from her. And he knew her well enough that he didn't have to ask her to keep his family's salacious secrets.

The moonlit drive to the lake house gave them time to form a strategy. The main goal was to figure out who the members were. Darias had already most of them by their voices or other mannerisms, and all were very prominent and wealthy members of Altaleone society—whose families and friends would have been shocked to know what they got up to in private.

Darias had been frustrated during his three sessions with the society because the members kept distracting him so he couldn't figure out who was who. Now his plan was to stand back and observe while Sandro kept their attention. He needed to figure out who the two remaining mystery members were.

On arrival, they parked in front of the lake house among the other black cars—their license plates blacked out—and Sandro took Serena's arm in his as they climbed the steps to the imposing double wood doors.

"Are you regretting coming?"

Yes. "No." She smiled, hoping to reassure Sandro. Her heart beat like a snare drum, rattling her nerves with each pulse. She didn't have a clear idea of what would happen tonight, but all the blurry ideas scared the heck out of her. Masked strangers? Edgy sex play? Murder?

But Sandro had brought her here to prove to her that he considered her his partner, his equal, welcome everywhere that he was welcome—whether the other people there liked it or not. She was determined to do her best to play her role.

Darias rang an ancient bell, and the huge wood door creaked open. Serena gasped as a masked figure in robes to the floor greeted them with a deep bow and a heavily accented "Welcome."

She couldn't fake a warm smile if her life depended on it. They were led into a huge, empty room with high ceilings. The only light came from candles that flickered menacingly in a draft. The house was empty of furniture and had a neglected air. These people had so many grand houses they didn't know what to do with them.

Where were the security force she'd heard so much about? She hadn't seen any cars on the road behind them, and she'd looked. What if they'd been intercepted and weren't coming at all?

Sandro took her hand and introduced her to the group—no names were mentioned. It seemed unfair that they should know who she was but not the reverse. There were drinks and even some platters of unidentifiable finger food that no one was touching. Given the threats she didn't plan to put anything in her mouth, and she hoped Sandro wouldn't either.

A masked woman spoke to her about Altaleone and its winter beauty—so Beatriz was wrong about women not being included—and she attempted to sound less terrified than she felt as she gushed over how pretty the snowy landscapes were. Then she and Emma were ushered into another large empty room, away from the private part of the ceremony.

Serena put her turned-off phone down on a window ledge and led Emma by the arm to the far side of the large room, with its dusty black-and-white stone floor. There was a single pillar candle burning in one corner and moonlight reflected off the white snow outside, but otherwise they were in darkness. They could hear muffled music from the room next door but nothing useful.

Serena leaned into Emma, finger to her lips. "Don't say anything audible. We need to monitor their meeting. Someone who wants the bank details is watching."

Emma frowned. "Gibran's men are watching."

"Are they?" Serena looked outside. "I looked for

headlights, and I never saw any."

"I presume that's because they don't want everyone to know."

"But what if they didn't make it?"

Emma bit her lip. "If we go outside we might be able to see in." Where was the "ghost"? Likely too busy watching the meeting to pay attention to her. There was an ancient paneled exterior door with a wrought iron bolt. "I wonder if we can get this door open?"

The rusted latch took some fiddling, especially in the dark, but they eventually got it to slide back and opened the door to the crisp night air. Serena decided to leave her phone behind in case it could be used to track her even while turned off. They stepped out into snow at least a foot deep—in high-heeled shoes—and crept along the wall to the room next door.

Serena peered through the window, heart pounding, and saw the cloaked figures standing in a circle. It was impossible to even tell which ones were Sandro and Darias, as they all wore hoods that covered their hair and creepy featureless masks.

"At least nothing terrible is happening," said Emma with a sigh. "Darias never seems to worry, but I often feel like I'm being watched by someone who wishes me ill."

"I notice how the family carries on as if the staff aren't there. No one has any secrets."

"Isn't it odd? I guess they're used to being surrounded by people all the time. At least in the castle Darias and I can live with only a guard or two, not a full retinue."

"And all the staff know the details of the

murders?"

"I don't know if they know about the sexual stuff. Darias has tried to keep that even from his mom."

"But they said it right in the car in front of the driver. He could tell anyone."

"I suppose they trust him. I know he's been with them for years."

Serena shook her head. "Maybe I'm just not a trusting person, but I'd be more wary."

The sound of crashing glass made them both jump, and Emma stifled a tiny scream. A black-clad figure had punched through the window on the far side of the room and now held a gun to one masked figure.

"Tell me the code and your king lives."

Serena gripped Emma's arm. "That must be Darias. Quick, call Gibran." Emma dialed and Serena heard her panicked whispered account. And a curse.

"They're stuck behind an avalanche over ten miles away. His men are coming on foot, but they're still at least twenty minutes out."

"Where's the driver, Wilhelm?"

"I don't know. I suppose he stayed in the car."

A grim thought crossed Serena's mind. "Do you think that's him?"

They stared at the man in black.

"Let me call him." Emma pulled up her phone. "I have his number in here somewhere. He helped me move a lot of stuff from the palace to the castle a few months ago."

"Wait." Serena grabbed her hand. "I have a weird theory. Look up his number but don't dial it."

Inside the hooded figures stood silently, no one moving. "Tell me the code," they heard him say.

Serena flinched as the black-clad man pistol-whipped the masked Darias.

Emma scrolled in her phone and found it. "Here it is. Wilhelm Rinald."

"What's the number?"

Emma held up the phone and the numbers glowed in the dark.

Adrenaline spiked through Serena as she recognized them. "That's it. The ghost." Serena grabbed her arm.

"What?" Emma winced as the stranger cocked his pistol at Darias head.

"Your king dies right now."

"We'll tell you," said a deep-voiced older man.

Serena crept along the window. If anyone was looking this way they'd be able to see them against the moonlit snow, but all eyes were on the assailant. "He's been texting me, threatening to kill the members of the royal family unless I cooperate." Her brain scrambled to come up with a plan. "I think that if you call him it might distract him enough for one of them to tackle him."

"Or he'll panic and shoot Darias," said Emma with a quavering voice.

"He might do that anyway."

"Tell me!" She heard the assailant yell. "Now!"

"When you dial him, I'll smash the window and we'll both duck right down, okay?"

"Okay." Emma's thumb hovered over her phone as Serena removed her shoe and pulled her coat down over her arm.

"Close your eyes, then push dial." Serena braced herself as she heard the dial tone in Emma's phone. She kept her eyes fast on the black figure and watched him flinch—his phone was vibrating! Gathering all her strength she slammed her shoe— heel first—at the window and watched it crack but not shatter.

Another robed figure rushed the intruder, and Darias dived to the side as a shot was fired. The breaking glass made the assailant swing to face her. She saw the gun aim at her before she dropped down into the snow. Glass shattered over her as she fell and a bullet whistled over her head.

She and Emma crouched face down in the snow, panting. Now they couldn't see anything but heard a scuffle and shouts, then two more shots were fired.

"Sandro's injured!" Darias's voice made Serena spring to her feet, a scream stifled in her throat.

"No," she rasped, heart clenched. Through the window she could see one masked figure sprawled on the floor, robe darkening with blood. *Sandro.* She could also see the assailant pinned to the ground, struggling with several others. Darias—hood thrown back and mask propped on his head—now held the gun. "Call for help."

Desperate, Serena smashed a bigger hole in the window, hiked up her dress, and carefully climbed through. "Gibran's men ran into an avalanche," she stammered as she rushed to Sandro's body. Darias had already removed his brother's mask. "They're on their way, but the road is blocked."

Darias ripped Sandro's cloak from him. Serena gasped to see that the wound was on his torso, a ghastly bloom of blood spreading across his chest. "We have to stop the bleeding." She pulled his jacket back and tore at his shirt. The wound was under his armpit, and she couldn't tell how deep it was. "Is anyone here a doctor?"

The robed strangers stood around like statues.

"Sandro, can you hear me?" He was unconscious, possibly from hitting his head when he fell. "Wake up!" The shot likely hadn't hit an organ, but what if help didn't come in time and he bled to death? There was no way to apply a tourniquet to this spot.

"Sandro." She touched his face. Her heart swelled with fear and panic. He'd done nothing but be honorable and kind to her. He'd showed her in so many ways that he was warm and caring and thoughtful—far more so than her supposedly sensible choice of partner.

Would he now be taken from her when she was just growing bold enough to care for him? "Sandro!" Did his eyelids flicker? "It's me, Serena. Come back to me...please." She could hear the desperation in her voice. "I need you..." She hesitated, screwing up her courage. "Our baby needs you. Don't leave us."

His eyelids flickered again and now opened slightly. "Serena?" His voice was barely a whisper.

She grasped the hand closest to her and squeezed it. "Yes, Sandro, it's me. Hang in there. Help is coming." She watched him struggle to open his eyes. "Come back to me..." She closed her own eyes for a moment, willing him back to health and strength even as she knew the blood was seeping out of him. "I love you."

Her admission fell from her lips and echoed in the air. She opened her eyes, half expecting to see shock on his face. She'd be grateful for any response, as it would show he was still conscious. His dark gaze fixed directly on hers. "I love you too. I won't leave you." His voice was cracked but steady. "I won't ever leave you."

"Listen!" Emma's bold voice rang out in the room. "Gibran says there's a medical helicopter on the way that will land in the courtyard within three minutes. Clear the way and get ready to lead them to Sandro."

The robed figures scurried out of the room. Serena held tight to Sandro's hand, his warmth giving her strength and courage. "You're going to be fine. They're almost here."

Sandro struggled to keep his eyes open. His white shirt was totally soaked in blood. What if he bled to death in the final seconds before the medical team got here? She put her hand over the wound and pushed on it with all her might. "Hold on, Sandro. Hold on!"

He didn't speak again, and his eyelids fluttered closed. "No, no, no." She leaned forward and kissed his face. His cheek was growing cold. "Sandro, I need you. Stay with me. I love you." Her own anguished whispers rang in her ears.

"They're here!" Darias' voice boomed. "Make way."

Serena didn't leave Sandro's side until the black-clad team thundered into the room, carrying a stretcher. Within seconds they'd taken Sandro's blood pressure and applied something to stop the bleeding. Sandro was rushed out to the helicopter and hooked up to equipment.

One of the medics barked something in their local dialect.

"He says he can only take one of us," said Darias. "Serena, you go with him."

Fear and panic made her knees weak, but she ran

toward the chopper and the medics pulled her in. That Darias would let her go instead of him—his own brother—touched her deeply. He must know how desperately she wanted to be there with him right now.

"We're starting a blood transfusion. He's lost a lot already," said one of the medics in halting English. "We'll be at the hospital in ten minutes."

Serena used the time to pray silently. She wasn't a preacher's daughter for nothing. And the medics allowed her to keep hold of Sandro's hand during the whole flight , which was only a few minutes but felt like an eternity. Right before they landed she felt Sandro squeeze her hand, and he rasped the words, "Thank you."

Thank you—for what? His words cut her like a knife—as if he were saying goodbye. "Sandro—" But the medics were already lowering the stretcher down off the helicopter. They ran into the hospital and she hurried behind as fast as she could, but when they wheeled Sandro into an operating room the door was politely but firmly closed in her face.

She realized with horror that her hands were covered with Sandro's blood. And she'd left her phone in the creepy mansion so she couldn't call anyone. Tears welled in her eyes, and she felt her knees finally buckle. Two nurses caught her and hurried her into an observation room where she was able to gather herself and wash her hands, but neither of them spoke enough English for her to get an update on Sandro.

She'd been so anxious to protect herself that she'd kept him at arm's length. She'd been so terrified of the sexual chemistry between them that she hadn't hugged him when she could have. He might be scared about the baby too. In some ways the uncertainty was much worse for men as she could move away and refuse to see him again.

She'd never assured him that she wouldn't do that. And now she regretted her defensive behavior with all her heart.

At least she'd told him she loved him. She meant it every fiber of her being and she didn't care who'd heard, either. She was done keeping secrets and hiding behind half-truths.

Please let me have another chance.

She sat on a row of chairs not too far from the operating theater, from where she could see anyone coming in or out. The door didn't move for a long time. They must still be working on him.

At last two men came out, removing their masks and scrubs, faces grim. She sprang to her feet and ran toward them. "Is he okay?"

They looked up, surprised, and she realized she might well look like a crazy person—despite the fact that little black dresses hid blood quite well—and was obviously not a family member. "Who are you?"

She stood, brain whirring, "I'm Sandro's...girlfriend." It was a bold thing to say, calling herself the romantic partner of this country's royal prince when he hadn't called her any such thing himself.

"Oh." They looked at each other. "He's very weak from loss of blood, and his right arm was broken by the bullet, but we expect a full recovery."

Relief swept through her at his last words. "Oh, thank God! Can I go see him?"

"He's being moved to a room. The nurses will

take you there when he's ready."

Chastened by their curt reply but elated that Sandro had survived the gunshot, she paced the hallway anxiously until the harried nurses ushered her to his room. To her surprise, Darias, Emma, his mom and Beatriz were already there. They exclaimed that they had been calling her and didn't know where she was. Sandro was awake and his eyes fixed on hers as soon as she came through the door. "Serena, you saved my life."

She barely heard his words as she rushed toward him, then hesitated, suddenly self-conscious in front of his whole family.

"I dived forward to get his gunsight off Darias, and as soon as he pointed the gun at me you broke the window and threw off his aim. The bullet grazed my chest and broke my arm instead of heading straight for my heart."

"I'm so glad you're both okay." So much emotion roiled through her that she could barely get the words out.

Emma had tears in her eyes. She turned to Sandro. "Thank you for risking your own life to protect Darias."

"Idiot," muttered Darias, with a half-grin on his face. "Typical, really."

"Serena, come closer." One of Sandro's arms was bandaged, but he reached the other one out to her. "I heard everything you said." He spoke softly, as if they were the only people in the room. "Did you mean it?"

"Yes," she admitted. "Every word."

"I love you too." His eyes sparkled with emotion. "I promise I won't ever leave you."

A thrill of emotion roared through her.

"Serena." He frowned. "Damn, I wish I could get down on one knee to say this, but they won't let me out of this bed and I don't want to waste another minute. Life is too precious."

She blinked as he squeezed her hand.

"Serena, will you marry me?"

It was a crazy question—too much, too soon and at totally the wrong time—but she knew there was only one possible answer. "Yes, Sandro, I will marry you."

She heard a sob behind her and turned, expecting to find Sandro's mom collapsing in tears at her son marrying a nobody. Instead it was Emma, blubbering into a Kleenex. Lina beamed. Tears hovered in her eyes, but they didn't look like tears of devastation. They looked suspiciously like tears of happiness.

"Congratulations, bro," said Darias gruffly. "Only you could turn an assassination attempt into a romantic occasion. My hat is off to you. Welcome to the family, Serena. It's a crazy place to be, but we love it."

The family.

Was she really going to become part of Altaleone's royal family? It seemed too impossible to imagine. But if they married in time, her baby would be born into a complete family unit and something about that appealed to her tradition-loving heart.

"Thank you for accepting me," she said quietly. "I suppose we should tell everyone we're expecting a baby."

She heard Lina gasp. "Oh, my goodness, I had no idea! Congratulations."

Darias and Emma looked at each other. She

stared at them. "Did you already know?"

"I swear, I didn't tell him," Sandro protested, face pained.

"He just guessed, right?" Serena couldn't help but laugh. "Never mind. I suppose everyone has to know sooner or later." She inhaled a quick breath. "Now I have yet another thing to tell my mom."

"I look forward to meeting your family," said Lina. "I hope they'll be able to come visit us here in Altaleone very soon."

Serena's eyes widened. What on earth would her parents think of her marrying royalty? On the other hand, they might be less shocked by that than by the prospect of her having a baby out of wedlock. "I think they'd like that. But I'd better call my mom and catch her up on my news before anything else happens."

EPILOGUE

Two days later Sandro was back at the palace, still bandaged and with one arm in a cast, but striding around one of the gilded living rooms as if nothing was wrong. "Wilhelm!" He shook his head. "He's been with the family since I was a teenager. He can't be more than a few years older than me."

"Yup," said Darias. "And this whole time he's been smarting over the fact that the Leones rule Altaleone and his family was driven into exile and lost all their money.

"But they were banished in 1848 right after the coup attempt. That's more than a hundred and fifty years ago!"

"You'd think they'd have moved on by now, but greed has a way of making people grasp at straws."

"But seriously, couldn't you have just given him that stupid code? It's not like it means he can go get the money."

"What makes you think it's money?" Sandro lifted

a brow. "I wish I could tell you, but I can't. You're not an initiate of the Cross of Blood…yet."

"Tell me about it. I think I've lost enough blood already. Maybe Rigo can join instead."

"He's coming here soon, he swears it. He's pledged to use his legal mind to get to the bottom of this mess—as soon as his big trial is over."

"That's something, I suppose. I bet it's diamonds. Is it diamonds?" He looked at Darias.

Who frowned at him. "No one in this family has any sense of tact. That's how Wilhelm knew far too much about us and about the Cross of Blood. He just listened quietly when we were flapping our lips."

"He swears he didn't kill dad?"

"He insists that he didn't kill anyone but that he's just the edge of a much larger conspiracy that did. Unfortunately, despite Gibran's best efforts, he won't reveal any more details about it. Gibran thinks that he actually doesn't know any more details. That they used him and his family grudge to further their own ends.

Throat clearing drew their attention to the doorway. It was Gibran. "Once again, I must apologize for not being able to protect you."

"You couldn't have known there'd be an avalanche," said Darias.

"I should have considered it as a possibility. It was deliberately set with dynamite."

"Wilhelm couldn't have done it," Emma cut in. "He was busy driving us. Someone else was involved."

"Yes, but unfortunately even Wilhelm himself does not seem to be privy to that information."

"I'll get to the bottom of this if it kills me,"

muttered Darias.

"Don't say that!" protested Emma.

"You know what I mean." He gazed at his wife tenderly. "I have far too much to live for. And thanks to Sandro and Serena drawing fire to themselves instead of me, I get to enjoy my life with you."

The sight of their love touched everyone in the room. And Sandro paced again. "When do I get to announce my engagement? Huh? I'm tired of waiting."

"You know there will be a media circus," said Lina. "So you need to be healthy enough to withstand it."

"I'm perfectly fine."

And you might as well wait until Maya Dunham crawls back into the woodwork. A pregnancy test proved she isn't pregnant, but she hasn't flown out of Zurich yet," said Beatriz. "Probably too embarrassed to show her face back in the U.S. after all her fake stories about you."

"Why don't you do an engagement photo shoot?" suggested Lina. "Then you can send out pictures to all the media outlets and they'll leave you alone for a few days at least."

"That's a great idea," said Sandro. "And Serena can vlog it. Aren't you supposed to be posting new content three times a week?"

"Are you serious?" She'd assumed privacy issues would mean she'd have to slow down her vlogging or quit altogether.

"Deadly serious," said Sandro. "How else are people going to discover that the Leones are the coolest royal family in Europe?"

Emma laughed, and Darias shook his head.

Serena bit her lip. "My followers would love it." She chuckled. "Especially if I showed the hair and makeup part."

"And we can tell them about the baby," said Sandro.

"It's not three months yet," she protested.

"Oh, come on. Haven't you learned to live dangerously?" He swooped in with a firm kiss on her lips.

Her pulse quickened and her skin heated. "I suppose I'm learning every day."

"Practice makes perfect." He took her hand. "Speaking of which, I need to talk to you alone."

Serena let Sandro lead her out of the room, across the foyer and up the stairs to her blue-and-silver bedroom.

"What are we doing?" she asked, perplexed, as he came in and locked the door.

"You don't expect me to wait until marriage, do you?" Fire smoldered in his dark eyes.

Heat flared in her core. "But you only have one working arm."

"Trust me, that won't slow me down one bit."

She laughed. "Your determination is always impressive." She'd fought the urge to make love to him for so long that the possibility of it happening unleashed a dangerous power surge inside her. "And I have an idea."

Together, using her two hands and his one good one, they unbuttoned and pulled off their clothes. The sight of Sandro's body—all chiseled muscle lightly sprinkled with dark hair—sent her core temperature soaring. She trailed her fingers over the

302

hard, flat expanse of his stomach, letting raw desire rise inside herself for the first time. She's spent so long being wary, afraid of getting out of her depth. Right now she could wade right in—the water was lovely.

"Lie down on the bed," she whispered.

Sandro's eyes flashed, and he quickly moved into position. His good arm rose to caress her as she climbed over him. She leaned in to kiss him and her breasts brushed his chest, causing him to inhale sharply. "Careful, things are getting explosive," he murmured, mischief dancing in his gaze.

"I'm getting used to living on the edge." She trailed a finger along the middle of his torso, between his hard pecs and down past his belly button, to where his impressive erection now jutted.

She lowered her hips over his. For an instant a thought of the tiny baby inside her flashed into her mind. Still too small to see but looming large in their lives, their baby had brought them back together and kept them there until she came to her senses.

"I promise to make you the happiest woman on earth, Serena." Sandro's husky voice tickled her ears.

"The weird thing is, I believe you." She glanced up, and the sincere expression on his handsome face made her heart trip. "I hope I can make you happy too." She knew she'd try her hardest. She always tried her hardest at everything, and sometimes it worked out and sometimes it didn't. And that didn't stop her from getting up the next day and trying all over again. "You're an amazing guy, Sandro."

"And you are a spectacular woman, Serena. I think I fell in love with you the moment we met."

She giggled. "When I smashed a vase over your

head."

"Yes. And why wouldn't you? I was invading your house in the middle of the night. I said to myself— this is my kind of woman." His eyes sparkled with mischief, and something deeper.

Her heart swelled with love for him. Meanwhile her nipples had tightened to hard peaks and her belly tingled with sensation. She craved Sandro's hard length inside her. "My situation is becoming dangerously unstable as well. Do warn me if I start to hurt you."

"Something tells me I won't feel any pain at all," he murmured, as she lowered herself onto his erection. Sandro's hips bucked as she sheathed him fully, and she watched his face contort with pleasure.

His hands rose to caress her as she moved over him, letting herself enjoy each sensation, every emotion that roamed through her. Just when she was at her lowest—her loneliest—Sandro strode into her life and turned it upside down. She should have had faith that even though things seemed like they were getting worse at every turn they were actually leading her down the path to perfect happiness.

"I love you, Sandro," she rasped, as unspent passion built to a crescendo inside her. She knew neither of them could last long. Desire gathered inside her like a giant storm cloud getting ready to unleash a mighty rainstorm.

"I love you too, Serena." A shout followed his words, and she felt him erupt inside her. Her own insides gripped him as the force of her climax flung her forward onto his chest. Together they rode out the waves of sensation that drew them closer and closer together with each moment. "I can't wait to be your husband."

The words sent a shimmer of emotion through her, and she kissed him softly on the lips. "I can't wait to be your wife and the mother of your child." Suddenly she remembered his injured arm and chest, and sprang back, realizing that she was pressing her full weight down on top of him. "Am I hurting you?"

"I don't think I'm capable of feeling any pain at all right now." A dazed smile lit up his face. "In fact I've never felt better."

She laughed. Typical Sandro to say what she wanted to hear. But strangely, now she knew him better, she also believed him. And trusted him.

And she couldn't wait to share her love for him with the world. "I can't believe my mom didn't freak out when I told her everything. And my oldest sister is already calling me Princess Serena. You'll like her, she's funny. My dad did say that titles meant nothing to him, and he wanted to know if you were a man of integrity. I told him you were."

Sandro grinned. "I take that as a great compliment, coming from you. Now you need to tell your followers. Make sure you make me sound better than that other loser."

"That won't be hard."

"I want a book about us too."

She laughed. "Weirdly enough there was a message on my phone this morning from my agent. She said the publisher is thrilled with my sales and wants to see a proposal for a new book."

"How to catch a prince," suggested Sandro. "Would that be a good seller?"

"Maya Dunham would buy it," she teased,

proving that she could even joke about her now. "Or maybe a book on planning our wedding?" Suddenly she felt shy. "If you want a big wedding, that is. I quite understand if you don't."

"Are you kidding me? I'm a Leone! We have a reputation to uphold. And purely out of sibling rivalry I need to one-up my big brother's wedding of the century, so there's that. I can't wait to see what you come up with."

"I have a feeling they'll like that idea."

Sandro closed his one good arm around her, drawing her closer to his chest. "I have a good feeling about spending the rest of my life with you."

They hadn't even talked about where they'd live. But for some reason that didn't matter anymore. "Me too. You would have been the man of my dreams if I'd ever dared to dream big enough."

"Instead you'll have to settle for me being your Mr. Right."

The title of her own book—and the subject of so much private embarrassment and recrimination—now seemed hilariously perfect. "You are my Mr. Right. I almost ignored my own advice and rushed my way into marrying Mr. Wrong when all along was supposed to wait that little bit longer to find you."

"I have a feeling our happiness will be worth the wait." He raised his head just enough to kiss her softly on the lips.

Warmth trickled through her, and a happy sigh burst from her chest. "I know it will."

Scratching and whining at the door reminded Serena that she'd forgotten all about Lucky. She eased herself off Sandro and opened the door just enough to let him in. Lucky took a running jump up onto the bed, where he ran right on top of Sandro—injuries be damned—and licked his face.

"Don't worry, Lucky," said Sandro. "You'll always be our first child."

Serena laughed. "We need to include him in the wedding."

"Perhaps he can be the ring bearer?"

"I love it!" She climbed back on the bed and ruffled his fur. "He was there at the beginning, and he is a core member of our family."

"Our family," said Sandro with a sigh. "I like the sound of that."

Serena smiled and kissed him softly on the lips. "Me too."

THE END

The complete Royal House of Leone Series:
The King's Bought Bride (Darias and Emma)
A Prince for Christmas (Sandro and Serena)
The Prince's Secret Baby (Sandro and Serena)
The Princess and the Player (Lina and Amadou)
The Princess's Scandalous Affair (Beatriz and Lorenzo)
Taming the Royal Beast (Rigo and Bella)

Join the new-release newsletter at www.jenlewis.com.

ABOUT THE AUTHOR

Jennifer Lewis loves heat in all its forms including spicy food, steamy temperatures and smoking hot heroes. She is a USA TODAY bestselling author and her books have been translated into more than twenty languages. She lives in sunny South Florida and when she's not sitting at her laptop she can often be found at the beach. Read more about her books and join her new release mailing list at www.jenlewis.com.

www.ingramcontent.com/pod-product-compliance
Lightning Source LLC
Chambersburg PA
CBHW031658170626
46808CB00005B/1506